THE OXFORD DESPOILER

and other mysteries from the case book of Henry St Liver

GARY DEXTER

First published in 2009 by Old Street Publishing Ltd
28-32 Bowling Green Lane, London EC1R 0BJ
www.oldstreetpublishing.co.uk

ISBN 978-1-905847-88-4

10 9 8 7 6 5 4 3 2 1

A CIP catalogue record for this title is available from the British Library.

Printed and bound in Great Britain by Clays.

AUTHOR'S NOTE

The sexologists mentioned in these pages were real people, although their work is not always accurately represented here, and there have been various shifts in chronology. I derived much of the detail here presented from Havelock Ellis's *Studies in the Psychology of Sex* (7 vols, 1897–1928). Readers interested in the period of the 'Creation of Love' in European sexology, when categories such as 'homosexual', 'transvestite' and 'transsexual' (among others) were largely developed, are directed to Ellis, as well as to works in translation by the trinity of German pioneers: Albert Moll, Magnus Hirschfeld and Iwan Bloch.

Contents

CHAPTER ONE

The Missing Flabellum

But I must not run ahead. The reader will have no idea of my personal connection to Henry St Liver, nor of the circumstances in which I first became acquainted with him.

I should perhaps very briefly sketch my early life. I was born in the little village of Summerseat, to the north-west of Manchester, in 1870. In my third year my family moved to Sydney, Australia, where my father took a job with a mining concern. At the age of seventeen I became a teacher at a rural school near Goongerwarrie, Queensland, and it was there, in the intervals of educating the children, that I managed also to educate myself, using some discarded volumes of Milton and Goethe, and a Latin grammar. I returned to England in August 1892, aged two-and-twenty, with the ambition of training to become a doctor.

I had seen photographs and engravings of London, of course, and read descriptions of it, and pored over maps. I had even tasted London gin. But I was not, inevitably, prepared for London. I did not anticipate, for example, the extortionate rents, the Irish bombs, murder stalking the streets, &c &c. On my very first day, as I disembarked at Tilbury, I was almost caught up in a riot. I believe those involved were dock workers: certainly it was very difficult to get away from the docks. The commotion had spread as far as Regent Street, where I later noticed that the windows of Mr William Morris's shop were entirely smashed in, sending rolls of wallpaper spilling in wild abandon along the pavement.

I found cheap lodgings in Hoxton, near to a penny gaff. I had nothing in my valise except a few clothes and books, and my manuscript, *The Story of an Australian Barn*. This latter was a record of my time in the vastnesses of the outback, which I began to circulate to publishers: after the seventh or eighth week it attracted interest from the firm of Drebber and Drebber, and the book was published in January 1893.

Not long afterwards Messrs Drebber forwarded the following letter:

16 Dover Mansions

Dover St

Shoreditch

12th February 1893

Dear Mr Iron,

I have been reading your *Story of an Australian Barn*, and it gave me so much pleasure that I could not resist giving myself the additional pleasure of telling its author so. I too came to an awareness of Mind and Spirit and Body in such an atmosphere as you describe, i.e.

a very dusty, grimy, impoverished place devoid of every material comfort, but under a sky so wide and blue that it gave one a feeling of perfect freedom, so that one was in almost an ecstasy of happiness every time one went out alone – and lit at night by stars such as we never see in London. If the experiences of life make us kin, then you and I are – dare I say it? – almost as brothers. Generally I would hesitate to write in this way but passages such as the following:

I stretch in passion on the red earth; the sap of pantheism rises in me... (pp 58, 345)

emboldened me to do so. Have you read Whitman?
I am, Sir,
With every good wish,
Yours sincerely,
Henry St Liver

The book had done very poorly in the month or so it had been on sale. The original run had been for five hundred, and I should imagine that in total it had sold forty copies. Ten of those had been bought by myself, at cost, to send to the press; it had managed to garner one review (in *The Hoxton Inquirer*: 'fresh... full of vigour... Mr Iron has uncanny insight into his female characters'). In short, it had sunk without a trace. This letter, then, was the sole, unsolicited, disinterested response, the one sign that it had moved any human heart, journalists not included. I studied it, as might be imagined, very carefully (here was an object that provided ample scope for the amateur sleuth), noting the quavering copperplate in which it was written (an old man?), the capitalized abstract nouns that seemed to belong to the correspondence of Pope or Macaulay, the nonetheless humble and measured tone, the envelope, which was manila and gave some signs of having been re-used (poverty? or parsimony?), and most of all, the intriguing name – St Liver – with its address in Shoreditch, not more than a quarter of an hour's walk away.

That evening I wrote a reply:

> 22 Bank St
>
> Hoxton

14th February 1893

Dear Mr St Liver,

I was very pleased to receive your kind letter, and to know that you understood my book and enjoyed it. It was written not in the country but in the town, in a Sydney suburb: I was at the time in a ferment of longing for the little farm in the bush where I had spent five wonderful years. You say you know this kind of life, so unlike London, where silence permeates everything and deepens hour by hour until one slips into a half-mystical reverie: were you in Australia?

I wish, however, to make a confession: I am not Roderick Iron. I apologize for the imposture but you must blame my publishers. They felt a male *nom de plume* would sell more books. It was absurd of them, but I was in no position to bargain. I should say that I was also asked to change some of the text – in particular the scene where

Emmie returns from Brisbane in the glow of her conquest of Mr Stirrup and obviously still unmarried – but on that I was firm.

I came here to London only recently and already long to go back to Goongerwarrie. I had nurtured hopes of becoming a doctor here but my asthma is bad and I am afraid the London air is making it worse.

Once again I thank you for your kindness.

Sincerely,

Miss Olive Salter

And that, for a while, was that. I fell ill (I suffer from asthma, chlorosis, eczema, hayfever, sleeplessness, migraines, neurasthenia, tachycardia and local physical disorders), fell also terribly in love and was bitterly disappointed, and gave little thought to Henry St Liver. Then, three weeks later, I received another letter:

16 Dover Mansions
Dover St
Shoreditch

8th March 1893

Dear Miss Salter,

I am sorry for not replying sooner but I have been unwell with a recurrence of the enteric fever I contracted in the otherwise paradisal surroundings of an upcountry village in the Karoo six years ago; I am now, however, fully recovered, and have had a chance to address myself to my correspondence, which is considerable. Several letters are still buried under a small ceiling collapse in the hall that occurred at the end of February, prompted by our little London earthquake. I believe it registered 5.2 on the Mercalli scale.

I was not entirely astonished to learn your sex, as your book deals chiefly with the life of a young woman in a small rural school, and, on a more thematic level, with the erotic, romantic, educational, intellectual and artistic rights of Woman.

As you are new in London, would it be impertinent of me to invite you to a meeting of the 'Fellowship of the New Life' in Bishops Street, Shoreditch (number 2)? The Fellowship has three tenets, arranged thus:

Object: To cultivate a perfect character for all.

Guiding Principle: The subordination of the material to the spiritual.

Practice: Strenuous and unwavering devotion to both the Object and the Guiding Principle.

One topic currently under discussion, which I mention because it may excite your interest as a commentator on rural matters, is whether to start a small farm where socialistic ideas could be implemented, perhaps along the plan of a medieval monastery – rather like Rabelais' Abbey of Thelema – where members would be able to work at some manual task during the day and devote the mornings and evenings to spiritual communion and fellowship between man and man, man and woman, and woman and woman. Of course this would all be done on thoroughly modern scientific principles of animal husbandry, agronomy, and so on: there would be scope to keep pigs, cows, goats, etc; there would also be a large library and an art club; and workers from nearby factories would be encouraged to visit and attend lectures.

Our next meeting is on the 13th, at half past seven in the evening, and I would be very glad to meet you and to discuss your book at length.

With every good regard,

Henry St Liver

Since coming to London I had attended numerous lectures and joined not a few societies: the Democratic League in Donkin Street; the Automatic Writing and Research Club in Geddes Row; the Men's and Women's Discussion Club in Chertwell Street; and the Brixton Applied Mathematics Club, which I joined on a whim, and left after one meeting, since the talk was purely mathematical. (A great disappointment: the young men through the window had looked so jolly.) The Fellowship of the New Life sounded interesting; I wrote back saying I would attend.

The next Thursday my chlorosis was so bad that I almost decided not to make the effort, but I had recently discovered Valentine's Egg White Elixir; and so, slipping a bottle into my pocket for emergencies, I set out for Shoreditch.

When I arrived, somewhat after the appointed time, I found that 2, Bishops Street was a Catholic chapel, and that the doors were locked. Exploring a little, I found a narrow side passage that led down, slightly below ground, to a door: I pushed at the door and walked along a corridor toward the only illuminated room. Knocking softly, I entered.

About twenty people were in the room, both men and women. There was uproar.

'No! No!' cried a tall young woman, made a foot taller by a peacock headdress, and with a cigarette in her hand. 'Russia must save herself! It is not in your gift!'

A young man in a fawn suit stood up. 'Then Russia will never be saved!' he thundered.

All eyes suddenly turned on me. I had the momentary sense of seeing myself through their gaze: a young woman with short brown hair under a plain black hat, startled hazel eyes and a long mouth. I felt unbeautiful.

Then, right at my elbow, a man rose from his seat like a rearing python. He was well over six feet tall, with an untamed chestnut moustache that stuck out in all directions and concealed the entirety of his lower face.

'How do you do?' he said in a high, effeminate voice. 'I am Henry St Liver.'

I offered my hand, though I could almost have wept with disappointment. 'Olive Salter,' I said.

'I am so happy you came,' the man piped. He gazed at me with watery eyes. 'May I introduce our members?' And with that he presented, in turn, each of the denizens of that underground chamber: Edith Nasmith (the peacock-befeathered one), Eleanor Marx (the daughter, I was astonished to learn, of the famous Karl), Edward Woodman (a writer with a languorous air), and several others.

'Miss Salter is of course the authoress of *The Story of an Australian Barn*,' Mr St Liver added belatedly.

There were interested murmurs.

'Did you meet any of the negroes there?' asked a young woman with lank hair.

'Yes: I knew several of the native people,' I replied. 'I lived in the country.'

'Miss Salter's book,' Mr St Liver put in, 'is, I think, one of the outstanding novels of the year, and I would urge everyone to read it. You will not find it on any railway bookstall. There is in it a burning, primitive sense of life almost unparalleled in writing today. It deals with the majesty of the rolling country, the relations between man and woman, feminine emancipation, and, though perhaps the authoress herself will correct me, it sounds a note of gymnemimetophilia... I have no doubt it will be one of the great successes of the year.'

'Almost good enough to eat,' said the peacock-befeathered Miss Nasmith. And she let out a booming laugh.

As the weeks passed and I began to see more of the circle, both at Bishops Street and at various at-homes and other meetings, I had several opportunities to converse with Dr St Liver (as I now knew him) alone – and among all the personages of that earnest group, it was Dr St Liver, more and more, who grew to interest me.

I found him not at all attractive. He was, I suppose, about thirty-two years of age, painfully thin and tall, and his moustache was excessive: behind it he seemed almost as a mild cow peering over a hedge. The hair of his head was long, flowing, disordered and chestnut, and his nose was very big and fleshy, almost tetrahedral. When deep in thought, his nostrils would dilate like those of an Ibsen heroine. He dressed very poorly, and was often to be seen for weeks on end wearing the same clothing, chiefly suits of antique vintage. There were not uncommonly food stains on his person.

I became aware, after a few weeks, that I had told him a great deal about myself, but had found out almost nothing about him. He seemed somehow to discourage direct questioning. I knew nothing of his background, nor his family, nor his profession, nor his relations to the other members of the society; and I soon came to see that his warm epistolary manner – his feeling that I might be a 'brother' to him – did not leak into his everyday manner. Perhaps he wanted a brother but not a sister?

It was as I was beginning to despair of learning anything of the real Dr Henry St Liver that a remarkable event occurred.

I had suggested to Dr St Liver that, since his house was on my way to the church, I might call on him one Thursday and we might walk together. He assented, and so it was that one April evening, as the last glimmers of sunset showed over the roofs, I found myself standing in Dover St in Shoreditch.

Number 16, Dover Mansions was a small terraced property. In the front garden was a folded dining table with one leaf missing, and on top of that a stack of sodden newspapers. A giant wild fennel, giving off a strong smell of aniseed, almost obscured the front door, which was slightly ajar. Taking this as a species of invitation, I put my head in. The sight that met my eyes was astonishing indeed.

In the narrow corridor was a great rolling mass of rubbish of all descriptions: a scarred pianoforte, a broken mirror six feet high, an ironing-board, an Eastman box camera ('You press the button, we do the rest!'), piles of mouldering periodicals, wooden battens and dowels, two typewriters, several rolls of rotting carpet, scores of tubs, tools, egg-cartons, coloured prints, picture frames, sacks, bottles, buckets, baskets, tins of paint, and on and on; and all about, on top of everything, plaster dust and rubble. I looked up, and saw that a four-foot section of the ceiling had come away, showing the laths underneath.

In the morning-room, visible through a door immediately to the left, the impression was the same, though with the emphasis on books: books filling all walls, heaped in tottering pinnacles on the floor, books on tables, chairs and window-sills, stacked on the mantelpiece and piled, like logs, perilously close to the fire. Two tanks filled with dark green water – presumably fish-tanks – stood at the far wall.

Then something moved. It was Dr St Liver. Detaching himself from the surrounding mass, he emerged from the morning-room, bade me greeting, gave what may have been a smile, and stood for a while in thought in the corridor, his moustache responding lightly to his respirations.

'I am sorry,' I said, 'the door was open.'

'Yes – it does not close quite to the jamb. Shall we go?'

He politely ushered me out, and we set off, leaving the front door still ajar. I was left amazed: I felt like the raider of an Egyptian tomb, with Dr St Liver the courteous mummy.

As we walked, and I listened to Dr St Liver talking, and we

passed along Old Street under the looming bulk of Shoreditch Town Hall, I ran over in my mind what I knew of him.

It came to a list as follows:

1. The extreme chaos of his mode of life argues against any conventional employment and suggests either that he has no profession or that he lives on a private income. The title of doctor certainly cannot denote a practising medical doctor.

2. The extreme precision of his manner of speech and fine turn of mind indicate a scrupulously methodical character, and are thus at maximal variance with his chosen environment and personal habits.

3. He has a trick of depositing cigarette ash on the floor in any location (even the private homes of others), which is occasionally surprising.

4. The use of strange words in ordinary conversation (that I am unable to find in any dictionary) is suggestive. Some of them appear to apply to myself. They include iatronudia, ecdyosis, and undinistic. This leaves unresolved the question of medical training.

5. His knowledge of literature and art is apparently wide.

6. His knowledge of psychology, spiritualism and mentalism, and phrenology, is also apparently wide.

7. At moments he appears to be contemplating something infinitely far-off.

8. He is around thirty years of age and has been in South Africa, where he has suffered from enteric fever.

But I put aside this mental analysis in disgust. It had brought Dr St Liver no nearer to me. I felt that if any further revelations were to come I would have to wait for them to arrive at their own speed.

This they immediately did.

As we arrived, a little early, at the church at Bishops Street, we were surprised to see a burly policeman guarding the side passage.

'May I enquire whether you are members of this Society?' he asked as we drew close.

'Yes,' I replied.

'I'm afraid there has been a break-in. One person has been injured.' The policeman referred to a notebook. 'A Mr Burlingame.'

'Mr Burlingame!' I cried. 'Hurt?'

'I'm afraid so, Miss.'

'Is it serious?'

'I can't say at the moment.'

'May we enter?'

'I'm afraid not. My colleague will call when he has finished.'

'I am sure he will,' I replied. 'But my friend here is a doctor. If Mr Burlingame has sustained any injury, you may be sure that he will wish to see him.'

The policeman examined Dr St Liver's ulster, which had at some point in its recent history been in contact with egg. Appearing to overcome his suspicions, however, he stepped aside. 'I beg your pardon, Sir, Miss,' he said. 'Please go in.'

We entered and hurried down the gloomy corridor and into the meeting-room, which held a small knot of people: Mr

Reginald Burlingame, our treasurer, a mainstay of our little group, much liked by all, lying in an armchair softly moaning; Miss Effie Dax, a young woman with exceptionally long honey-coloured hair; Mr Manley, a youth; Miss Genevieve Pfister, originally German, I believe, an older woman of perhaps seventy, but remarkably active and quick-witted; and the churchwarden, who lived next door to the chapel and had, it seemed, been just that moment informed of the incident. He was standing listening to Mr Manley. Miss Pfister, by the fire, was comforting Miss Dax under a small reproduction of Holman Hunt's *The Scapegoat*. In the centre of the room, notebook open, stood the second uniformed policeman, who glanced up as we entered. He was a man with a look of beef-witted devotion to duty that seemed rather out of place in a room that had seen so much talk of utopias.

'Dr St Liver,' I said quickly, 'is here to help Mr Burlingame.'

The policeman gestured towards the recumbent form of the treasurer and Dr St Liver trotted over. Going down on one knee, he began asking questions of his patient in a low voice. Mr Burlingame soon indicated the main location of the injury, in the lower abdomen, and Dr St Liver began gingerly to feel the stricken place.

Miss Pfister sidled over to me. 'We sent for the police,' she whispered, 'as soon as we saw what had happened, and we summoned a doctor, who has not yet come. It is fortunate Dr St Liver is here.'

The policeman, evidently having finished taking evidence from Miss Dax and the others, now walked slowly across to Dr St Liver and Mr Burlingame.

'Is there any serious injury, Doctor?' the policeman enquired.

Dr St Liver stood up. 'There is some bruising to the abdomen, but nothing of any seriousness. There appears also to be some shock. Some brandy would help.'

'I'll go,' said Mr Manley, and slipped out.

The policeman fixed his eyes on Mr Burlingame. 'Could you tell me what happened, Sir?' he said. 'I have it already from Miss Dax that you were attacked by ruffians.'

'Yes,' Mr Burlingame said in a wheezy voice. 'Two. They overpowered me.' He shut his eyes and made a gesture of pain. 'It is all as Miss Dax has said.'

'Could you tell me in your own words, Sir?'

The treasurer hauled himself up and spent some time tucking in his shirt. 'Very well,' he said at length. 'Let me see... We came early. We were rehearsing a duet – there is my flute, on the piano. I find the flute is good for my chest. We rehearse each Thursday, a little earlier than the main meeting. We give baroque concerts at the Guildhall. At around half past six, I think, we heard noises in the corridor.'

'In the corridor. Was the door to the street unlocked?'

'That is just the point. We always keep the door to the street locked until around a quarter past seven, when we unlock it to allow our friends to enter for the meeting at half past seven. It was impossible that anyone could have entered without a key at that hour. It struck me immediately therefore that we must have left the door open by mistake. I peered out into the corridor but all was darkness. Then I heard a... a tinkling coming from the chapel. I started down the corridor to the right, which leads into the chapel, and I saw coming towards me two men.'

'Could you describe them, Sir?'

'One was short, and the other of medium height, and with a beard.'

'And their clothing?'

'I am afraid I did not notice. I think, though – yes – the taller one wore a heavy coat.'

'Did you notice its colour?'

'Dark blue.'

'Were they carrying anything?'

'The smaller of the two was carrying something of brass or gilt.'

The policeman wrote in his notebook.

'I blocked them in the corridor,' Mr Burlingame continued. 'There was a struggle. The two miscreants forced me into this room, and, once we were all inside, locked the door behind us. I told them in no uncertain language that they must return the property and leave. Then the taller of the two took a grip on Miss Dax. He told me that no harm would come to either of us if we did what they said. For Miss Dax's sake I refrained from any further action, and...' – he swallowed – 'the two ruffians tied Miss Dax to this chair, here.' Mr Burlingame indicated a plain wooden chair with a railed back. 'With these two scarves.'

'Are these your scarves, Sir?'

'Yes, the *crêpe de chine* one belongs to Miss Dax, and the woollen one is my own.'

'Go on.'

'They were on the point of tying me up when we heard

footsteps descending the passage, and voices. I saw that help was at hand, and raised a shout. The men, seeing they were trapped, broke out through that window.' He indicated a large window, still slightly open, about four feet high by two wide, at the back of the room, and giving out onto the church grounds. It was quite high up but accessible via a row of tables. 'They disappeared through the window and I went to the door to admit Mr Manley and Miss Pfister. And the rest you know.'

'Alright, Sir, thank you,' said the policeman. 'So – the two men forced you into this room and held you here.'

'Yes.'

'Rather than simply run out the way they had come?'

'Yes. I imagine they were unwilling to meet our friends.'

The policeman again took some time to write something.

'You say that the two men entered from the side passage through the door you had left open?'

'Yes.'

'But this lady' – the policeman indicated Miss Pfister – 'has told me that the door was locked when she arrived, and that she and the gentleman used the spare key hidden under a stone.'

'Then the thieves must have forced it. It is a weak door. The mortice is loose, I think. They must have opened it with a kick or a blow.'

'In that case this lady and gentleman would have found it open.'

'Well, perhaps they closed it behind them to escape detection. If the mortice was weak it would not necessarily be apparent to Miss Pfister that this had occurred. Or perhaps they did not enter via the side passage at all. I did not see them come in, you must remember. I merely heard them in the corridor. You must examine the door.'

He stopped, and wheezed a little.

'You say that the men were carrying a single item of plunder from the chapel. What was that item?'

'A candlestick, I think.'

'Mr Haire' – the policeman gestured toward the church-warden – 'tells me he could find nothing of that description missing.'

'I tell you they were carrying something!' Mr Burlingame said, his face reddening.

The churchwarden spoke. 'Ah... it may be of some significance,' he said, 'that there is a flabellum missing.'

'A flabellum,' repeated the policeman.

The churchwarden peered with a kindly expression at Mr Burlingame. 'If I may explain,' he said, 'a flabellum is a sort of fan... or whisk... used to keep insects or other undesirable... ah... things... from the species of the Eucharist. It is rarely used in winter. I am sure it was in the aumbry. The aumbry is... '

'I think we all know what an aumbry is,' Mr Burlingame said testily. 'It is a sort of cupboard, is it not?' I was surprised to see the anger in his face. The churchwarden murmured something and the policeman studied the treasurer carefully.

'Now, Mr Burlingame,' the policeman continued. 'You stopped the men and they brought you in here and locked the door.'

'Yes! I have told you.'

'Still carrying this flabellum?'

'Yes.'

'And they tied Miss Dax to this chair.'

'Yes.'

'Using these scarves.'

'Yes.'

'And they were about to tie you up too – when they were disturbed.'

'Yes.'

'They used both the scarves on Miss Dax?'

'Yes!'

'Then what were they going to tie you with?'

Mr Burlingame set his jaw in an apparent attempt to control his feelings. For a moment he did not reply. 'With her hair,' he said, at last.

There was a gasp from those present. The policeman's pencil froze. 'With her hair?' he asked finally.

'Yes. They sat me in a chair – that one you see there,' Mr Burlingame said grimly, '– and positioned Miss Dax behind me, in the chair they had tied her to, facing in the same direction.' He paused. 'Like... train carriages. You see what long hair she has. Then they bent her forward so that her head was... in the requisite position. They were intent on using her hair – which as you can see is of exceptional length – to fasten my wrists to each side of the chair. The rogues seemed to find great entertainment in it. They were laughing. But I could do nothing. One of them stood over me with the flabellum.'

'This flabellum is, as I understand it, a whisk,' the policeman said.

'Yes... You must understand, constable, that I had Miss Dax to think of. I was afraid they might harm her. I thought it best simply to do as they ordered and allow them to leave with the stolen property.'

'The whisk.'

'Yes! Certainly the whisk.'

'Very well. And did they manage to tie your wrists in this fashion, with Miss Dax's hair?'

'They did not, as I have said. Through an act of providence, Miss Pfister and Mr Manley arrived.'

'And as you heard them you raised a shout?'

'Yes.'

The policeman turned to Miss Pfister; Mr Manley was still in search of brandy. 'And you heard this shout?'

'I did,' Miss Pfister said in forthright tones. 'A loud cry.' She considered briefly. 'Almost a howl. I tried the handle of the door but it was locked. I rapped on it and demanded to be let in.'

'And how long was it before you were admitted?'

'Not above a minute.'

The policeman turned back to Mr Burlingame. 'What occurred between Miss Pfister trying the door and your opening it?'

'I have told you. The thieves made their escape. I tried to stop them, and received some blows for my pains.'

'And that was all?'

'I tried then to assist Miss Dax but could not immediately get the knots undone,' said Mr Burlingame. 'There was only a short delay – a matter of seconds.' He glanced quickly at Miss Pfister.

'You did not then succeed in untying Miss Dax before unlocking the door?'

'No.'

'I see. Well, that all seems clear, Sir. Thank you.'

'Thank *you*, officer. And I hope you catch these men. They are dangerous.'

At that moment the doctor arrived. Again Mr Burlingame's shirt was loosened; again his abdomen was inspected. After a minute, the doctor reassured Mr Burlingame that there were no bones broken nor damage to any organ, and, as Dr St Liver had been, was then questioned by the policeman. I was standing by and heard the exchange: the doctor reported, as had Dr St Liver, that there had indeed been some bruising, adding that it had possibly been caused by some weapon, rather than by blows or kicks; he asked the policeman whether there had been any weapon involved in the case, and was told that the focus of the dispute had been an instrument by name a flabellum; the doctor asked for a description of it, and received in reply that it was a whisk- or fan-like object with a handle. A sturdy handle? Yes, the policeman said (after consultation with the churchwarden), a sturdy handle, somewhat encrusted with gems, though of little value. Then that, the doctor said, if used rather in the manner of a truncheon, might have been responsible.

At length the policemen withdrew, giving assurances that the matter would be looked into. The doctor too departed, leaving a bill in the hands of Miss Pfister. Immediately the room began to fill up with the other members of the Fellowship, who had been kept waiting outside. They all had to be apprised of what had taken place, and in a few minutes the room was loudly buzzing. Mr Burlingame and Miss Dax seemed to have recovered and were chatting to the others. Mr Manley had still not returned with the brandy.

A little afterwards – at around eight o'clock – I noticed Dr St Liver taking Miss Dax and Mr Burlingame aside, and then leading them from the room into the corridor where the struggle had taken place. Miss Dax's long hair, I noted (as indeed I had many times before), was very beautiful: it swept down in a gorgeous curling cascade, soft and thick and honey-gold.

Drawn partly by the hair and partly by curiosity, I too slipped from the room and was just in time to see Dr St Liver ushering the pair along the corridor to the chapel. Intrigued, I followed. The trio passed through a heavy red-velvet curtain which cut the corridor off from the chapel; a short time after they had passed through, I stealthily slipped in behind them, nestling into a corner shielded on one side by the curtain and on the other by a heavy stone wall. Through a narrow gap in the curtain I was able to see into the chapel unobserved. The three figures stood before the high altar with its reliquary: Dr St Liver, towering thinly; Miss Dax, delicate of lip; and the round-bodied, rubicund Mr Burlingame. I had missed the earlier part of the conversation, but the first two sentences that I managed to overhear – from Dr St Liver – were striking indeed.

'I have one question for you, Miss Dax. Where is the missing flabellum?'

Miss Dax tossed a brief, panicked look at Mr Burlingame. 'The flabellum?' she asked in a fluttering voice.

'I told you,' Mr Burlingame put in quickly, addressing Dr St Liver. 'They took it. At any rate, I assume it was this... instrument that they took, for I have never heard of such a thing... a whisk... before.' He gulped.

'I trust you will not think me overly persistent,' Dr St Liver said, 'but I would ask you to remember the Object of our Fellowship – the cultivation of a perfect character for all; and our Practice – the strenuous and unwavering pursuit of that Object. I am forced to put it to you – all the while humbly recognising my own faults and failings – that the appropriation, even temporarily, of the property of another, does not live up to this high standard. I would ask you to reconsider, and to apprise me – or any other official with power to rectify this matter – of the location of this flabellum, so that we may restore it to its proper and sanctified place.'

'I have no idea what you are talking about,' said Mr Burlingame wrathfully.

'Oh, heavens, Reginald, tell him!' cried Miss Dax. 'It is obvious that he knows everything. I cannot continue deceiving everyone like this.'

Mr Burlingame glared at her.

'I quite understand,' Dr St Liver said to them both, 'that you were forced into this... little deception by events earlier this evening. I certainly will not reveal to anyone what I know. But I must insist that you restore the flabellum.'

Mr Burlingame continued scowling. Miss Dax, on the other hand, seemed quite prepared to take matters into her own hands. 'I agree,' she said. 'Please both turn your backs.'

'Certainly,' Dr St Liver replied, doing so.

Mr Burlingame too, reluctantly, turned. I was astonished to see, through my chink in the curtain, Miss Dax reach beneath her skirts, and, with a slight effort, produce an object which I can only describe as a bejewelled fan.

'Here it is,' the lovely young woman said. The gentlemen turned back. 'I will replace it.'

'Might I suggest that you put it in somewhere other than its accustomed place in the aumbry?' asked Dr St Liver. 'That would explain its apparent disappearance more convincingly than if it were to reappear in a location that had already been searched.'

'Very well,' said Miss Dax, chewing slightly on her lower lip. 'I will put it beneath the altar, here, above this box – and well to the back.'

'Excellent,' Dr St Liver said. 'And now I think we might return to our friends.'

Mr Burlingame, however, was bristling visibly. He had not spoken since Miss Dax's revelation, and it was clear that he was far from ready to return to the meeting-room: something in him was about to 'give'.

'One moment!' he cried. His words rang out among the hallowed stones. 'One moment, please, Dr St Liver! I wish to speak! You... obviously do not believe us. You think, as I see it, that this *flabellum*' (I have rarely heard the word uttered with more venom) 'was not stolen by the ruffians, but by ourselves.'

Dr St Liver widened his eyes.

'Perhaps,' Mr Burlingame continued, 'you think that there were no ruffians.'

'That would seem to follow,' said Dr St Liver slowly.

'And, *ergo*, that there was no scuffle.'

'Of course, that conclusion would also be suggested.'

'Neither was there any attempt to tie Miss Dax to the chair.'

'No...'

'And no flight through the window.'

'Such is the inference I must take.'

Mr Burlingame stood puffing out his chest. 'Then what, may I ask, do you feel *did* happen?'

'I do not think we need go into that,' Dr St Liver said. 'I am prepared to consider the matter at an end.'

'Wait,' Mr Burlingame said quickly. 'You examined the outside door. That must have been it. You saw that it could not have been kicked down – or was not kicked down. Is that how you knew?'

'No, I did not examine the door.'

'Then it was the flabellum,' interjected Miss Dax. 'It must have been Reginald's uncertainty as to the... the nature of the object that gave us away.'

'No,' said Dr St Liver after a space. 'That had not occurred to me.'

Both Miss Dax and Mr Burlingame now seemed keen to play the part of detectives in their own crime.

'Then was it,' Miss Dax offered with an appearance of thought, 'Reginald's unreasonably long delay before opening the door to admit Miss Pfister? A delay that might be better explained by his *tying* me to the chair rather than attempting to *untie* me?'

Dr St Liver considered.

'Or the detail of my hair?' Miss Dax continued, earnestly fondling a strand of her locks. 'It *is* impossible to tie people up with hair, you know. I have often tried to tie my sister up, but it always comes undone. How did you know that?' She smiled winningly.

'No,' said Dr St Liver, 'though I am grateful for the information. No, I rather feel that these are corroborative matters only.'

'Then what?' asked Mr Burlingame.

'It was on examination of your injuries that I saw the truth.'

'What do you mean, Sir?'

'The truth regarding the nature of your activity in the meeting-room when Miss Pfister called.'

'I deny any such activity,' declared Mr Burlingame.

'That is your right and privilege,' Dr St Liver replied equably. 'And, as I have said, since the property has been returned, I have no reason to elicit any further statement from you on this matter.'

'But this is all unfair,' Miss Dax cried, her face aglow. '*What* do you know? I must ask how you did it. Are you like Maskelyne and Cooke, and do not give away your secrets? I want to know what you think happened.' She cast her long lashes down. 'I would wish you to understand,' she went on, 'that there was no... impropriety in that room. None. Reginald and I...'

'Effie!' cried the treasurer.

Miss Dax held out one slender arm. 'Is it not best, Reginald, to tell Dr St Liver everything? Otherwise... he may think something altogether different.'

Mr Burlingame looked away. When his words finally came, they were addressed not to anyone present but to a small statue of St Teresa of Ávila on the far wall. 'Yes,' he said at last. 'Yes, you are right.'

'But first we must know how you did it,' said Miss Dax firmly.

There was a slight pause. 'Very well,' said Dr St Liver. He pressed his lips together (at least, I felt he was doing so, since his chin moved, and there were ancillary motions of his jaw; his lips were naturally invisible under his luxuriant moustaches). 'We have only a brief acquaintance,' he began, 'and neither of you, perhaps, know the nature of my work. I am a student of that part of man's being connected with the instinct of love. I hope this does not shock you unduly.'

'Not at all,' Miss Dax said, looking at Dr St Liver with a species of delighted horror.

'Ah,' Mr Burlingame said slowly.

'Yes. I have, over the past few years, acted as an informal consultant, both to private individuals and to the police, on these matters. The two constables we met tonight were, fortunately for us, unaware of my identity. When I examined you, Mr Burlingame, I at once began to form a picture of the evening's events. This picture was rather at variance with your story. My examination showed a multitude of small reddish circular bruises, all fresh; they were each about a half-inch in diameter, and studded over your lower abdomen. Upon a more extensive examination I have no doubt I would have found the same marks on your thighs and chest. This multiplicity of bruises was caused by a small blunt instrument impressed repeatedly and violently into the flesh. The bruises were not, however, attributable to the handle of the flabellum, as hypothesized by my colleague Dr Mainprize. Two facts served to convince me of this. Firstly, on a close inspection, numerous similar bruises were evident – faint to be sure, but evident nonetheless – that were older: some were days older, some weeks. And secondly, Miss Dax is wearing a pair of attractive shoes with remarkably high and narrow heels – Louis heels, I think. I should imagine, to judge by the tooling on the uppers, that they were expensive. A gift, perhaps?'

Mr Burlingame's eyes gleamed feverishly. 'I believe you know everything,' he said. 'You are a wizard.'

'Not at all.'

'Go on,' said Miss Dax.

'I had, then, established the nature of the activity in the meeting-room – and the reason for the cry that Miss Pfister and Mr Manley heard as they unexpectedly came upon you at half past six. It became clear therefore that the story of the thieves could not, strictly, be considered truthful. It must have been you, Sir, who tied Miss Dax to the chair as soon as you realized your cry had been heard, in order to establish an alibi. The flabellum could not have been taken by the thieves, since they had never existed. Therefore it must have been removed by another. The only persons with a motive for theft were yourselves – the motive being to make your story of the thieves more convincing. The removal of the flabellum must have been carried out by you, Miss Dax, because you, Mr Burlingame, were confined to your couch, the cynosure of all. I would imagine,

Miss Dax, that after conferring hastily with Mr Burlingame, you made some excuse and went quickly to the chapel, at some point after the advent of Miss Pfister but before the arrival of the police, where you found that the flabellum was the smallest portable object of value that you could quickly take. You then returned with it hidden about your person just as the police arrived.'

'Oh, bravo!' cried Miss Dax.

'Indeed. Bravo,' said Mr Burlingame.

'As you can see, the whole picture emerged simply from the marks on your abdomen.'

'Yes, it seems simple as you describe it,' Miss Dax said. 'But it is still astonishing – is it not Reginald? – that in complete disdain of all other evidence that might have implicated us, Dr St Liver chose to focus on one area of a purely... specialized nature.'

'I find, on the contrary,' Dr St Liver said, 'that it is only by concentrating on this one area that I can penetrate to the solution of any mystery.'

'Well, I suppose we must congratulate you,' said Mr Burlingame. He gave a brief, nervous chuckle. 'This... will go no further, then?'

'I see no reason why it should.'

'And... ' He paused. 'And this... this activity is nothing new to you?'

'By no means,' replied Dr St Liver. 'Taking an historical view, it is remarkably common.'

'I am amazed to hear it,' said Mr Burlingame. 'I thought I was almost the only one.'

For the first time, Dr St Liver permitted himself a laugh. 'No, no. May I speak freely?'

'Certainly.'

'Miss Dax?'

'Please.'

'Thank you. Well, then... interest in the foot – perhaps I may put it like that – may be discerned throughout history and throughout the world. Indeed, the whole field has been thoroughly explored and tabulated. Retif de la Bretonne built his entire literary career from his fascination with the lower leg. I refer you to his *Le Pied de Fanchette*. It is in his honour that foot fetichism is often called Retifism, although there are other terms.'

'I had no idea,' said Miss Dax.

'Certainly,' Dr St Liver replied. 'In Southern China today we find a population almost entirely in thrall to a mania for the female foot, or as they term it, the "Golden Lotus". Tatar women in the Southern reaches of the Russian empire will happily bare almost any other part of their bodies, but never appear in public unshod. In our own European societies one has only to turn to our Cinderella stories – which exist in hundreds of variants – to see the part the pretty patten plays in courtship. Cinderella's shoe fits her foot, but in the context of erotic symbolism both shoe and foot are representations of more basic realities. In the Jewish wedding ceremony the groom breaks a glass symbolizing virginity – but where does he break it? Under his heel. And so on and so forth.' He paused. 'Since you have already mentioned your willingness to speak further on the subject, Mr Burlingame, and if Miss Dax has no objection, may I ask when these feelings made their first appearance? My interest I assure you is purely occupational, and I gladly withdraw the question if you find the least particle of embarrassment in speaking of it. I am fully cognizant that this is a most personal and private demesne.'

It was interesting now to see the glimmerings of professional curiosity in Dr St Liver's eye. There was, indeed, a certain banked-up power in the man which, for the first time that evening, I could sense radiating strongly from him. He seemed stronger, broader, more commanding. I believe Miss Dax felt it too, since she gazed at him with an expression little short of rapture.

'Yes, please!' she breathed.

'I have said I wish to speak,' said Mr Burlingame, 'and I will.' He gazed at Miss Dax. 'Miss Dax has always been so kind to me,' he said. 'So kind. Yes. But I have not always been so fortunate. My early years were dominated by feelings that it seemed I would never either understand nor assuage.'

'Do you date them then from your earliest childhood?' asked Dr St Liver.

'Yes. They are present in my earliest memories. My mother was, I remember, always fascinated by my feet: she would often play with my toes and tickle them. She enlisted them in a hundred games. And when I grew older I found she also had a special fondness for her own feet. She had a particularly shapely lower leg, ankle and foot, and bought only the prettiest and most expensive shoes. Fortunately we were not short of money, and my father allowed her a very extensive wardrobe, much of which was composed of footwear of various sorts. I remember with particular vividness a pair with high green pompadour heels and a blue border: I would often steal into her room when she was out and admire them. I can still recall how my heart beat as I handled them, sometimes still warm from her foot, listening intently for any noise that might bring discovery.'

Watching from behind my curtain, I was, as the reader will imagine, not a little astonished. Mr Burlingame had always seemed to me a rather bluff and plain-spoken character, yet here he was confessing to this extraordinary interest in shoes and feet. It was the first time I had ever heard him say anything in the least bit interesting.

Dr St Liver, however, merely nodded.

'But you will think that these feelings were conditioned entirely by the influence of my mother,' Mr Burlingame continued. 'I do not believe it was so. When I was thirteen or fourteen, I struck up a friendship with a servant girl, and it was she who truly initiated me into these mysteries. One afternoon, as we were sitting opposite one another at a table – I was watching her peel beetroots – she extended her leg and – I beg your pardon, my dear – laid her shoe over my organ (still, of course, covered by my breeches).'

'Oh!' cried Miss Dax softly.

'Immediately on contact with the heel I felt a sensation that now I recognize to have been my first sexual crisis. You have heard how a photographic plate may be "fixed" in a dark room: in the same way, at that moment I believe my own preferences were themselves unalterably fixed. I was too ashamed to speak to her about what had happened, and afterwards avoided her, as we often avoid those persons who excite the greatest desires in us, as objects not only of longing but of terror; and soon afterwards she left our employ. I have reason to think my father may have had something to do with it. At any rate I was left alone. It was not until my sixteenth year that an event occurred that helped me gain a greater understanding of these desires.

'As children we were often visited by another local family with whom my mother and father were on very friendly terms. They often stayed for several days. The children consisted of three brothers and two sisters, and one of the daughters was a girl of about my age whom I shall call K. I was especially drawn to her because of her feet, and, I think, after a time, she noticed my glances. She had a very delicate foot, and, not surprisingly, was fond of showing it off in the prettiest footwear: she had a large collection of shoes of all types, and she took to bringing a selection of them with her on her visits. I did not encourage her to do so; she simply brought them as other people might bring a change of clothes, and changed into and out of them several times a day. Given my mother's enthusiasms, that was nothing out of the ordinary in our household; but even so I remember K.'s brothers laughing at her, and referring to her as a "shoe-maniac". I came to feel that she changed just to delight me. Indeed many of these slippers were extremely impractical for our games, since they were for indoor wear, and much of our play was outside in the garden and orchard, but this did not prevent her from wearing them. She seemed to take great pleasure in stepping and stamping on things. On one occasion, while we were playing on a paved court after rain, some tiny snails, of a variety I had never before seen, made their appearance, and she began stepping on them; they were so small it did not seem a very great matter to end their lives, I suppose, and K. seemed to enjoy the crunch they made. I watched with fascination and almost hatred, for I felt in some obscure way that the snails were myself.

'One night I was outstretched on a chaise longue in the library, perusing a book. The day's play, and my little companions, had induced in me a sort of sick longing for I knew not what, feelings at once sweet and terrible... K. came into the room, alone; she saw me stretched out by the bookcase, and walked over to me. She looked very beautiful. She was wearing a cerise gown with a frothy underskirt, and her calves were encased in light rose stockings, with, over the foot, a patterned black, slim-heeled shoe with a single strap. She wanted a book high up in the stack behind me, and as she pointed up she asked me to move from the couch so that she could stand on it. I laughingly refused, saying she would have to stand on me instead. With a look of mischief, she placed her foot on an exposed portion of the couch, hopped up, and then, finding that she was still not high enough, experimentally placed her right foot playfully on my midriff, saying that she would do so but that I would get dirty.

'I responded with equal good humour, taking hold of her foot and pressing it into me. As I gripped and held her foot, she shifted more and more of her weight onto it, perhaps to see how I would stand it; and then, after a half a minute or so of this, with my encouragement, she transferred its entirety – perhaps nine stone – onto me, and so was balanced completely upon me. The heel dug in with some ferocity, but I tried not to give any indication of the pain, continuing to smile and encourage her. Then I reached out for her left leg and tugged it gently to signal that she should place it on me also. This she did, uttering a little cry, as I, in my turn, attempted to contain my tormented ecstasy. Seeing my face suffused and rosy she must have understood that I was in the grip of powerful feelings, though must at the same time have been unaware of their true nature. By now she was standing upon me with both feet, still half-pretending to search for the book she wanted; she began to tread upon me in an exploratory fashion, while I strove to give every appearance of being completely unaffected. This encouraged her to tread more boldly, and it was not long before she was marching carelessly up and down all over my chest, belly and upper legs. I was by now in a state of considerable excitement. Perhaps what came next will not surprise you. I took her little foot and placed it on top of my organ, which was in a state of the most savage erection. She pressed on it, at first tentatively, and then with all her weight, as if to determine what it was. And it was at that point that an orgasm flooded over me, which, because of the pressure she was exerting on the penis, partially restricting the emission, was drawn out to the point where I thought I would faint. She felt the organ throb and looked at me at first wonderingly and then, with a cry, disgustedly; she stepped off, stood for a while, then turned and walked quickly from the room.

'I was left lying there with mixed emotions, as you can imagine. Chief among them were self-disgust, shame, fear of possible consequences, physical agony (I was bruised all over for days) and delight in my new and terrible self-knowledge. It will not surprise you, Doctor, that our friendship was never the same again. We never spoke of the events of that evening. I believe she later married and went off to Birmingham, where she caught diphtheria.'

'Poor boy,' said Miss Dax.

'Your story is of extreme interest,' said Dr St Liver.

'There is a great deal more,' said Mr Burlingame, 'though I am afraid I bore you.'

'Not at all,' said Dr St Liver.

'Well, I will make a précis. Miss Dax is in possession of most of the facts. I hope I do not appear in these remarks to traduce or insult the female sex. That is far from my intention; on the contrary, I have the highest respect for women. I have often formed friendships with women of good breeding and heredity, and valued them as companions and intellectual equals. I have often, however, also desired that they trample me.'

Miss Dax's nostrils dilated imperceptibly.

'Like any other man,' Mr Burlingame continued, absently tracing a pattern with his finger on the stonework of the altar, 'I appreciate beauty in woman, and elegant manners, and so on. But this is all from the aesthetic point of view. However beautiful any woman may be, there is but one aspect of her person that I find attractive, physically: the lower leg and foot. I have no interest in anything above the knee, so to speak. If anything of that upper region is revealed, my ardour is immediately cooled. Consequently I prefer heavy skirts, preferably in rich patterns and brocades. I admire all styles of hosiery, the finer the weave the better. As for shoes, I particularly admire high, slender heels,

– what is sometimes called the stiletto or Louis heel. The shoe must be expertly fitted: nothing repels me more than a shoe into which the foot is either crammed, so that it bulges against the leather and distorts it, or is loose, and does not move elegantly with the foot. My desire is in fact in proportion with the beauty of the foot and leg and its tasteful and expert covering. If these points are addressed, my desire rises almost to volcanic proportions. The sight of the naked body of a woman would offer me absolutely nothing. I am aware that this is abnormal. I simply state it as a fact.

'Now to my life experiences after my sixteenth year. I soon discovered that it was a comparatively simple matter to persuade ladies, many of good heredity and intellectual attainment, almost all of them married, to trample me. To Miss Dax I have made full confession of my experiences. I have in the past had a wide circle of acquaintance and I would estimate that fully fifty women have stood on me. I have been very careful to become intimate with them in advance so as to ensure that my invitation will not be rejected; husbands, also, I have carefully cultivated. When I am certain that the lady in question will not be offended or outraged by my suggestions, I contrive it so that they come upon me in a reclining position. That is an easy matter. It is then also comparatively easy to tempt them to walk upon me. Many women, once the strangeness of it has worn off, are quite ready to trample on a man, often quite pitilessly. They find a great deal of amusement in it. But when the true meaning of my invitation becomes clear, the reaction is almost always negative. The trampling therefore usually takes place only once. Sometimes the friendship is terminated; occasionally there have been serious consequences, though no prosecutions.

'This was the state of affairs before I met Miss Dax. You will know that Miss Dax is, of course, unmarried, and I most earnestly desire that one day she will enter the conjugal state. She will not mind my saying this; we have often discussed it. I should be very sorry to lose her. But I hope I would continue to retain her friendship.'

'Yes indeed,' murmured Miss Dax.

'Miss Dax plays the pianoforte to a high standard, and it was in her capacity as my accompanist that I first invited her to trample me. Her reaction to the proposal – at the Fawncote Rooms – was not anything out of the way: she agreed, as most ladies do, as if humouring a silly whim. When, however, she saw the pleasure it had given me, her reaction was most unusual. Unprecedented, I may say, in my experience. But there I must leave it, for I cannot presume to describe a lady's feelings.

'Needless to say, during these... ah... sessions we both remain clothed throughout. For the last few years Miss Dax has graciously agreed to trample me almost every day; sometimes, after a prolonged absence, she will trample me several times in a single day. On such occasions my body is so covered in bruises that I can barely move; yet each fresh application of pressure is a delicious purgatory.'

Mr Burlingame seemed finally to come to a halt, and there was a brief, profound silence in the chapel, as befitted these extraordinary revelations.

Unfortunately at this precise juncture I was forced to sneeze. I have said before that I suffer from numerous allergies, and the combination of velvet and dust had inflamed me to such an extent that I was unable to hold back any longer. A violent paroxysm shook me, and, though I attempted to contain it, the escape was clearly audible in the quiet of the chapel.

'Who is there?' cried Dr St Liver. And, taking two decisive steps forward, he wrested the curtain aside.

'Miss Salter!' he ejaculated.

'Yes,' I said meekly.

Miss Dax and Mr Burlingame stared at me in extreme disquiet.

'How long have you been there?' roared Mr Burlingame.

'Not long,' I said. 'I was looking for Dr St Liver and heard you talking.'

'How much did you hear?' Mr Burlingame asked.

'Nothing, indeed,' I said. 'Nothing that would reflect ill on anyone present.' I collected myself and took a few steps from my hiding-place. I drew myself up. 'I am, as you may be aware, Miss Dax, Mr Burlingame, the author of the little book *The Story of an Australian Barn*, which deals with the truest relations between man and woman...'

'Yes, yes.'

'I am a student of the human heart – an humble one. Nothing that I have heard – by mistake – tonight reflects dishonour on anyone present. Quite the contrary.'

'That may well be true,' began Mr Burlingame, but he was interrupted by Miss Dax.

'You will not tell anyone what you have heard?' she quavered, taking a half-step toward me. 'I beg you, Miss Salter.' Her long locks, swaying slightly, glowed gold in the little candlelit chapel.

'I hereby vow,' I said, holding up my palm, 'to reveal none of this either in speech or in writing.'

'Well, then,' said Mr Burlingame gruffly. 'I suppose that will have to do. We cannot do anything else, at any rate. I know Dr St Liver will not speak of this. I trust his professional credentials. As to whether we can trust a lady novelist... well, that is a different matter. But I will choose to believe your assurances, Miss Salter. Please do not think that I will forget your vow. What you have heard concerns things unknown to anyone apart from we four gathered here tonight. I would wish to bind all present with a vow of the most solemn variety.'

And that was that. It was my introduction to Dr St Liver and his work.

Dr St Liver's profession, such as I now knew it to be, interested me extraordinarily, since it was closely related to my own literary concerns. The whole problem of man's erotic life had preoccupied me continuously in the outback, and I had resolved to do whatever I could to understand it. It was truer than Dr St Liver had ever meant it – though perhaps, all things considered, he *had* meant it – that we were as kindred spirits.

The events of that evening drew us together somewhat, and I began to learn more of the man and his work. I came to accept and to understand his mode of life, in which quotidian concerns played no part. I discovered that it was he, and no other, who had helped the police with the strange affair of the ship *The Grafenberg*, found drifting out of Rotterdam with a crew made up entirely of women; he who had finally cleared up the murderous secret at Buske Hall in Northumberland; and he (and no other) who had resolved the mystery of the racehorse 'P'tit Indiscrétion', the favourite of the Countess of B—. I became a frequent visitor at 16, Dover Mansions, and as our friendship deepened, Henry (as I now knew him) and I would often stay up all night talking. As dawn broke, I would try to find a space to stretch out, which, among all his books, accoutrements and frank rubbish, was not always easy.

It was not long before I began to accompany him on some of his adventures.

CHAPTER TWO

The Oxford Despoiler

I had never really felt at home in Hoxton, and had wearied of my landlady, who practised as a medium, and who in the intervals of communicating with the departed was almost perpetually drunk. The penny gaff was noisy – three times a week it staged something called 'La Traviata', though it was certainly not the opera – and the house itself was in a state of some putrefaction: the walls dripped. As soon as was practicable, therefore, I moved and took rooms in Grosvenor Road, Shoreditch. This new accommodation, as well as possessing a view of the park, had the advantage of being closer to Henry.

I had by this time postponed any active idea of undergoing medical training, and was instead concentrating on producing a sequel to *The Story of an Australian Barn*. It was essential to my literary work, as in the past, to keep a detailed journal, in which I recorded my experiences and the doings of my friends and acquaintances.

Naturally Henry's cases came to dominate my journal. In that first year of our acquaintance there was, for example, the strange affair of the Eastcheap Geishas, which exercised the prints for weeks and is perhaps still too painfully fresh in the public mind to dilate on here. I also see from my journal that it was in the July of that year that the case of the Disturbed Baker came to Henry's attention. But perhaps the most remarkable of all his cases in 1893 concerned the singular events which took place at the University of Oxford.

I well remember the first we heard of it. It was late in the afternoon of a dull, rainy September day, and I was suffering from asthma brought on by the damp. I had been forced to stay at Dover Mansions for three nights together due to the impossibility of venturing out in the rain, and had managed to clear some space for myself in Henry's second bedroom, where I had found a tolerable divan hidden beneath several stacks of sexological journals.

We had both nodded off in front of the fire when we were roused from our daydreams by a knock on the door. Soon a familiar form made its appearance: that of Inspector FH Pelham Bias, Henry's chief contact at Scotland Yard.

Pelham Bias was a curious fellow. I never met a single person in whom he did not inspire at least some degree of repugnance. His body was very fat and fleshy, and he kept his hair extremely short, so that it stood up in three-quarter-inch-long spikes all over his head, extending down to the roll of fat on the back of his neck. On his chin he sported a chinchilla beard carefully barbered to the same length. He habitually dressed entirely in brown – he was, of course, a plain-clothes officer – and his movements were somewhat slow and gelatinous, so that he called nothing to mind so much as a large, bristly, brown slug, of the type found in damp vegetation near watercourses. I have in fact heard several mutual acquaintances describe him as a 'slug'. Henry, though, seemed to get on with him famously. He was the only person, to my knowledge, who did.

On the credit side of the ledger, the Inspector's methods were highly innovative. He was prepared to employ any means, however experimental or untried, to bring forth results; and in many cases his investigations had met with spectacular success. His use, for example, of the medium James Anatole to channel messages from the victims of the unknown Winslow Woods murderer was at first laughed at, but when it was proved that Anatole was in possession of specific details of the killings that had been known only to the police, the case was finally solved and Anatole himself was arrested for the murders, and later hanged.

Henry's advice had enabled Pelham Bias to 'bag' several important cases, and the two often joked that if Henry solved one case too many he might also fall under suspicion.

'Bias! Take a seat, my dear fellow!' Henry cried.

I cleared a chair of its plate and our visitor subsided into it with a mucilaginous expression.

'I see everything here is much as I left it,' he observed.

'I think the stuffed snow leopard cub is an addition,' I said, pointing to the object in question.

Pelham Bias turned slowly. 'Ah yes,' he said. 'A recent acquisition?'

'Yes, quite recent,' Henry replied. 'It was a gift from the

Maharao of Cutch after that little business of the asphyxiation of the Commissionaire Kitwan.'*

'Ah yes.' The other paused. 'Well, it is in regard to a similarly intractable matter that I come here today. It seems to be in your line, St Liver. I like to think I am schooled in your methods, but I admit I am baffled in this case – as we all are up at the Yard – as to the possible motive of the criminal.'

'You interest me greatly.'

'Well, you shall judge for yourself. It concerns some disturbing happenings at Oxford in recent weeks, among the student body there. The local constabulary can make nothing of it, and when it came to London it was farmed out to me. Considering the nature of the affair, my first thought was to seek your opinion.'

'Go on.'

'The beginning was trivial enough. It was at Somerville Hall. Somerville is one of the two women's halls, as I am sure you know – its main entrance is just on the Woodstock Road.'

'I know it well.'

'You were up at Oxford, I believe?'

'At Balliol in '79. Briefly.'

'Just so. Well, it was there, at the main entrance to the Hall, that the first incident occurred, in the second week of last month. Ink was thrown over a young lady student's dress.'

'Ah.'

'This was repeated on two further occasions. On the third

---

* An intriguing case: it was solved by reference to the lunar timetable, and to the fact that the commissionaire's pockets contained a suicide note countersigned by his wife.

occasion, however, the matter took a more serious turn. Instead of ink, a different substance was used – vitriol.'

'Vitriol. I see.'

'Vitriol, of course, is highly dangerous. If it falls on skin – a naked arm, perhaps, held out in defence of a dress – it can cause serious disfigurement. It was only by luck that this failed to occur.'

'Quite,' said Henry. 'What were the exact dates of the respective incidents?'

Pelham Bias referred to a notebook. 'The first was on Monday the 12th of August, when a Miss Bastable had black ink thrown upon her dress. A similar attack occurred the following Monday, the 19th – a Miss Hunt-Furze, also black ink. And it was the Tuesday after that – Tuesday week, the 27th of August – that the vitriol-throwing occurred. Miss Mary Massey, a history student, was on her way into Somerville at around nine in the evening, after paying a visit to a friend, when she noticed a small dark form hurrying past her. She did not pay it any attention, as she was in haste to enter the Hall before the curfew, but as she passed the porter's lodge she became aware of a strange odour. Looking down, she saw that her dress was sending out little clouds of smoke, and had been eaten away in several areas. She batted at it with one hand and immediately felt a stinging on her fingers. She then called for the porter, who rushed out of his lodge; the fellow perceived what had happened, and, knowing that if the acid were allowed to eat right through the dress Miss Massey might be seriously injured, he advised her – while of course averting his eyes – to remove the dress there and then in the lodge. Relief came after a message was dispatched to another friend at the Hall, a Miss Eleanora Moss, to bring a replacement dress. Miss Massey and Miss Moss then retired, much distressed, to their chambers.'

'And that was the most recent assault, on Tuesday the 27th of last month?' Henry asked. 'That is over three weeks ago.'

'No, I am afraid not. I have said that there were three throwing or spraying incidents; but there were later two further assaults of an entirely different nature, at exactly the same spot.'

'I see.'

'On Monday the 9th of this month, at around 8pm, a Miss Lettice Angel was entering the Hall when she became aware of a dark form rearing up behind her. By now the Hall students and staff were coming to expect these attacks. Miss Angel screamed and tried to gather up her skirts in the hope of saving them from ruin, but the attacker had another object in mind. Bringing out a shining implement, he swiftly lopped off a large hank of Miss Angel's hair.'

'Was the girl just inside the gate, next to the porter's lodge, or was she at some remove from the gate?' asked my friend.

'From what I can gather she was some ten feet short of the gate on the street side.'

'Very good. Pray continue.'

'Her hair was cut with an instrument that may have been a pair of large scissors or shears, though Miss Angel could not specify. She simply saw the blade flash. It is possible it may have been a sharp knife of some description, which of course lends the affair a more sinister dimension. The attacker then fled immediately, at high speed, clutching the hair, and disappeared around the corner of Little Clarendon Street. Now, at 8pm, in that location, there should have been plenty of witnesses – there are several public houses there – but the fact is that we could not find one solitary person who could corroborate Miss Angel's account. However, there is no doubt that her locks were very gravely mutilated. Her hair is now cut short in a bob, and very miserable she is. And then, yesterday, the 13th, the most recent attack occurred. This was perpetrated upon a Miss Belinda Buss-French, a young woman of good family, of Lincolnshire gentry stock, and a student of philosophy.'

'And was that attack also at dusk, and some distance from the gate?' asked Henry.

'It was,' said Pelham Bias. 'It was at around 8.30 pm – and at around the same spot as the attack on Miss Angel. Miss Buss-French was also favoured – until recently – with a magnificent head of long, curling, dark hair. A two-foot section of it was brutally hacked off by the attacker. Miss Buss-French then ran into the Hall screaming wildly.'

'Did the porter come to her aid?'

'As soon as her screams were heard the porter ran out of the Hall and into the street, brandishing a life-preserver, but of the attacker there was no sign.'

'Thank you.'

'And so to the miscreant.' Pelham Bias paused and studied his notebook afresh. 'The girls are agreed that he was dressed from head to foot in dark clothing and appeared to run doubled up, almost as if loping on all fours, at very high speed. He seems also to have worn a mask. In all five cases, no sooner had the attack been committed than the assailant had made himself almost invisible. This is one of the very remarkable features of the investigation.'

'Yes.'

'All five attacks took place at or near dusk, in low light. This, combined with the speed of the attacker and his dark clothing and mask, have rendered identification difficult. A final singular detail is that the attacker was heard to utter a cry as he escaped: something like "Boojoo!"'

'Might it have been "Loo! Loo!"?', I put in. 'That is a hunting cry.'

'Yes, that occurred to us,' said Pelham Bias, swivelling torpidly in my direction. 'It has led the local police to look into the hunting fraternities around Oxford, and to make enquiries in the various students' clubs. The "Beaters" in the Cowley Road have come under suspicion.'

'Yes, I know the "Beaters"', said Henry. 'From what I know of their main preoccupation, I think you are wasting your time.'

'Yes, they do seem to have proven a dead end.'

'No other suspects?'

'Just one – and it is in my opinion a long shot. At Somerville there is a junior lecturer in fine art by the name of Mr Edgar Rampoe. He is a young man of very eccentric habits – what Oxfordians call an "exquisite". He habitually dresses entirely in velvet, and he affects a baboon. He walks out with it on a leash.'

'A baboon, you say?'

'Yes. It is a female baboon, and very tame. It climbs anything

– lamp-posts, walls, the chandeliers in restaurants – and is very popular with the students.'

'And what is it that has excited suspicion against Mr Rampoe?' Henry asked.

'Nothing, as far as I can see,' said Pelham Bias, 'apart from prejudice.'

'Then I think we may eliminate him,' said Henry. 'There are other forces at work here.'

'Indeed?' asked Pelham Bias.

'I am sure of it,' Henry said, 'though it would be a mistake to theorize further at this stage.'

'You will look into it, then?'

'It promises to be a most interesting problem.'

'Excellent.'

'Yes – most interesting. The fusion of hair and ink.' Henry turned to me, his moustache a little buoyed. 'And ink is your medium, my dear Miss Salter. If you will accompany me, then, I think we will catch the Oxford train early tomorrow.'

So it was that the following morning we found ourselves on the 9.20 from Paddington. I was, as the reader might imagine, much intrigued by the case. The acts that Pelham Bias had brought to our attention seemed to have originated in a mind in which the erotic winds had freshened to gale force.

As the train pulled out, Henry was uncommunicative, and, not liking to disturb him, I took out my copy of *Snowden's*. Fifteen minutes into the journey the sight of a flock of sheep led Henry to expatiate on some habits of the Montenegrans, but after this he again lapsed into silence. It was not until we were almost at Oxford that Henry produced a small book from his jacket pocket and, opening it, flattened it on his knee.

'"Somerville Hall,"' he read, looking aside at me and pointing to a small steel engraving of a solid building with a tower like a pepperpot. '"It was founded in 1875, the second women's hall in Oxford. Strictly speaking, it cannot boast the title of College, but does retain some of the academic privileges of the colleges. Its foundation came about as a result of sororal conflict with the older Lady Margaret Hall.

'"The Hall [he continued] is named in honour of the mathematician Mary Somerville, whose international reputation as a scientist was gained in the intervals of raising a large family of sixteen children. Largely self-taught, she published her first book, *Population Growth and Statistics*, in 1857. Her last book was *Malthusian Speculations*, in 1876. On her death in 1877 her place was taken by Mrs Serena Paine, and in 1892 by the current principal, Mrs Philippa Oth. The Hall's motto is *Donec rursus impleat orbem*, which is apparently impossible to translate.

'"The college is bounded by Woodstock Road to the east, where the main entrance is situated, by Little Clarendon Street to the south, and by Walton Street to the west. Each of the south and west streets has a gated snicket entrance. To the north, the property adjoins estate land of the Duke of Northumberland, and is cut off from it by a high wall."'

'It would seem to be well protected,' I said.

'Indeed,' Henry replied. 'The flaw, I suppose, is that the

young ladies persist in leaving and entering. But I see here we are at our destination.'

The towers and spires of the famous university had come into view. The train drew slowly into Oxford station.

After negotiating our way through the crowds of students and visitors we made our way to our hotel in Beaumont Street, and on arrival settled down to unpack our few things. We had been allotted adjoining rooms on the third floor of the hotel, with a commanding view of the teeming lower part of St Giles. Despite the season, my room was a little chilly, and so I rang for the fire to be made up. It was while I was waiting for the maid, and not five minutes after my ring, that I heard a loud commotion coming from outside my room. I put my head out of the door.

In the corridor, his fist still raised in the act of knocking, was the most extraordinary person I have ever seen. He was dressed entirely in viridian, with a soft viridian hat, viridian jacket, viridian cravat, viridian cloak, viridian breeches buttoned at the knee, and viridian leggings. His costume gave out a feral smell. The only touches of colour that were not viridian were a white lace collar and a large sunflower in his buttonhole. Physically he was small, with short legs even for his diminutive height, although his arms were long. His face had a simian aspect, with an upper lip that held a pair of moustaches separated by a wide gap.

At that moment Henry too opened his door.

'My name,' the personage announced in a loud, ringing voice, 'is Edgar Rampoe. I am the assistant art master at Somerville Hall. And I must ask that you leave me alone.'

Henry's eyes bulged slightly. 'Certainly,' he said. 'If you wish it.'

'I am dangerous if provoked,' continued Mr Rampoe. 'I warn you. I will not tolerate further harassment in this matter.'

'The matter of... ?' Henry began.

'Do not dissimulate, Sir.' Our visitor's lips twitched. 'Ever since this business started I have been hounded, positively hounded by the police and the newspapers. And now I hear that you are involved. I know of you, Dr St Liver. I have heard of your branch of science – if indeed it deserves that name. I wish to make it clear that I am innocent, and do not take kindly to base-less suspicions.' His voice rose to a scream. 'I give no interviews! Today I have left Boojum downstairs in the lobby, but the next time you see us, have a care! You will see us both bare our teeth!' He snarled, exposing dun-coloured fangs and a liberal amount of gum. He looked utterly deranged.

Henry's moustache trembled slightly. 'Boojum?' he asked.

'Boojum, Sir, is my baboon! Do not say you have come to Oxford and do not know of Boojum! Do not attempt to deceive me! The whole *world* knows of Boojum!' Mr Rampoe snapped his green cloak about him, widened his eyes and threw us another gingival snarl. 'Do not trifle with us, Doctor!'

And with that, our visitor stalked away down the hall. Turning at the stairwell, he descended and was lost to sight.

Henry remained with his head poking wordlessly out of the door. There was a long silence.

'Did you remark the name of the baboon?' I said at length. 'Boojum. Very similar to the cry of "boojoo!" heard after the attacks.'

'Yes,' Henry said. He emerged from his door. 'But baboons, as far as I am aware, are not able to manipulate scissors and vitriol.'

'Could it not be trained?'

'I doubt if any baboon could be trained to lie in wait for attractive females of another species, carry out an assault of this kind and flee, uttering its own name.'

'Do you have any other theory?' I asked.

'Let us follow Mr Rampoe to Somerville Hall.'

Somerville Hall is, as already mentioned, on the Woodstock Road, only a little up from St Giles, and so not more than three minutes' walk from the hotel in Beaumont Street. The entrance was a sub-ecclesiastical affair in brick: looking further in we could see the window of the porter's lodge.

Henry took some time to examine the pavement outside the Hall, at one point going down on hands and knees. He then walked to the opposite side of the road and stood for a time, looking, as far as I could make out, at nothing in particular. Returning, he pointed over my head, where a wing of the main building jutted up close to the wall, overlooking the road.

'Do you see that?' he asked.

I replied that I did.

'And there is no streetlamp outside the gate,' he added, indicating the place where a streetlamp would have been, had there been one there. 'The only lamp is on the opposite side of the pavement. Rather inconvenient for the young ladies, would you not say?'

'Yes, perhaps a little.'

'Very well then, let us enter.'

Henry stalked past the porter's lodge, in which the porter himself was not in evidence, and made directly for the Hall itself. The main building was a massive rotunda of red brick, quite new-looking, and rather ugly. In the tiled hall-way was a desk; and behind that, a woman with close-set eyes and a long, thin nose, in which several gradations of colour were visible.

'I am here to see the Principal,' Henry said.

'Who shall I say?'

'Dr Henry St Liver and Miss Olive Salter.'

'Is she expecting you?'

'No,' said Henry. 'But I think she will wish to see us.'

'Very well,' said the thin-nosed woman. 'Please wait.' She rose from her desk and disappeared up a side-staircase, and for a long time there was no sound but the tinkling of a piano from across the quad: it was rather a melancholy sound, as if the pian-ist had suffered a romantic disappointment. At length, the door to the staircase re-opened and the thin-nosed woman came out, followed by a personage we assumed to be Mrs Philippa Oth.

Mrs Oth was a tidy little person of around five-and-thirty years of age, with an unlined, intelligent face and an eye in which a mordant humour seemed to gleam. Her hair – very slightly sil-vering at the temples – was tied back in a bun. Pince-nez, with a spare pair around the neck on a gold chain, bespoke the scholar; and indeed, as we later discovered, she was the distinguished authoress of several textbooks on palaeobotany, the investigation of decayed plant matter. Her career, as I also later learned, had not been exclusively academic: she had won a 'blue' for the high jump, the first female to do so, when she had herself attended the Hall as a student in the late 1870s; and after leaving college she had trodden the boards as part of an ensemble known as 'The Heat Girls'. She had been married, but her husband, Dr Oth, a divine and watercolourist, had died when snow fell on him from the roof of Lincoln Cathedral as he attempted to sketch it. One son had been the sole issue.

'Terrible events, Dr St Liver,' began Mrs Oth briskly.

'Terrible indeed,' Henry replied. 'May I present Miss Olive Salter?'

Mrs Oth smiled politely: she did not appear to recognize the name. 'Delighted,' she said.

'You have spoken to my friend, Inspector Pelham Bias?' asked Henry.

'Yes. I will do all in my power to help.'

'Then I have, if you will allow me, a few brief questions.'

'Certainly.'

'Firstly, whose window is it overlooks the gateway?'

'It is my own. It is useful to overlook the entrance. Occasionally a girl is late and a fine must be exacted.' Mrs Oth smiled a little, though the expression soon faded. 'Of course, it has been useful in recent weeks for a more unhappy reason. I have found, on some nights, at about eight or nine in the evening, that I am almost unable to tear myself away from the window – though at the same time fear to look out in case there is a recurrence of these dreadful acts.'

'Might I see the gateway from that vantage point?' asked Henry. 'I think it would help greatly in my investigation.'

'Certainly, if you wish it,' Mrs Oth said.

We ascended the main staircase, and, passing along several corridors, arrived at the east wing, which overlooked the gate. On the way we brushed past numerous of the young ladies of the college, most of them rather plain girls. All looked quizzically at Dr St Liver. I wondered whether we might once again encounter the interesting Mr Rampoe, perhaps this time with Boojum, but neither the art master nor his pet were in evidence.

Mrs Oth's rooms were comfort itself. Ranks of carefully dusted volumes, small tables on which glowed little lamps, and the occasional curve of a marble statuette made up a most agreeable and tasteful picture. Sumptuous curtains and rugs deadened the clatter of wheels from the street. The living-room had but one large window, curtained and more than seven feet in height, which proved to be the very same that Henry had seen from the road; but to my surprise Henry gave it but a cursory glance.

'And your other rooms?' he asked.

'I hardly think they can help you,' Mrs Oth returned, the beginning of a challenge in her tone. 'They do not give out onto Woodstock Road.'

'No, no,' said Henry. 'That is right. I had not yet entirely found my bearings. Well, that is all I require, Mrs Oth. Thank you very much. I have just one duty left to me while I am here at Somerville, and, as I am sure you are busy, I will not delay further. I wish, if possible, to speak to the girls who have been the victims of these attacks.'

'Miss Bastable went down from Oxford to the north of Scotland,' Mrs Oth said briskly, 'immediately after the first assault. Miss Hunt-Furze and Miss Massey are both studying in their rooms, and I would beg you not to disturb them: both have an important examination tomorrow to prepare for. Of the capillary victims, Miss Buss-French, never very stable, seems to have gone completely out of her mind. She is being treated for neurasthenia in the John Radcliffe. That leaves only Miss Angel.'

'And where is Miss Angel?'

'Here, at the Hall. She shares with a Miss Purkiss.'

'Thank you. I will visit her, if I may.'

'You have finished here?'

'Thank you, yes. I will not trespass further on your time.'

The three of us descended again to the first floor, and Mrs Oth led us, via some stone steps, down a low corridor, to a row of small oaken doors. She rapped on one, and after a short delay the form of a girl with cropped blonde hair appeared. She was tall and full in figure, and wearing a crumpled cotton dress. Her bright green eyes, slightly shadowed beneath, were open wide in surprise at the unexpected visit of her Principal.

'Mrs Oth!'

'Lettice, this is Dr St Liver, and Miss Salter, his assistant.'

'Oh! How d'you do?'

'I am sorry to disturb you, Miss Angel,' Henry said soothingly. 'I have formed a theory concerning the origin of these attacks, and wish to ask you one question that may aid me in my researches. It is this.' He paused. 'Are you fond of cured meats?'

'Cured meats?' asked Miss Angel. She looked thoughtfully

for a while at Henry's moustaches. 'Yes... though no more nor less than anyone else, I think.'

'Ham?'

'Yes.'

'Very good. And other cured meats?'

'I once tasted salami, on a visit to Verona. In Italy,' she added.

Unlike her fellow student Miss Buss-French, Miss Angel appeared to be a person of some composure. Neither did she seem, as Pelham Bias had said, 'very miserable'.

'Quite so,' said Henry courteously. 'Well, that is all I wished to say. No doubt you think my questions strange.'

'I am sure that you had a good reason for them.'

'I did. I did indeed. I think it will all become clear very soon. Well, I will let you return to your studies. My deepest thanks.'

Mrs Oth, unspeaking, escorted us to the gate, where we said our goodbyes. Her manner as we parted, in testament to her good breeding, appeared not to have altered greatly toward us, but this latest display on Henry's part seemed almost beyond the bounds of reason. Bottling up my questions I accompanied him back to our rooms.

'Did you notice the carpet?' Henry asked me as we sat down together on his bed. He lit a cigarette.

'Which carpet?'

'In Mrs Oth's room.'

'No. I confess I did not.'

'It was streaked all over with parallel marks.'

'Marks?'

'Yes.'

'Henry, you must tell me what you know.'

Henry looked at me in a rather pained manner. 'At the moment I do not know anything. I have formed an idea, that is all I can say – an idea that came to me as soon as Bias told me of these events – and the only thing to do is to put it to the test.'

'How?'

'Your cooperation, I think, will be required.'

'Very well.'

'What I suggest is as follows. Firstly, we must ask Bias to put a policeman at that gate. We will leave a constable there every evening for a week, between the hours of six and ten. And then, on the eighth day'– he let out a substantial nimbus – 'which, if we begin tonight, will be a Wednesday, we will withdraw the policeman. The perpetrator will see his chance, and, starved of his own peculiar form of gratification, will strike. You must be the victim.'

'I?'

'Yes. It will be necessary, I think, to make a small foray into your repertoire of disguise. You have a blonde wig?'

'Yes.'

'Long?'

'I can put my hands on both a long and a short, as needed.'

'If you can find one of unusual luxuriance, that will serve our purposes best. The suspect will strike at your hair.'

'And then?'

'I and the police will lie in wait.'

'I see.' I paused, wondering what possible bearing the cured meats, the parallel tracks, the disposition of streetlamps, &c &c,

had on the case, which, it seemed, had now descended to my acting as a decoy for a man who was in all probability insane.

'Please do not worry,' said Henry, divining my thoughts. 'I would not ask this of you if I thought there was the least possibility of your being harmed. I think I can guarantee that the perpetrator is as sane as you or I.'

'That, at least, is a comfort,' I said.

Henry insisted that we leave Oxford during the week he had mentioned, and we took the next train back to London.

On our return my asthma reacted very badly to the dreary fogs that curled around Grosvenor Road, and I immediately confined myself to bed. While I lay there I continued work on my new book. I had by now roughed it out in my mind: it would follow the same young woman, or a remarkably similar one, to a large city – possibly London – where she would attempt to make a life for herself, possibly as a woman doctor, all the time much afflicted with sleeplessness and melancholia and the pain of leaving behind the scenes of her childhood and their rather more bracing climate.

After a few days of rest my asthma improved – although my eczema was at the same time worsening, exacerbated by the large amounts of bromide I was taking to combat a related problem – and I left my bed to begin preparations for the coming adventure. I had managed to borrow a blonde wig from a theatrical acquaintance, and also found a dress that I thought might suit the occasion: it was a pink house-dress, the sort of crumpled and unfashionable attire habitually worn by the ladies of Oxford. Over it, I thought, a similarly rumpled and slightly stained cape, with perhaps a bulky jet necklace, would complete the picture of an amorous bluestocking in a fever of impatience for her sizar lover.

Wednesday arrived, gloomy and fog-bound. Purely from an atmospheric point of view, I was looking forward to our return to Oxford, even though it meant placing myself in close proximity to a madman with a pair of scissors. We took the 2.20 from Paddington, and on arrival at the little hotel at Beaumont Street, I hurried to change for the evening's undertaking.

'Excellent,' Henry said, as I displayed the complete ensemble. You are transformed. That is important. The attacker must not recognize you.'

'Why?'

'We have already been much in evidence around the Hall. If the attacker were to become suspicious that a trap had been set, then the whole venture would certainly fail.'

'Of course.'

'Now, at half-past eight I will give Bias instructions to withdraw the policeman; you will then take your place.'

'I understand.'

'You should wait facing the road, around ten feet from the gate, and to the left side, unmoving, and should not under any circumstances turn around. I will be watching from a hansom on the corner of Little Clarendon Street. One constable will be with me, and two other plain-clothes men stationed nearby.'

'Very good.'

'You should make some show of looking at your pocket-watch from time to time, as if waiting for some meeting or assignation.'

'Yes.'

'Excellent. Well, I think we might start.'

It was now eight fifteen. As we made our way from the hotel, I trying not to scratch (the wig was very irritating, and, as I have said, I suffer from eczema), my mind was still rather full of my new book, which, I was starting to think, might include some more adventurous element (in addition to its medical theme), perhaps even some element of criminal romance. As I took my place outside Somerville Hall, I had almost forgotten about baboons and scissors. It is very odd how sometimes literature seems almost to be a substitute for life.

For perhaps twenty-five minutes there was nothing except itching. Students passed in and out of the gate, a few glancing idly at me; a group of Italian nuns stopped to gape at the monument at the top of St Giles; and a group of rowdies coming out from Keble College made some remarks. A bill-sticker had posted a notice on some hoardings opposite: 'BOO FOR SAB', it read, in huge letters: a legend entirely impenetrable, to me at least. Was there a link between 'Boo' and 'Boojum'? And what was 'Sab?'

The minutes continued to tick by in the gathering gloom, and I was beginning to think that it was perhaps all for nothing, and when all of a sudden I saw out of the corner of my eye a small dark shape creeping along the pavement. My senses were instantly afire. It was all I could do not to recoil or run; but I affected to pay it no notice, and instead turned slightly away from the shape, presenting my hair. In a moment, with a sudden shuffling sound and a cackle, the creature was on me. Revulsion overtook me as I felt hot breath on my neck, and the hands of the thing grasp my wig. I jerked my head in panic. The wig came entirely off, and I stumbled forward with an inarticulate cry. The creature too uttered a shrill of surprise, and then, pausing briefly in confusion, scampered rapidly away from me, clutching the hair in its left hand. As it flashed past me I had a brief opportunity to observe it: it was a low form of indeterminate sex or species, possibly wearing black clothing and a mask. In its left hand (or claw) was the hair, and the right held a pair of wicked-looking shears. But, as I say, this was a brief impression only, for the creature accelerated astonishingly quickly away from me; and as it ran, quite clearly gave tongue to a cry of 'Boojum! Boojum!' It then sped up Woodstock Road, away from Henry in the hansom, and toward Observatory Street. Soon it had entirely disappeared from view.

I heard a police whistle, and Henry ran up and stood before me gasping.

'You are unhurt?'

'Yes!' I cried. 'Did you see it? And did you hear –?'

A plain-clothes man puffed towards us from the direction the creature had taken.

'What news?' Henry shouted.

'What?' asked the policeman in dismay. 'Didn't you catch it?'

'No!' groaned Henry. 'The miscreant ran in your direction!'

'I heard the whistle and came directly!' the policeman replied. 'It must have got over the wall!'

'Then there is not a moment to lose!' Henry cried. He sprinted into Somerville Hall, past the porter's lodge (the porter had now emerged and was gazing stupidly), and into the main building.

Ignoring the thin-nosed woman, Henry clattered up the main staircase, with myself and two of the plain-clothes men in hot pursuit. Screams and shrieks erupted around us as we elbowed our way past particoloured bevies of young ladies to arrive at Mrs Oth's rooms. Henry, his eyes blazing, pounded upon her door.

'Mrs Oth! Mrs Oth!,' he shouted. 'Open up!'

The door opened and Mrs Oth stood before us.

'What has happened?' she asked, staring at the four of us. 'Another attack?'

'Yes, Mrs Oth,' said Henry grimly. 'Another attack. And I must ask to search your chambers.'

'Why?' asked Mrs Oth. 'What could you possibly think to find here?'

'I think you know, Madam,' Henry said. He pushed past her. The policemen and I followed. Henry rushed to the further of the two doors leading off from the main room and threw it wide open. Mrs Oth uttered a sob. In the middle of the little bedroom, gazing at us in terror, was a young man seated in a wheelchair. On his lap was the yellow wig.

The policeman took one look. 'Mrs Philippa Oth,' he said, showing his badge, 'I arrest you on suspicion of assault on five students: Miss Jemima Bastable, Miss Titania Hunt-Furze, Miss Mary Massey, Miss Belinda Buss-French, and Miss Lettice Angel.'

At the little café in Walton Street the waiter brought us each a celebratory glass. Mrs Oth had been taken into custody, along with the boy, her son. It had been pitiful to see how he had fretted and mumbled at the wig as he was wheeled away.*

'Mrs Oth,' said Pelham Bias, fingering his wine disbelievingly. 'I would never have thought it possible. And now her career is in ruins.'

Henry took a small sip of his cassis.

'The time has come, Henry,' I said. 'How on earth did you know?'

The corners of Henry's eyes moved. 'It was chiefly a matter of considering the psychological origins of the crimes,' he said. 'In a case such as this, the investigator should be able to take an initial compelling fact and work through to the sole and inevitable solution. The pursuit of a single line of logic, ignoring other considerations – that is the key.'

'I am not sure I understand.'

'The crimes were ones of despoliation.' Henry put down his glass, though not quite on the table: it fell and broke. 'Two ink-throwing incidents, one vitriol, and two incidents of capillary kleptomania. On the surface perhaps quite disparate: but at a deeper level very much of a piece.'

'But why Mrs Oth?' asked Pelham Bias.

'Mrs Oth was not acting for her own gratification, but that of her son. Confined to his wheelchair, he was able to observe the events outside the gate. That was the meaning of the parallel tracks in the carpet near the window: they were the marks of his wheels.'

---

* Unfortunately the wig had been borrowed and I would now have to find a replacement.

'So the shape that we thought was a baboon was in fact Mrs Oth?'

'Yes – although I am sure I never thought it was a baboon. Mr Rampoe is an unpleasant man, to be sure, and it is tempting to make any man with an ungovernable temper and a baboon into a suspect. But I soon realized that the location of the attacks was the key to uncovering their perpetrator.'

'Why?' I asked.

'Someone who wished merely to despoil the females of Oxford could do so anywhere. The maids of Oxford do not confine their existence to a small spot ten feet from the gate of Somerville Hall.'

'That is true.'

'The location must therefore have been chosen for a reason; and the most likely reason, it seemed to me, was that the despoiler wished to be observed there. It was certainly a grave risk for him – or her – to repeat the attacks in the very same spot each time. Only an overriding necessity forced the choice: the necessity of being observed by a confederate, whom the attacks were designed to stimulate. The most intriguing aspect of the case, therefore, was that the despoiler was not in the strict sense a despoiler, but a despoiler-by-proxy.'

'Ah,' sighed Pelham Bias.

'The best vantage-point,' Henry continued, 'for observing the attacks, and thus the hiding-place of the confederate, was, naturally, the window overlooking the gate. That was my main reason for eliminating the porter. He could not see the attacks as they happened: they took place ten feet outside and to the left of the gate. Even if he had been in league with the despoiler-by-proxy, he could not have witnessed them. And although he was doubtless granted an erotic windfall when Miss Massey was compelled to remove her clothing in his lodge, immediate undressing was not necessitated in either the ink-throwing or hair-removal attacks. The porter was therefore without possible motive.'

'I see,' said Pelham Bias. 'What then of the time? The attacks all took place at dusk.'

'Indeed they did. It was only then that the low light would offer some cover for the assailant. If they took place later, at night, conditions would be favourable for an attack, but since there was no streetlamp outside the gate – a circumstance I noted on our first inspection of the scene – the despoliations would be of little use to the hidden spectator.'

'So let me, if I may, summarize,' I said. 'Mrs Oth, for the entertainment of her son, who was watching from the window overlooking the gate, came out on five occasions, dressed in dark clothes and a mask, and defiled the lady students of her own college, before fleeing and uttering the name of Mr Rampoe's ape?'

'That is correct. Mrs Oth, as we discovered, had some reputation as an athlete in her former days, and could put on a formidable turn of speed. She had competed as a high jump specialist; too late I realized that she must have used this skill to get over the wall and elude our plain-clothes man. Her theatrical experience, too, came in useful, enabling her to disguise her appearance.'

'Then why the cry of "Boojum!"?'

'A transparent attempt to throw investigators off. Given his aggressive and surly mien, Mr Rampoe would inevitably become a suspect in any investigation. It is quite possible also that Mrs Oth found him an embarrassment to the Hall and wished to incriminate him.'

'I see,' I said. 'I see. Well, then, only one thing remains. Why did you ask Miss Angel whether she was fond of cured meats?'

'Ah... that was for Mrs Oth's benefit. If Mrs Oth had not been there, I would certainly not have asked the question.'

'So it had no significance?'

'None, except to throw off Mrs Oth's suspicions. Mrs Oth is a highly intelligent woman. We had that moment visited and inspected her rooms; it was quite possible she was beginning to think we were on her trail. I knew that the next phase of the investigation would involve a decoy. If she suspected a trap, all was lost. With that in mind, I wished her to think that we were following an entirely erroneous line of reasoning, and this I attempted to achieve with the mention of cured meats. Clearly there was nothing in the case connected with cured meats. But as long as Mrs Oth thought that we were under the misapprehension that cured meats played any part, our work would be easier. Cured meats were *outré* enough to encourage Mrs Oth to think that my methods were eccentric, erroneous, perhaps even insane.'

'First class,' said Pelham Bias, shifting slowly in his chair. 'The general footing of your method seems very firm. But I am still not very clear on the whole matter of... despoliation, as you put it.'

'Surely it is obvious?'

'Not to me, I am afraid,' said Pelham Bias. 'I confess I find it quite incomprehensible.'

'It is a central tenet of the erotic symbolisms that what is incomprehensible to one individual might form the centrepiece of the erotic life of another.'

'The attacks were symbolic attacks?'

'In a sense. The normal man finds the act of sexual conjugation at the focus of his desires. But for others, symbols of that basic conjugation substitute for the act itself. For example, a desire for self-gratification in a municipal rose-garden might originate in the correspondence between the shape of a rose's petals and a woman's external genitalia. Thus it is with the despoiler: his acts are an attempt to mimic coitus. Let us take first the ink-throwings. Krafft-Ebing presents a typical case. A young man of twenty-five, of good heredity, has acquired, as a child, a fetich for women's linen underclothing, after having observed the underclothing of his sister and her friends while they were romping on a bed. Afterwards he can only become excited by women wearing white dresses. One day, when walking out with a young lady so attired, it happens that a cart comes past and spatters her from head to foot with muddy water. Soon afterwards he begins fantasizing about a repetition of these events, and leaves his job in the city to become a cab driver. His method is to lie in wait near large muddy pools at the side of the road until ladies in white dresses are strolling by, then to drive rapidly alongside them, sending torrents of fluid spattering all over their virginal garments. This activity is usually accompanied by erection and ejaculation, and sometimes the loss of control of his vehicle. Eventually he abandons his cab and extends his activities to the throwing of fluids onto the dresses of young ladies as they pass him in the street: his favoured substances are ink, perchloride of iron, and sulphuric acid, the defilement thus extending to the destruction, not simply the dirtying, of the clothing. I believe the case was in the *Zeitschrift für Medizinalbeamte*. The symbolism of the ejection of fluid, the marking and the possession of the object, et caetera, is too obvious to merit comment.'

'Quite,' I said.

'What is perhaps less obvious is the continuity of symbolism in the case of hair despoliation. Hair is a normal focus of sexual desire, of course. Hair, though, is quite unlike most other parts of the body in being intermediate between a living and a dead state: it can be removed painlessly from the body in the same way as clothing. Thus, psychologically, it may be treated as an item of clothing, as if it were a dress, or a shoe, or a glove; and obsessive fascination with it falls into the category of clothing fetishism we have just been discussing.'

A woman wearing a magnificent crimson ball gown passed, doubtless on her way to some University function. Her dark hair, tied up, was intricately interfolded in the style known as the 'porter's knot'.

'Hair despoliation,' continued Henry, 'is common in all countries. In France the despoiler is known as a *coupeur des nattes*, and in Germany as a *Zopfabschneider*. The despoiler will typically follow a woman with exceptionally long or beautiful hair, worn either loose or plaited. When he sees an opportunity, he will snip off a piece – perhaps a few strands, perhaps a generous hank – and run with his prize. An illustrative case appeared in the *Annals de Hygiène* of – if my memory serves me – some time in 1890: a young man of below average cranial development, married with no children, suffered a fever, and after his recovery was overtaken by a mania for hair. He took to following women in the street, pouncing on them and cutting off their braids, which he would either take home to enjoy, or throw away before reaching home. He was eventually caught after perpetrating more than a hundred such attacks, and sentenced to five years in prison. The cutting of the hair is the same as the ink upon the dress; the destruction of an object intimately associated with woman, though not the woman herself, and thus at one remove from the aggressive and despoliative aspects of coitus. In Pope's *Rape of the Lock* we have a mock-heroic treatment of the subject.'

Henry had made these remarks in a loud, high voice, and had attracted considerable interest from the other patrons of the café (it was Oxford, after all): several people had moved their chairs nearer to our table, and, as he delivered his peroration, there was a smattering of applause. The waiter then approached with an apologetic air and asked us to leave.

The three of us walked slowly down Walton Street, where the sad stones of the University Press buildings glimmered black and gold in the fading dusk. Another huge poster reading 'BOO FOR SAB'* was plastered around one of the pillars at the entrance.

'And it was all for love,' I said, breaking the meditative silence that had descended on us.

---

* A 'Sab', I later discovered, is a student 'sabbatical' officer. Evidently it was an election poster.

Henry turned to me with a tender glance.

'Yes,' he said feelingly, 'with your customary insight, my dear Miss Salter, you have hit on the phenomenon that truly lies at the heart of this case. A mother's love for her son. What else was open to him, a cripple, in the sphere of sexual relations? For him, fetichistic symbolism had entirely taken the place of the sexual act. He must have confessed his desires to his mother, who then resolved to do whatever she could to help him, even at the risk of her own livelihood. Love, yes; and mingled inextricably with it, darker forces.' He paused. 'How does Pope begin his poem? "What dire offence from am'rous causes springs?"'

CHAPTER THREE

The Well-born Client

In late 1893, temporarily putting aside my sequel to *The Story of an Australian Barn*, I set myself the task of sifting through the mass of material I had collected concerning Henry's cases, with the idea of presenting each in a narrative form. There were five cases in that year which, for their intricacy and novelty, I thought might be laid before the public: they were 'The Case of the Three Lemons'; 'The Case of the Disturbed Baker'; 'The Case of the Missing Flabellum'; 'The Case of the Crimson Box'; and, of course, 'The Case of the Oxford Despoiler'. I soon worked them into shape, discarding some of the wilder speculations with which Henry sometimes embellished his investigations, and they duly appeared in the *New Age* in the February, March and April of 1894. They were an immediate success.

It was while I was occupied in further perusal of my notes in the late April of 1894 (the dramatic points of the affair of the Fruiterer's Toe had particularly caught my eye) that I realised with a start that I knew next to nothing of Henry's earliest life. My readers, I felt, would be sure to want details of it. Henry, however, had never shown the slightest inclination to talk about this period. I resolved, therefore, to quiz him on the subject as soon as possible.

The opportunity came a few days later. It was a warm spring afternoon, and we were sitting amid the burgeoning shrubs of Henry's little back garden. All around was the smell of the awakened earth; insects were flitting hither and thither, and so on. I and Henry were reclining in deckchairs, writing, reading and talking in a desultory fashion. After a time I brought up the subject of my own childhood, and told him a little of my youth in Australia. Then, as casually as I could, I turned the conversation to Henry's own early years, asking him in general terms about his family. To my great pleasure, he seemed perfectly willing to talk.

I learned that he had been born in Croydon. His father had been a sea captain, and Henry, as a child of no more than six, had in fact sailed with his father around the world, and put in at all of the ports of the Indies, Africa, and the Far East. At this time his only education had been acquired by means of a collected Shakespeare and one or two volumes of the Lake poets, as well as the *Biographia Literaria*. However, when Henry reached the age of nine, the trips were curtailed and his mother sent him away to a small boarding school in Wales. Oxford followed, though for one term only: Henry left Balliol without a degree and went to London to undergo medical training. It was at this time, I supposed, that he had developed his rather specialized interests. By the age of four-and-twenty he was an M.D., though, due to circumstances he always seemed rather to skate over, he did not practise. Instead, his imagination fed by memories of Callao, Shanghai and Trincomalee, he set off once again tramping around the world, and after many adventures settled in South Africa, at first in Cape Town and then with the native peoples of Ndeleleland, near Potchefstroom.

'And did you truly live as a native?' I asked him.

'Certainly,' Henry replied, his eyes closed against the weak spring sun. 'I joined in all the customs and traditions of that remarkable people.'

'You dressed in native costume?'

'Yes: I lived as an Ndelele. It was not always an easy existence, of course. The Ndelele, you know, live to a large extent on the discarded products of our industrial age. They take the refuse of others and rehabilitate it for their own purposes. In Ndeleleland everything is of some utility. A blunt razor, a piece of string, a cardboard box, et caetera – all can be reclaimed and re-used in some way or another.'

'Ah.'

'I learned to respect this mode of living. And after I had been with them for a year I endured the *bela*, or male initiation ceremony.'

'What did that involve?'

Henry's hand shot out as if involuntarily, and knocked over a small table piled with sexological papers. He opened his eyes. 'The ceremony involved a small physical modification,' he said, 'followed by a period of seclusion. I was confined to a cramped and sweltering hut for three days. While there, I was expected to meditate on various tribal ancestors and their doings. As I did not have any tribal ancestors, I had to resort to memories of my own family life.'

'In Croydon?'

'Yes.'

'I see.'

'When they took me from the hut I was almost insensible.'

'And was your life much changed after the *bela*?'

'Certainly. I was now a full-fledged member of the Ndelele, and took up a post as an advisor to a local nobleman, a young man by the name of Gosi. The Ndelele live as scavengers, but they still have a functioning hereditary aristocracy. I was not much help to him, I fear. A problem involving the theft of some artificial legs went unresolved; at the time it cast rather a cloud over my career. A year after my *bela* I was already back in England.' Henry sat up suddenly in his deckchair. 'But talk of Gosi rather reminds me of something.' He poked around in his clothing and produced a grubby piece of paper: by the look of it, a telegram. 'I think that if you had not reminded me of Gosi I would entirely have forgotten. We are to be favoured today with the visit of a princeling of a home-grown variety.'

I was rather annoyed that our talk had been cut short, but could not help feeling curious as Henry handed me the telegram. I studied it: it was dated that morning, and read as follows:

SHALL BE PASSING THIS AFTERNOON ABOUT 3 STOP WOULD GREATLY APPRECIATE YOUR HELP AND ADVICE IN DIFFICULT MATTER STOP MAY HAVE READ ABOUT IT IN THE NEWSPAPERS STOP CANNOT SAY ANYTHING FURTHER NOW STOP MATTER OF NATIONAL IMPORTANCE STOP ABOUT 3 THEN IF IT IS CONVENIENT STOP YOURS N—

'What do you make of that?' Henry asked.

'The communication has a rather hectic and babbling tone,' I said.

'Yes.'

'The sender is not short of money.'

'Our client is of high rank, yes.'

'Yes. Well, then... The mention of the newspapers – there have been several cases in recent weeks of members of the aristocracy – if such he is – getting into difficulties of one kind or another.'

'Can you think of any of relevance to my field of enquiry?'

'Not immediately.'

'Then the name N—?'

'Could it be the Lord N—?'

'Well, you will soon have a chance to decide for yourself,' Henry said. He rose from his seat. 'For, unless I am mistaken, here comes our visitor now.'

Turning in my deckchair, I saw a figure crunching towards us on the little gravel path. I was greatly astonished. It was indeed Lord N—, that illustrious scion of the N—s of R—.

The name of N— will be familiar to many readers. It was the same Lord N— who later held a cabinet post in the government of Lord M—, and was so prominent in the coalition of L—G—. In person he was every bit as imposing a presence as his portraits made out. As tall as Henry, he was broader in every direction, and was dressed, as might be expected, with faultless elegance: long frock coat, pale yellow silk waistcoat, striped trousers, high-buttoning spats and shining Oxford boots. Although not yet five-and-thirty, his mode of life, in which every pleasure had been repeatedly gratified, had left its mark on him. There was a voluptuous decay in the soft lines and folds of the face.

We went forward to meet him. Henry shook his hand.

'I do hope you will forgive my coming in,' Lord N— said. 'I knocked and received no reply. But I heard voices. So I thought I would investigate.' He smiled.

'You are very welcome,' said Henry. 'Please join us – we have an extra deckchair.'

'Thank you,' said Lord N—. 'But I will stand.' He glanced at me.

'My apologies,' Henry said. 'This is Miss Salter.'

'Ah, Miss Salter,' said Lord N—. He extended a plump hand. 'I have read your accounts of Dr St Liver's cases in the *New Age*. Very entertaining. But this is not a matter anyone can read about, you know. I cannot have this turned into a short story.'

'Oh, certainly not, if you do not wish it,' I said.

'You give your word?'

'Of course.'

Lord N—, still grasping my hand, regarded me soberly. Then his mood seemed to lighten. 'Excellent,' he said.

'Shall we go into the house?' Henry asked.

'Yes, yes,' said Lord N—. 'I think it would be preferable if we discussed this matter in a more intimate setting.'

We filed into the comparative gloom of the house and soon were seated around the small dining-table that had been the scene of so many remarkable revelations. Lord N— shifted a little uncomfortably in his place by the stuffed snow leopard.

Whether his unease was due to Henry's domestic arrangements, or to the dark secret he had doubtless come to reveal, or to the fact of my presence, or to his large size, or the circumstance that his frock-coat had now picked up a certain amount of plaster dust – or some combination of the five – it was difficult to say. He kept glancing out of the bay window to the street, where a smart phaeton and a pair of greys was waiting.

'Yes. I have a most difficult matter to communicate,' Lord N— said at length. 'Very difficult. I think I mentioned as much in my telegram. It is truly a matter of national importance. On the other hand – if this is not a paradox – it is also a matter of a most private and personal nature. I must ask you to give it your most serious attention.'

'I will give it the attention I reserve for each of my clients,' Henry replied gravely.

'Well, I cannot ask for more, I suppose,' said Lord N—, looking a little surprised. 'I will lay the salient points before you, then. You are aware that I am about to be married?'

'The press coverage has been remarkably full,' Henry said.

'Indeed. The bride of course is Lady Violet L—R—, of the Berkshire L—R—s. I have known her since we were children. Her father and mother are Lord and Lady J—, of U— Hall in Warwickshire.'

Henry gave a nod.

'As you say, it is difficult to be unaware of the preparations. The papers talk of nothing else. Westminster Abbey. The Bishop of London. The hundreds of guests, the cake, two junior members of the royal family among the guests, Prince F— and Princess

C—. The government represented by the Foreign Secretary and the Chancellor. In brief, it is to be the society wedding of the year. *Tout le monde.*' Lord N— made a sweeping gesture. 'And all would be well,' he sighed, '– all would be well – if I did not have the irresistible urge – ' He paused and sucked in his lower lip – 'to display myself.'

Henry gazed at Lord N—. His moustache twitched. 'You refer to –?'

'Yes.'

'You desire to exhibit yourself?'

'Yes.' Lord N— passed his hand over his forehead and uttered a small choking sound. 'In churches. I have an uncontrollable tendency to display myself in churches.'

'I see,' said Henry.

Lord N— looked up. 'It has been this way with me ever since I can remember. I have no idea how or why – or even when – it started. Possibly it had to do with a game we played as children. We would all go down to the servants' hall and march around, pulling up our smocks, and the servants would clap. But these memories are very faint. And perhaps they are not so dissimilar from the general run of childhood experiences.'

He paused, collecting himself.

'Was your childhood otherwise happy?' asked Henry.

'My home life was in every respect a healthy and a happy one,' Lord N— said. 'I am an only child, and my parents were both exceptionally kind and loving. I should perhaps tell you though that my father suffers – to this day – from epilepsy, and that one of my aunts too has some of this congenital affliction. In other branches of the N— line there is also a strain of idiocy. Perhaps that is of relevance, perhaps not.'

'You are not yourself epileptic?'

'No.'

'Thank you,' said Henry. 'Please omit no detail, however insignificant it may seem to you. Your case is of exceptional interest.'

'Yes. Well I too find it of some interest, Doctor,' our visitor said bitterly. 'Unless you can help me, I am about to suffer the most complete public disgrace in the history of the English aristocracy.'

'Forgive me,' Henry said. 'Please continue.'

'Very well then,' said Lord N—, a little mollified. He paused. 'What is there to tell? I began yielding to this temptation in perhaps my fifteenth year. I suppose I have displayed myself on dozens of occasions. I find I am more attracted to the larger sort of church. I do not favour either the young or the old as witnesses: as long as the persons to whom I display myself are of the female sex their age does not greatly matter. I usually strike while they are in attitude of prayer. I wait until I am sure of being seen, and then I walk over to them. As they look up, I display myself. I observe their faces very carefully while I am doing this.'

'Yes.'

'I believe it is the interchange of ideas that I desire more than anything. My organ is not in a state of excitement. It is quiescent. The atmosphere is sombre. I seek to communicate something – I hardly know what... I watch their faces to see if they understand. I see shock; surprise; horror. Sometimes I imagine them talking about it afterwards. *Did you see it? Have you ever seen anyone do anything like that? And in church?* And so on.

'My intention is not sacrilegious. Far from it. But the act must take place in church – if it does not, the act does not have its full significance. I know of men who feel compelled to display themselves in school playgrounds to little children, or in Harrods to shopgirls. I find their behaviour incomprehensible, and not a little tasteless. I repeat: in my case, without the religious aspect, the act is robbed of its meaning. Please imagine the scene: the women are praying; they kneel; their minds are on higher things. Then they look up, and see me before them. They must know that, if I display myself in this manner, it is done in full seriousness. It is not merely to gratify myself. I wish to lead them to a conclusion that they might not have arrived at without my intervention.'

'May I ask a question?' said Henry.

'Certainly.'

'You have never been apprehended in this activity?'

'By the police? Once, many years ago. There was some unpleasantness, but charges were never brought.'

'And, since then, you have continued in this practice, as you say on numerous, dozens of occasions, without any scandal attaching to you?'

'Not quite. You run ahead of me, Doctor. I realized that if I went on with it, I would sooner or later make the mistake of displaying myself before some woman who would not rest until she had dragged my name in the mud. I considered using a mask or a disguise of some sort – but decided that such a thing would utterly impede my primary purpose, that of the interchange of ideas. And so I arrived at the only possible solution.'

'Which is?'

'I go abroad, I go abroad,' he said with an airy gesture. 'I have not displayed myself in an English church for two decades. I have, in fact, not been in an English church. If I had, I would undoubtedly have given in to temptation. No: France, Italy, Spain, the Catholic countries. The idea of displaying myself in a Lutheran church has little appeal. Fortunately, on the Continent, they take a liberal view. A few francs or lire generally helps smooth the matter over.'

'But now you will be forced, for the first time in many years, to enter a church at home.'

'Yes. And I am sure the temptation will be too strong. It is not that I have no fibre whatever, you know. I struggled for years before I yielded to the temptation to visit St Peter's in Rome. But this – Westminster Abbey, the Chancellor – it is too much, too much. I know, when the time comes – and in front of the Chancellor! – that I shall simply be unable to resist.'

'I do not wish to intrude,' I said, 'but might I make a suggestion?'

'Certainly,' said Lord N—.

'Does your fiancée know anything of these... compulsions?'

'An excellent question. No, Lady Violet is in complete ignorance. I have never discussed the intimate aspects of marriage with her in any way.'

'Could not she – soon to be your loving wife – help and guide you through the ceremony?'

'Much as I love Lady Violet,' said Lord N—, 'I do not think

there is a woman or man alive in the world who could prevent me from committing the act of self-destruction that is inevitable on Sunday the 7th of May this year, in just ten days' time – unless it is Dr St Liver.' He threw a look of appeal at Henry. 'You, Sir, are my last hope. I admit that I was not even aware persons such as yourself – with your particular specialization – existed, until recently. It was Miss Salter's essays that kindled the flame of hope in my breast. I was immensely relieved when I discovered that you were not a fictional character.'

'Yes,' Henry said doubtfully. 'Well, I am much gratified by your confidence.'

'Can you help me?'

'Ten days, you say.' Henry considered for a moment. 'Well, it is a not an unique case, and is one on which the literature is unlikely to be entirely silent.'

'Very good.'

'I will look into it, certainly. But I am afraid I cannot give an immediate answer. I must think.'

'Then think, Doctor, think! Ten days! Ten days to avert a scandal that would rock the nation! Not to mention the dire personal consequences – would the marriage not be annulled there and then on grounds of insanity? And my career? Everything, everything is at stake!'

'Yes. Yes, it is as you say.'

The Lord N— got up from his chair. 'If you could solve this conundrum I would gladly part with a thousand pounds. But perhaps it is beyond even your powers. Well, I shall look forward to hearing from you, Doctor.'

He bowed in his courtly way to me, then to Henry, and made his way with a preoccupied shaking of the head out of the morning-room and down the front path. Henry and I watched as he stepped into his phaeton; then the liveried driver whipped up the horses and the Lord N— was borne off at a brisk trot.

'What on earth are we to do, Henry?' I asked as we watched him go.

Henry sat down heavily, raising a small cloud of plaster dust. 'This is indeed a difficult case,' he said at last. 'And with so much at stake. If only Christianity did not take such a narrow view of the exposure of the sexual parts.'

'What do you mean?'

'The noble Lord's behaviour, and the sacerdotal manner he seems to adopt on these occasions, recalls the phallic cults of the ancient Mediterranean. In these ancient cultures the "display" he speaks of would be regarded as quite orthodox during the performance of religious rites. Indeed its absence, one might go so far as to say, would be remarked upon. Bloch has some illuminating remarks in his *Beiträge zur Psychopathia Sexualis*.'

'But this is not the ancient Mediterranean, Henry. Nor is it Germany. This is England. And of all the possible solutions, the complete overhaul of the Anglican liturgy in the space of two weeks seems to me the least practicable one.'

'The situation also rather calls to mind the predicament experienced by the poet Coleridge.'

'Coleridge?' I said. 'Did Coleridge too… ?'

'No, Coleridge was not afflicted with this particular mania.'

'Then why do you mention him?' I asked.

Henry looked at me imperturbably with his moist hazel eyes. 'It seems to me that our noble visitor is experiencing a dilemma in which two opposing states of mind are in conflict,' he said. 'On the one side are the sexual and emotional centres, which demand the gratification he spoke of. On the other side are the higher centres of reason and wisdom. But the higher centres have been weakened. They are no longer able to counteract the deep compulsions of the sexual centres. The mention of epilepsy was, I believe, significant: the epilepsy and the other heritable mental disease mentioned by Lord N— may have been responsible for the weakening of the higher centres.'

'But how does this relate to the author of "Christabel"?'

'Ah yes. Coleridge was, of course, an opium addict. His favoured method of ingesting the drug was in the preparation known as laudanum, a tincture of alcohol and opium. De Quincey relates that Coleridge once attempted to wean himself from his addiction by hiring a man to prevent him bodily from entering any druggist.'

'I still fail to see... '

'The hired man, symbolically, was Coleridge's higher self.'

'Oh.'

'Coleridge, you see, had failed to deploy successfully his own higher centres, his own powers of rational control. But he tried to, as it were, buy this agency back, by having another act as his ratiocinative self.'

'And did it work?'

'No,' Henry said. 'No, such a scheme was doomed, of course. As the man's employer, Coleridge could at any time countermand his own orders. But Coleridge was nothing if not ingenious. He went one step further. He settled on a password which he agreed to use only in desperation, formulated so that he would shrink from uttering it, and only on its production would the man be permitted to let him pass into the druggist. I do not know what the password was, but I imagine it reflected badly on Coleridge himself: "Coleridge is an ass", or something of the sort. Unfortunately however Coleridge broke down and had recourse to this password in the first half-hour of his self-imposed forbearance. As a consequence he was forced to devise ever more absurd and humiliating passwords, ending, inevitably, in a form of words which commanded the man to attend him post-haste in the performance of an obscene act. This caused the man, a leech-gatherer by profession, so much confusion that he became irrecoverably insane within a few days of Coleridge employing him.'

'Then how does this help?'

'Help? I am afraid it does not help – except perhaps to re-state the problem in a different way, which is occasionally useful.'

'I see.'

'Lord N—, like the poet, can, at any time, reverse the decision of his rational self. As long as the primitive side of his being is the stronger, the voice of reason will always be stilled, despite the very highest stakes; perhaps, indeed, *because* of the very highest stakes. He seemed to suggest, did he not, that it was the very magnificence of the occasion that made the act a foregone conclusion.'

'So there is nothing to be done?'

'The Coleridgean route may have something to offer us, even if only tangentially. The notion of a drug, for example. If Lord N— could be sedated sufficiently, so that he would be capable of uttering the marriage vows, but disinclined to display himself...'

'But who knows what effect an untried sedative might have?' I said. 'Might it not relax him still further?'

Henry considered. 'Well, I shall have to think,' he said. And he rose and clumped up the stairs.

For a day or two I did not see much of Henry. I was at the time much involved in various clubs and societies. I had joined more of these than I could strictly keep up with, and listened to innumerable talks on vegetarianism, the salvation of the working man, polygamy, four-dimensional space and so on and so forth. It was at the Progressive Association, I think, the day after the visit of Lord N—, that I met Mr Karl Keane.

Mr Keane surprised me by telling me he had read my book, and his comments showed that he had done so with some attention, though he seemed to have drawn something of a mono-dimensional message from it, viz that 'sex intercourse is the great sacrament of life'. I replied that I was not sure that that was *entirely* the moral of my book, and that I was concerned more for true and right relations between man and woman.

'Yes. Right relations. Very good,' he said. We were rather hemmed in together under a spiral staircase in the busy meeting-room. 'But do you not seek release from the snare?'

'The snare?'

'The snare that imprisons us in habits of thought foreign to our true natures. The snare tightened by mothers, fathers, priests and prophets. The snare that limits true burstative power.'

'I confess I have never heard the word "burstative" before,' I said, backing away slightly and holding up my glass of shandy.

'It is my own coining,' he replied.

Karl was in some ways my ideal man: virile, passionate, handsome, radical in politics, unafraid to speak his mind – and also, as I later learned, suffering from a wasting disease that would kill him within the year. We fell madly in love, and the next three days were perhaps the happiest of my life. I soon resolved to tell him of the problem concerning Lord N—, and to elicit, if possible, his help.

It was on the Monday after Lord N—'s visit, I remember, that Karl dropped by at my rooms in Grosvenor Road. I had already told him of Henry St Liver and his work – he had been skeptical, I remember, but that was the common reaction of many – and I now took the opportunity of apprising him of the grave danger looming at the nuptials of Lord N—. Karl's response, I was utterly dismayed to witness, was to burst into gales of laughter.

'Lord N—!' he shouted. 'He likes to…!'

'Yes,' I interrupted. 'It is a problem ingrained since youth.'

'Ha ha ha! And in front of the royal family! And the world's press! I hope the cameras are out in force! Ha ha ha ha!'

'Really, Karl, how can you joke?'

'You press the button, we do the rest! Ha ha ha ha ha ha!'

'It really is no laughing matter,' I said. 'These are dangerous times. What of our reputation abroad?'

'I cannot think of anything calculated to do it more good!'

91

'I cannot agree!'

'Come, come,' said Karl. 'On the Continent they think us dead from the waist down.'

'And Lord N—'s career?'

'I'm very much afraid I don't care greatly for Lord N— or his career. Lord N— and his type are inbred fools. We are better off without them.'

'It is not only Lord N— who will suffer. Think of his family.'

'I cannot feel much sympathy for his family – or indeed his entire caste,' Karl said. 'My concern is for the working man. We have put up with fools like Lord N— for long enough. And if your Dr St Liver thinks otherwise, he is a fool too.'

'Henry is many things, but not a fool.'

'Well I say he is.'

And it was that point, I think, that I asked Mr Keane to leave.

That same morning, determined to stimulate Henry into action over the Lord N— affair, I rushed to Dover Mansions. Such was my state of agitation that I barely registered the presence outside Henry's house of a fashionable gig.

'Henry!' I called out as I strode through the perennially open door of number 16, and into the morning-room. And there, sitting with Henry at the dining-table, was a woman in her early thirties, of very great beauty, with light auburn hair and large, spirited brown eyes. A delicate flush, as of some moderately strong excitement, suffused her cheeks. She was dressed entirely in blue chiffon, which complemented her eyes exceedingly well, and around her neck diamonds sparkled.

'Miss Salter,' said Henry. 'You join us at a fortunate moment. May I present to you Lady Violet L—R—?'

'How do you do?' I stumbled out.

'Miss Salter!' cried Lady Violet, rising to her feet. 'How do you do? How wonderful to meet you! I know all about you. I have read your marvellous stories in the *New Age*. "The Three Lemons" is I think my favourite. Who would have guessed where they were hidden?'

'I certainly did not,' I said.

'Lady L—R— has just this moment arrived,' Henry put in.

'Yes,' said Lady Violet, 'I have come from Hugh.'

'Hugh?' I asked.

'Lord N—. He confessed everything to me. Of course, I had been aware of it for a good while: we were childhood friends, you know. But I was so touched that he chose to confess. It gives the strongest indication that our union will be a strong and a happy one.'

'Indeed,' said Henry.

'He told me of his visit to you, Dr St Liver,' Lady Violet continued, 'and of the consideration you are currently giving to his case. I want to thank you from the bottom of my heart' – she pressed both hands to the organ in question – 'and to say that we have full confidence in you.' She gazed winsomely at me. 'Lord N— and I have both been reading your stories, Miss Salter, and – what do you think? – were all the time unaware we shared the same tastes. It is one more pleasant interest that unites us. However,' – she paused significantly, pursing her lips – 'I *think* I may have come up with a solution. I wanted to make sure of the

St Liver seal of approval.' She resumed her chair and reached into a bag by her side, from which she produced a leather garment reminiscent of the short-legged breeches seen in certain parts of Bavaria. 'Leather!' she cried, her eyes shining.

'Leather...' said Henry meditatively.

'Yes,' said Lady Violet. 'This is a pair I had made up for demonstration purposes. We used to wear something similar as children, at night. Of course, these are no ordinary breeches. You see, at the front, that they are laced with extremely thick, strong leather cords. Once carefully fitted and properly tied, they are impossible to get undone. I can personally testify to that.' She held out the laces: they were about a quarter-inch in diameter and, as far as I could judge, extremely robust. 'We will, I think,' Lady Violet continued, 'have two pairs made: an inner and an outer. One will lace at the front, and the other at the back.' She smiled. 'Both will be made-to-measure and tightly laced. They will be absolutely impossible to get off at short notice.'

'Hum,' Henry said, gazing at the article, his moustache blowing forward. 'An intriguing idea.'

'Do you really think so?'

'The essential task,' said Henry, 'is to get Lord N— up to the point in the ceremony where the exchange of vows can take place.'

'That was my feeling.'

'And these garments may well help us achieve precisely that. Yes, Madam, I think you may have hit on it.'

'Wonderful!'

'Lord N—'s higher centres,' Henry said, 'will be responding

to the bishop: the lower centres will at the same time be trying to rip off his clothing. But these garments will be impervious to any manual removal, at least in the short period of time available to him. My advice would be this. Tell Lord N— of the plan in advance. I imagine he will accept, seeing its advantages. However, do not be deceived. Your husband-to-be is likely to exhibit some cunning. He will go along with all the making-up and fitting, but when it comes to the morning of the ceremony, do not let him put the breeches on by himself. Supervise the operation yourself, or employ someone you can trust. Left to his own devices, Lord N— may be tempted to put them on in such a way as to make it possible for him quickly to unlace them. Of course, your future husband knows the advantages of *not* disgracing himself, of *not* creating an international scandal, and so on; that is why he came to me. But other, potentially more powerful parts of his person-ality will be ceaselessly working to counteract all the things his conscious mind desires to safeguard: the nation; yourself; your married happiness; your future progeny.'

Lady Violet blushed a little. 'Hugh was right in what he told me,' she said. 'I believe you are the best and wisest of men.'

And that might have been that, had it not been for an interven-tion of my own, shortly after the departure of Lady Violet.

Henry had, I thought – and perhaps rather unusually – exhibited a certain degree of complacency in his dealings with Lady Violet. Perhaps it was owing to the charm of Lady Violet's person; or perhaps a certain degree of capitulation to the first superficially attractive solution that presented itself after his own failure to find one. At any rate, an obvious objection was apparent.

'Could not,' I said casually as we sat down to our modest luncheon, 'Lord N— use scissors?'

Henry paused with a cracker half-way to his mouth. 'Scissors?'

'Yes, or a knife. It seems to me,' I said, 'that the situation is still somewhat analogous to that experienced by the poet Coleridge. Lord N— can still countermand his own orders. He merely needs to conceal a pair of scissors about his person to be able to cut through the leather cords.'

Henry put down the cracker untasted. 'You are right,' he said, his cheeks ashen. 'He will employ scissors. Of course. Of that there is not the smallest doubt.'

'Then should not Lady Violet be informed?'

'Certainly. I will do so directly.' He fished in his clothing and produced one of the innumerable dirty scraps of paper he habitually carried about him: turning it over, he began writing feverishly on the back.

'What are you doing?' I asked.

'Another wire,' he said. 'This time to Lady Violet.' He looked up at me: something about his eyes now seemed to suggest amusement. 'This works to our advantage. Lord N— will certainly – perhaps not immediately, but some time before the ceremony – be struck by the very same thought. He will meditate scissors. He will then secrete these articles about his person *after* he has been dressed by Lady Violet. He will go to the church tightly bound up, but possessing the antidote to that binding-up.

His person in fact will be a symbolic representation of his mental state, in which two halves will be locked in psychic opposition. But once again we shall forestall him. At the point of his entry into the Abbey, we shall search him and remove the scissors.' He finished writing with a flourish. 'Both symbolically and actually, we shall castrate the lower centres.'

Henry held up what he had written:

```
LORD N— WILL USE SCISSORS STOP ST LIVER
```

'That seems adequate,' I said.

'Yes, I think so.' Henry folded the paper and returned it to his pocket. 'I shall send a letter later today, to follow this telegram, outlining in detail the measures Lady Violet should take.' He took up his cracker once more. 'If England is saved this disgrace, then you, my dear, will be heroine of the hour.'

Sunday the 7th of May dawned bright and clear. There was a general public excitement and anticipation in the air, and as we made our way to Westminster Abbey, crowds thronged the streets and pavements.* It was impossible to travel by 'bus or cab in the crush, and we were forced to walk the last mile, with the result that by the time we arrived at the Abbey, approaching from the Great College Street side, we were half an hour late.

---

* I later found that demonstrators had arranged, also on that same day, the funeral of a young man who died after being mauled by a police dog; Annie Besant was the principal speaker. At the time I thought that the many placards with slogans on them such as 'Hang the Rich' were in protest at Lord N—'s nuptials.

The main entrance to the Abbey, as Londoners know, is remarkably narrow for such a magnificent church; it is, in addition, railed off from the paved court that sweeps in front of it. This fact, and the huge welter of people around the Abbey, combined to make access impossible. Among the crowd were flocks of wheeling and darting children, shock-headed and ragged, attaching themselves to any passer-by with appeals for their 'poor little sis' or 'dying ma' – this despite the fact that these persons were themselves almost certainly at that very moment engaged in the same activity elsewhere in the crowd. Various dirty-looking women in tattered plaid shawls strolled hither and thither. Henry and I were therefore forced to stand outside and await events. It was not long, however, before we and the watching crowd were privy to a remarkable spectacle.

At precisely thirty-nine minutes past ten, confused shouting began inside the Abbey, and a woman with a tiara shot out into the open air, uttering as she did so a thin, piercing scream. A horse then reared up and knocked over a man with a sandwich board on which the words 'Red Revenge' were painted. This was the signal for general tumult, which rose to a roar when two further personages flew out through the archway of Westminster Abbey, seemingly locked in mortal combat. One was Lord N—, his pinstripe trousers destroyed and hanging in tatters, though underneath, completely intact, a pair of knee-length, severely-laced brown-leather breeches was visible. The other, whom I could not identify, was a tall man in morning dress with a spatulate chin and a Roman nose. Lord N— and his co-combatant were almost a blur as they tussled their way through the crowd,

Lord N— shouting something incoherent over the screams and ejaculations of the crowd, while Roman-nose repetitively shrieked 'Hugh! Hugh!' The tumbling pair passed close by us, but there was no flicker of recognition from Lord N—, whose face was distorted into a savage mask. Roman-nose bundled him into a coach, which immediately took off.

Then, to the delight of the crowd, another pair of combatants made their appearance at the mouth of the Abbey. This time they were two equerries in gold-braided uniforms: one wore a red-and-gold tricorn hat; the other, who had either lost his hat or had not been wearing one, was bleeding profusely from a cut to his hand. With a shock I saw that the first one (with the hat) was holding a pair of gold scissors. Attempting to separate them were five or six nuptial celebrants, most without hats, some without other articles of clothing, all fighting and struggling. The rougher elements of the crowd then joined in the affray, which after a minute was broken up when a small cohort of policemen pushed their way through the mob, separated the various parties and dragged them away.

The remainder of the guests began to spill out from the Abbey towards their conveyances, all talking in animated fashion. I noticed the Countess of B—, to whom Henry had rendered such a service in the matter of the racehorse 'P'tit Indiscrétion', as well as the Duke of D—, his son the Hon. O— G—, the Marquess of M—, and others less well known. At length Lady Violet processed out, arm in arm with her mother Lady J—, and was on the point of mounting the steps to her carriage when she saw us at the barrier. She skipped rapidly over to us.

'It all went off swimmingly!' she cried. She kissed Henry on the cheek. 'And it was all thanks to you!'

'No, no,' said Henry, his moustache rising with, perhaps, a reflex of pleasure. 'The inspiration was yours. And Miss Salter added the final touch. I claim no credit.'

'But the second telegram! That was the master stroke!'

'Second telegram?' I asked.

'If it had not been for the second telegram, all would have been lost! But we must talk later,' she said. 'My mother is eager to avoid the traffic. Will you come and see us?'

'I should be glad to,' said Henry.

'Then good-bye!' gushed Lady Violet. And she ran on light feet back to her coach, waved at the crowd, stepped in, and was gone.

'I confess I do not understand, Henry,' I said, after we had stared at the departing Lady Violet for a time.

'Understand what?' asked Henry.

We turned and began to walk slowly back to Victoria.

'Lord N— obviously managed to remove his trousers,' I said, 'and moreover was carried off screaming. How can that be judged a success? And what was the meaning of "the second telegram"?'

'I think I can reconstruct the play of events,' said Henry. 'Lord N—, as you said he would, anticipated that he could cut through the leather cords with scissors. He therefore secreted scissors about his person. Lady Violet, however, had been warned by my letter, and had him searched as he entered the Abbey. But Lord N— is a person of some ingenuity. He guessed that he would be searched, and hired a man, dressed as an equerry, to supply him with a spare pair of scissors when the crisis came. I anticipated that he might do this. After dispatching the letter with your warning about the scissors, I sent a second telegram to Lady Violet, advising her to hire another man to disable Lord N—'s man if this plan came into operation. Not knowing whether the precaution would be strictly necessary, I did not inform you of it.'

'So –'

'So to the events as they unfolded. The two men in the first skirmish were Lord N— and his friend and best man Lord V—. He owns substantial mineral deposits in Dyfed, I believe. The two men in the second battling group were the first hired man and the second hired man. The first hired man obviously attempted to present Lord N— with the scissors at the crucial moment of the ceremony: the second hired man was there to prevent him. There was a struggle, and the second hired man was injured, though not, fortunately, permanently disabled. Lord N—, seeing his ruse frustrated, began tearing at his clothing, while his own best man attempted to restrain him. Other sections of the congregation joined in the melée. As this was happening, however, the service continued. I had instructed Lady Violet to warn the Bishop that something of the kind might occur, and his brief was to carry on come what may. The sacrament was, it seems, effected.'

'I see,' I said. 'But surely this behaviour is disgrace enough? Is not a career in public service now barred to him?'

'Not at all. It will hardly be remarked,' said Henry. 'It will all be put down to an epileptic fit – there is epilepsy in the family, you remember.'

We walked for a space, passing down Tothill Street and Petty France, where in the gardens a 'Pantheon of Lux' had been erected; the notice outside said that 'Professor Thomas Tamer' promised that 'all comers will be astonished by this new and exquisite apparatus, which causes phantasms to materialize with every appearance of reality... Professor Tamer accompanies each showing with a "Unearthly Lecture" explaining the exchange of impressions.' The billboard was accompanied by a picture of a woman with an enormous half-nude behind, though I could not see its relevance.

'Then Coleridge was of some help after all,' I observed. 'In the matter of the hired men.'

'Exactly,' Henry said. 'The problem was to put an exact quantum on Lord N—'s powers of anticipation. Had I estimated his cunning any higher, I should have hired a fourth man to counteract his own putative third man. In fact, theoretically, there could have been an infinite regression of hired men, each one paid to counteract the actions of the one immediately preceding him in the chain.' He glanced at me, his moustache suddenly jovial. 'It is a lesson to our politicians and policy-makers. Let us never neglect the poets if we would wish to give a rounded education to the young.'

Chapter Four

The Boy Explorer

❧

So far in these little case histories I have concentrated on the successes of Henry St Liver, and on the insights that enabled him to solve problems intractable to more workaday intellects. Nevertheless there were times when he, like other mortals, tasted failure: and these disappointments, cul-de-sacs and unprofitable dribblings-away of time and effort tend not to feature in my accounts, for obvious reasons (i.e. that the public tends to be more interested in stories with some point to them). Only where the details of these failed investigations are particularly notable does the present author presume to lay them before the public; and, even though the case I am about to describe ended in defeat for Henry – in that he utterly failed to illuminate it in any way – it is, I think, of such interest that a full account of his career would be incomplete without it.

The case was also notable in that it had its origin partly in my own personal circumstances. I must briefly describe these, then, before I go any further.

I have mentioned that by the middle of 1894, two years after my arrival in London, I had halted work on my sequel to *The Story of an Australian Barn*. My first book had fared badly in the shops, and I was, in truth, much dispirited by the experience. I was beginning to feel that the public had little taste for whatever I could offer in the way of delineating true and right relations between man and woman. And I would almost certainly have persisted in this belief, and abandoned any idea of penning a sequel, had it not been for a most unexpected upsurge in my book's fortunes. In the early summer of 1894, eighteen months after its first appearance, and thanks almost entirely to the efforts of Henry to recommend it to his friends, the book was reviewed in no less a publication than *Woman's World*.

Moreover, to my astonishment, the reviewer was no less a person than Mr Oscar Wilde.

The review was a generous one. It was entitled 'A HIT ON THE BARN DOOR', and read as follows:

> There has been a glut of colonial narratives in recent months, most of a depressing nature. Who could have failed not to thrill to the recent offering of Mr H. Rider Haggard: *Gold, Diamonds, Ivory, and other Natural Wonders of Southern Africa*? Or to the strange and purposeless peregrinations in voluminous clothing of Mrs Henry Teague throughout the former Dutch East Indies, whose title for the moment escapes me? [*Wanderings Throughout the Former Dutch East Indies* – Ed.]
>
> But here is a narrative that offers a respite from tales of 'adventure' – adventure that cannot fail to be felt as inconvenience by those in whose lands the adventure takes place.

Mr Roderick Iron's new novel strikes an unusual note. It is written by a native of the colonial territory in question, that of Australia. That in itself sets it apart and stamps it with authority. Moreover Mr Iron has restricted himself to a remarkably small number of native bearers, obviating the need for them to die like flies and be left with sun-blackened lips by the side of the road, a mainstay of the conventional narrative of adventure as we understand it at present. 'Man's misery may be traced to his inability to remain quietly in a room,' says Pascal. In this case the room is one of large dimension – a barn – but it is a room notwithstanding, and the principle holds. Mr Iron demonstrates how one may remain quietly in a barn; and the description of the Barn, and the conditions in which the heroine remains in it, at close quarters with four strapping young lads, is most inspiring.

Also refreshing is the book's account of the native peoples of the Goongerwarrie district. Many of these, it appears, have a definite mechanical turn. They enjoy repairing machinery and getting their hands dirty. These are not effete young men and women but energetic persons, full of horseplay. They give every good hope for the productive development of this outpost of the Empire.

It seems also that the political systems of the district are remarkably well developed. Universal suffrage has been here in operation for several thousand years, having been instituted not only when London was a collection of mud huts, but when Rome was a marsh, Athens a field and Nineveh a dune. One thing to note in passing is that village counsels are held *tout nu* – perhaps a custom that could be imported for use by our own Parliament.

This is a book with one other remarkable quality. It deals particularly with feminine themes, among them the educational, political, romantic, and erotic rights of Woman, as well as others I have forgotten. This shows remarkable sensitivity on Mr Iron's part. Rarely can the name of that metal associated so often with inflexible masculinity – iron – have been so inappropriately bestowed on any individual (though Mr Iron may have sisters, say Jane and Jennifer Iron, for whom it would be still more inappropriate; and I suppose his mother too, and paternal grandmother, if still living, are both Mrs Iron – but perhaps the point should not be laboured).

I eagerly await the sequel to the *Story of an Australian Barn*, since I learn that Mr Iron is now among us in London and might therefore be expected to direct his energies to themes closer at hand – perhaps a study of English haylofts, ricks, byres, sheds, hangars and shelters, and the doubtless interesting and instructive things that go on in them.

My delight, as readers will imagine, was intense. It was only matched when, almost immediately on publication of this piece, sales of the book sky-rocketed. Drebber and Drebber rapidly ran through the remaining few hundred of the first edition and were compelled to rush out a second. In that June of 1894, all London, it seemed, talked of nothing but the Barn, the machinations of Emmie and the come-uppance of Mr Stirrup. Soon a third edition of my book was called for; and then a fourth. The word 'sap' – which I suppose I had employed more than once, as a colloquial Australian term to describe spunk, energy or attractiveness in persons – gained a wholly unexpected, and, to me, frankly incomprehensible vogue; the public seemed to find a great deal of amusement in it. It even found its way into the title of a burlesque song, 'Give Me a Girl with Some Sap', by Mr Titch Bunker.

One consequence was that my identity as author could no longer be concealed. The matter had, of course, already substantially leaked out: Henry had long since taken to introducing me to friends as 'Miss Olive Salter, the authoress of *The Story of an Australian Barn*'; and after a brief flirtation with the notion of 'Rodericka Iron' as a feminine substitute, the second edition was published under my own name. Far from quelling the surge of speculation, this only seemed to add oil to the flames. *The Times* asked: 'If the author's name is not to be believed, why should not the whole thing have been written from an armchair in Hampstead?' and *Lippincott's* even claimed to have discovered the 'real' author (which was rather odd, since I had already admitted to being that person). They informed their readers that she was a dressmaker in Princes Risborough, Oxfordshire, by the name of Jennifer Iron – a 'discovery' obviously prompted by an inattentive reading of Mr Wilde's original article.

Aside from Mr Wilde's review, the general tone of the remarks in the press was mixed. There were accusations of 'rushed and sloppy writing', 'sensationalism', 'recycling of motifs', 'inconsistency and implausibility', 'laughable melodrama' and so on, but none of this seemed to have any effect on the sales of the book, other than to increase them. Perhaps headlines such as 'Eros in the Desert' and 'The Case for a Nude Parliament' were responsible, together with the success of 'Give Me a Girl with Some Sap'.

For his part, Henry seemed pleased by the *éclat* I had made. It sometimes happens that a sudden success impairs relations between friends, but in our case it did nothing of the sort. The friendship was, if anything, strengthened. When I was asked to speak at meetings – a now frequent occurrence – Henry always attended; and even when I was asked to give my opinion on questions of the day as they related to erotic, amatory or reproductive themes, Henry never once intimated that my expertise was any less than his own – a display of tact quite astonishing for a man of his achievement.

In the course of speaking at meetings, attending parties and so on, I met many celebrated figures of the day. Perhaps the most illustrious of my new acquaintances was Mr Wilde himself.

By 1894 Mr Wilde had achieved immortality as a playwright, society wit and leading light in the Aesthetic movement. Nevertheless he was still a working writer, and forced to pen much cheap and shoddy journalism to make ends meet. The occasion of our first meeting was a small luncheon given by Mr Wilde himself at the Holborn Cricket Club (not many know that Oscar was a great cricketer and golfer). I was, as the reader will imagine, extremely apprehensive at the prospect of meeting this great figure. I well remember my first glimpse of him as I entered the tearoom. Mr Wilde is familiar from his many portrait photographs, so there is no need to describe the expansive head with its piercing brown eyes, sensual lips and domineering chin, nor linger over the soft, flowing locks, swollen fingers, astrakhan-collar coat, cravat, Malacca cane and green carnation. But perhaps the reader *will* be surprised by one detail: his utter want of conversation.

This was apparent as soon as I approached the table. The gathering was hectic with the shrieks of cricket-loving aesthetes, but at the centre of it, like a brooding brown insect, Mr Wilde sat wordless and almost motionless. He gave no sign, in fact, that he had even seen me. Instead, a young man wearing a yellow morning-suit rose to greet me.

'Miss Salter?' he asked, with a charming smile. 'May I introduce myself? I am John Gray, Oscar's private secretary. One of several.'

(I had heard of Mr Gray, the author of such lyrics as 'My love has sickened unto loath' and 'Rancid are the buttercups', and was surprised to find how very young he was. Not more than twenty-one, I would have said, and a person of some beauty, with a very white, smooth skin, curling russet hair, and large dark eyes with long lashes.)

'Oscar told me particularly to invite you,' Mr Gray went on. 'Such a triumph with the *Barn* – never has agriculture seemed quite so indispensable.'

'Thank you,' I said.

'And your admirable stories of detection! I think "The Oxford Despoiler" is my favourite. I was up at Oxford myself at the time. Who would have guessed that the principal of a girls' college could convincingly imitate a baboon?'

'I certainly did not,' I said.

'Now – do not be surprised at Oscar.' Mr Gray said. 'He may seem a little withdrawn.'

'Oh... I hope he is well?' I asked, glancing again to where Mr Wilde sat with his vast expanse of face. He now seemed to have noticed my presence, but gazed at me as if I were not a person, but some natural object – a mountain range, perhaps.

'He is in excellent health.' Mr Gray smiled once more. 'But I should tell you that you are unlikely to get much from him. I know you will expect great things from Oscar – everyone does – but the real Oscar is rather different to, let us say, the Oscar of legend.' He smoothed the backs of his yellow gloves. 'Oscar is renowned for his wit. When people first meet him they think he will discourse like a character from "A Woman of No Importance". He will not. I have known Oscar for two years, and he is perhaps the most uncommunicative person I have ever met.'

A loud outbreak of shrieking, which ended as precipitously as it had begun, rang through the tearoom. Mr Gray appeared not to notice it. 'He has declared war on conversation,' he continued. 'You are unlikely to meet a more solemn fellow.'

'But surely...' I stuttered.

'No,' Mr Gray said firmly. 'No. You must believe me, Miss Salter. Oscar's is the most carefully manufactured reputation in England. It is perhaps his greatest work. He is *capable* of utterance, of course: he is not dumb. He will even say the odd good thing if you poke him – though he needs a lot of time and perhaps an envelope to work it out on first. "True spontaneity springs from deep wells of preparation" is one of his maxims, and I vividly remember the time he spent coming up with that one. No, Oscar is only any good with a pen. I guarantee that today you will hear him utter but three words: "yes", "no" and "I'll have the trout".'

I was deeply astonished. Could Oscar Wilde's reputation for the brilliant paradox, the iconoclastic epigram, the lightning riposte, be nothing but the fruit of a clever campaign of publicity?

But it was all as Mr Gray had said. Mr Wilde remained silent throughout the luncheon. Everyone present seemed entirely at ease with this state of affairs. In a rather remarkable fashion, Mr Wilde seemed, through sheer massiveness of face and body, to be able to exercise a greater influence over his coterie of hangers-on than he could ever have done by means of brittle and flamboyant repartee.

Mr Wilde's taciturnity notwithstanding, the luncheon was a most enjoyable occasion. When the time came for me to take my leave, I stood and, looking over at Mr Wilde, reiterated, in as loud a voice as I could manage over the general laughter and talk, my thanks for his generous review of my book. I was determined to wring at least one word from him.

Mr Wilde looked absently at me.

'Well, then, goodbye!' I shouted.

Mr Wilde waved a hand, but not in farewell; rather as if declining an offer.

It was only later I realized that he thought I was the waitress.

Several days passed. It was about a week after my meeting with Mr Wilde – if indeed it can be accurately described as such – that the event occurred which brings me to the true commencement of the case of the Boy Explorer.

Henry and I were settled comfortably one afternoon among

the rubbish at Dover Mansions, Henry occupied in the inspection of some unpublished aquatints of Burton, and myself in
answering a letter (a young man had written to me asking if I
thought that the sex relation was 'the chief purpose of human
life,' and I was carefully considering my reply), when, at around
four o'clock, I heard steps on the path outside, and a brisk pound-
ing at the outer door. Before either of us could rise there bounced
into the room a slender form dressed entirely in cream. It was Mr
John Gray.

'I do hope you will forgive me,' Mr Gray began breathlessly,
'but I saw the door open and took the liberty of looking in.'

'You are very welcome,' said Henry, getting to his feet.

'Henry,' I said, 'Might I present Mr John Gray, the poet? Mr
Gray is a friend of Mr Wilde.'

'Delighted to meet you,' said Henry, offering his hand.

'And I you, Doctor,' Mr Gray replied, taking it. 'I admire
your work greatly, Sir. I have read every one of Miss Salter's stories in the *New Age*. There was much for us all to learn in the case
of the "Disturbed Baker". And it is your expertise that I hope to
draw on today. I am convinced that the events I have to relate are
quite as serious as any of the case-histories I have so far read.'

'You interest me very much,' Henry said.

'Very well, then: I will come to the point.' He brushed a stray
curl from his cheek. 'I am afraid Oscar is in some distress.'

'Mr Wilde?'

'Yes. He asks if you will see him.'

'With pleasure,' Henry replied.

'Thank you. Well, then – he is outside.'

'Outside?'

'In the four-wheeler.'

Henry and I both involuntarily glanced through the bay window. In front of the house, hard up on the pavement, was a cab; both green blinds on the pavement side had been drawn.

'I see,' said Henry. 'Would Mr Wilde care to come in?'

'I think it unlikely,' Mr Gray said. 'I think Oscar would prefer, if possible, an interview *in situ*. In the cab itself.'

Henry considered a moment. 'Very well,' he said.

'Excellent,' said Mr Gray. And so, in a moment, the three of us were striding up the front path towards Mr Wilde's conveyance. Mr Gray tapped on the door, and there was the click of a lock.

The door swung open.

Bent like an elderly marquess – a massive one – in the far corner of the cab, was Mr Wilde. His enormous face had, in the low light, acquired a tint of green; an intimation of cruel sensuality flickered about the mouth. Not for nothing, I thought, as I beheld him there, had he been dubbed – I forget by whom – 'the third most sensual man in London'. With a bejewelled paw he motioned us to enter. We clambered in and seated ourselves: Henry and I on the right-hand bank seat with our backs to the driver, and Mr Wilde and Mr Gray opposite on the left. The air was heavy with an unidentifiable scent. 'Perhaps,' Mr Gray said, adjusting his cravat, 'I should explain the situation. Mr Wilde is concerned for the safety of a friend. He saw him last at the Aeolian Hotel in Islington.'

Mr Wilde regarded us with burning eyes.

'I see,' said Henry. 'Might I know the name of this friend?'

'His name is Vivian Mbati,' Mr Gray said unsmilingly. 'Known as "Cheeky" Mbati. He is fifteen years old.'

'He is of African descent?' asked Henry.

'I believe so,' replied Mr Gray.

'And – Mr Wilde, it would help greatly in my investigation if you could find it in yourself to answer my question directly – this young man was a particular friend of yours?'

Mr Wilde stirred. 'Yes,' he replied in a low voice.

'He was staying at the Aeolian Hotel?'

'Yes.'

'And you were accustomed to visit him there.'

'Yes.'

'I see. May I ask how often?'

Mr Wilde regarded Henry with an expression I have never before seen on any human face. There was intelligence there, certainly; interested enquiry; a hint of challenging humour, too, perhaps, as well as a touch of mockery. An expression that was, in short, redolent of full comprehension of Henry's question, but which, at the same time, held not the smallest hint that it would be favoured with an answer.

'Every week?' Henry asked.

Mr Wilde did not speak.

'More often?'

'Yes.'

'Every day, then?'

'No.'

'Once or twice a week?'

'Yes.'

114

'Did you see him yesterday?'

'No.'

'The day before yesterday?'

'Yes.'

'And he was not in his room?'

'No.'

'What leads you to be concerned for his safety?'

Mr Wilde's only other known utterance apart from 'yes' and 'no' – that regarding trout – was obviously incapable of doing justice to the situation.

'Perhaps I might step in,' said Mr Gray. 'Oscar informs me that on repairing to the Aeolian Hotel the day before yesterday, with a friend, Mr Shannon, he noticed that Mr Mbati's name had been removed from the door of the room where he customarily resides. Despite the fact that he was a well-known and well-liked guest, none of the hotel's staff appeared to know anything of his whereabouts. All of Mr Mbati's personal effects had been removed from the room: his clothes were gone from the wardrobe, and his assegai was missing from the corner. The walls had been freshly painted, the linen changed, and, in fact, every effort had been made entirely to efface Mr Mbati's presence. Oscar does not have a forwarding address for Mr Mbati, nor does he know of anyone else who does. Mr Mbati has disappeared from off the face of Islington.'

'How did Mr Wilde inform you of this?' asked Henry.

'In a note.'

'You have the note?'

'Certainly.'

Mr Gray produced a sheet of thin blue notepaper. He handed it to Henry, who took a long time reading it.

'Yes,' he said finally. 'It covers the main points you have mentioned.' He handed it back. 'On which floor was the young man's room?'

'The third floor. Number eighty-six,' Mr Gray replied.

'Number eighty-six. I see. One thing springs to mind, Mr Wilde – are you certain that you had not simply strayed into the wrong room?'

'Yes,' Mr Wilde said.

Henry considered briefly. 'Well, then. If you will instruct your driver, Mr Gray, I think we will pay a visit to the Aeolian Hotel. Perhaps Mr Mbati left some trace behind him before so unaccountably departing this existence.'

The Aeolian Hotel is situated in Myddleton Passage, Islington, just off the Pentonville Road, and and so is about fifteen minutes' drive from Shoreditch, in moderate traffic. The journey, and the silence of my companions, gave me time to think about the singular matter that had just been presented.

The case was a perplexing one. The fact that no member of the hotel staff had been able to furnish any information concerning the young man's whereabouts was undoubtedly sinister. On the other hand, it seemed to me that the mystery could not long survive a concerted interrogation of the hotel staff, and perhaps also some of its clientele. My experience so far of Mr Wilde's powers of speech did not lead me to think that he had extracted the maximum data possible from these sources. And in the very presentation of the case there were odd lacunae. What of Mr Wilde's frequent contacts with Mr Mbati? Was there a literary reason for these? And how could such a young boy afford to stay in a hotel?

The afternoon was now shading into evening, but the weather was warm and the canopies of the planes dappled the street pleasantly as we stepped from the cab into Myddleton Passage. The Aeolian Hotel was a four-storey affair in rose stucco with, over the doorway, a representation of an angel playing a harp, picked out in leaded lights. Henry spent a short time observing the building from outside, then, appearing satisfied, led us in a group through the double doors.

The small lobby was deserted, and at the desk the sole member of staff – a young man standing under a notice that read: 'Visit the Bowers of Telemachus, where you can receive a shampoo in the limpid foam of the Aegean' – inclined his head respectfully as Henry strode past. We proceeded to the main staircase and ascended to the third floor, where Henry made his way down a corridor, stopping in front of room eighty-six. There was, as Mr Gray had said, no nameplate on the door.

Henry pointed. 'This is the room?' he asked Mr Wilde.

'Yes,' Mr Wilde replied.

'You remember particularly the number eighty-six.'

Mr Wilde gestured to the door immediately to the left, number eighty-seven. It had a small nameplate on it, with the legend 'Willie Loades'.

'You remember particularly that Mr Mbati's room was immediately to the right of Mr Loades'.'

'Yes.'

Henry tried the handle.

The door opened onto a quite ordinary hotel room, about twelve feet long by ten wide. A bed covered in a red organdy cloth lay to the right side, under a window that looked out onto an unalluring rear courtyard. A stream of sunlight illuminated a sideboard with a washbasin, an oval table with two chairs, and, at the far end of the room, a wardrobe and chest of drawers with a revolving mirror. The walls were a light pink, and there was a definite odour of paint. We three entered, leaving Mr Wilde standing massively in the doorway. He seemed more than ever dour, perhaps even grim. The appetency had now left his face. He seemed less the third most sensual man in London, and perhaps only now the ninth or tenth.

Henry, however, had no time for observing Mr Wilde. He had set about nosing into the wardrobe and the chest of drawers. Mr Gray, meanwhile, his head tilted upward, examined a print on the wall.

Rarely, I think, in my accounts of any of Henry's cases, has there been as little dialogue.

After examining the bed, and then standing for a while at the window observing the scene in the courtyard, Henry turned and announced briefly that he had completed his investigations. We four then descended the staircase to the lobby, and, walking out the way we had come, emerged into the street.

'Well, Doctor?' asked Mr Gray, as we stood once more under the seraphic harpist.

'Intriguing,' said Henry.

'You do not wish to question the staff?'

'I am sure it would be quite fruitless.'

'Indeed?'

'I think we must start from the very obvious fact that Mr Mbati has been abducted. A very great effort has been made to cover up his abduction; and any deputation made by anyone connected with the Aeolian Hotel would therefore be utterly meaningless. I will admit, however, that I have no present theory. I beg that you will leave this matter with me for the time being; I will give it my full attention. You have not yet informed the police. There may come a time when that will be necessary.'

'Very well,' Mr Gray said thoughtfully. He plucked a microscopic fleck of red organdy from his cream jacket. 'We shall hear from you, then.' He turned to me. 'I hope it goes without saying, Miss Salter, that this is a case of extraordinary delicacy.'

'Naturally,' I replied.

'You would naturally never consider entertaining the public with an account of it. Even trivial-seeming disclosures may have unforeseen ramifications.'

'Of course,' I said. 'Please rest assured that I will exercise the utmost discretion.'

'Thank you.'

And with that we parted.

The next evening, at Dover Mansions, Henry sat in his armchair looking through the crumbling pages of a journal.

I will admit that I felt, not for the first time, some impatience at Henry's working methods. I knew that he was apt to solve cases such as the one before us – considerably more baffling ones, indeed – by a sudden deft sexological lunge; but still, the utter blankness of the whole business revolted me. A boy was missing; no one knew where he had gone; there were no clues; the main witness would only say the words 'yes' or 'no', despite being the most gifted talker of his generation; no one had been interviewed; and Henry had, for the moment, no theory. What the pages of a German periodical published three decades ago could offer, I had not the smallest idea.

At length Henry looked up from the Gothic script, his moustache thoughtful. Seeing my puzzled expression he reached into the top pocket of his jacket and held out a small rectangle of card.

'Please read it aloud,' he said.

I took the card. On one side were a few lines of text, embossed in red; on the reverse was the familiar design of the angelic harpist.

'"Mr Digby Probyn,"' I read. '"This accomplished young man has just attained his sixteenth year, and, perfect in character as in form, enters as a volunteer in the field of Uranus. He plays on the mandolin, sings, dances, competes in contests of cricket and golf, and converses with wit and taste. He is five feet eight in height, with brown eyes, dark golden-brown hair, and a manner brimming with amorous excitement. Every movement of his form is gracious and symmetrical."' I handed the card back. 'Where did you find this?'

'In the lobby,' he said, 'on a table. It was one of numerous examples of its type.'

'What does it mean?' I asked.

'Why, prostitution,' Henry said briefly.

'Prostitution?'

'Certainly.'

'Of men?'

'Certainly,' said Henry.

I knew, of course, that Mr Wilde was a leading Aesthete, although I admit I had not made the connection.

'I see. Then that young man –' I pointed to the card – 'is a... a boy prostitute?'

'Yes.'

'And the Aeolian Hotel...?'

'Is a brothel. There are several brothels in London catering to Uranians. I could name three within a few minutes' walk, although I admit that the Aeolian was new to me.'

'If that is the case then it was all remarkably discreet.'

'Of course. The hotel does not wish to frighten its customers by too great a display of ostentation.'

'I am astonished.'

'It is really nothing unusual.' Henry tapped the periodical on his lap. 'The boys' brothel is attested to throughout history. It is found everywhere in the ancient world: in Constantinople, Rome, Greece... Boys in many cases were prized above female prostitutes, and commanded higher fees. They were often the favourites of wealthy men who would provide for them an excellent education in singing, dancing, poetry, and so on.'

'Yes, I see...'

'The poet Theopompos in the *Comicorum Atticorum*

Fragmenta writes that one of the most celebrated boys' brothels was on the summit of Lycabettus: "On my rocky height boys willingly give themselves up to those of the same age and to others.'"

'But of our own times? Are we not in danger of romanticizing the matter? Are not many of these creatures forced by economic necessity into the sale of their own bodies?'

'That is often put forward.'

'Is it not true?'

'In a recent study by Plock,' Henry began, with characteristic command of the minutiae of his branch of science, 'in the *Monatsschrift für Harnkrankheiten und Sexuelle Hygiene*, 3,516 female prostitutes working in the environs of the Tiergarten in Berlin were asked to complete a questionnaire. Of these, 1,215 confessed that economic hardship had led them into their profession; 1,442 attributed their career to their own uncontrollable desire for pleasure; 434 said that it was due to bad company; 367 blamed drink; 34 said they had taken it up to spite a lover; 23 had been sold into sexual slavery by their parents; and one confessed she had embarked upon prostitution as a newspaper stunt, and found she could not stop.'

'In that case fully a third were in serious want.'

'Yes, but the phrase "economic hardship" must be further examined. I doubt whether in most cases there was a threat to actual survival. Most, I would contend, were tired of a life of unremitting drudgery on small wages. They were motivated by a desire for betterment, not a need for food or shelter. Most prostitutes are recruited from the ranks of those already employed, after all – factory hands, domestic servants, and so on.'

'I suppose so.'

'If my memory serves me aright, that figure of 1,215 was further broken down. 771 admitted that prostitution enabled them to buy finer clothes, jewellery, sweetmeats, presents and so on; 201 said that the work was altogether easier and less demanding than what they had been doing previously; 140 said they were saving up for furniture; and 103 could give no convincing response.'

'You seem to be saying that prostitution may, in some cases, be the rational choice of any man or woman.'

'I do not deny that there is much in the present system that could be reformed: but even as it stands I do believe prostitution may work to the good. It may have a civilizing aspect.'

'Civilizing? How so?

'There is much in life that is monotonous, laborious and humdrum. Dull work; tiresome responsibilities; insipid pleasures. The prostitute, no less than his or her client, is a creature who desires release. You will have noticed that in the *Monatsschrift* survey fully 1,442 said they had taken up their current mode of living out of a love of pleasure. The prostitute exists in a world of excitement, of danger, in which considerable sums of money continually change hands. In many cases he or she will be surrounded by all that art and wealth can provide. It is this atmosphere, perhaps as much as the desire for illicit sexual contact, that the prostitute and his or her client craves. It is craved indeed by many who never come into contact with prostitutes directly at all. Prostitution supplies the materials for innumerable fantasies: what else do we find in the romances of Monsieur Zola or

Mr Gissing? The world of the prostitute, with its *frisson* of the forbidden, penetrates the novel, the theatre, the music-hall...'

'Yes. I see.'

'When one puts together the promise of luxury, excitement, gaiety, riches, and the *tabu* of various pleasures that dare not speak their names, it is not surprising that the career of a prostitute attracts a hard-pressed farm-hand or tweeny as a lamp attracts a moth, especially at a time of life when the young boy or girl is just beginning to feel the stirring of his or her own orgiastic impulses.'

'I confess I had not thought of it quite like that.'

'If you still have any doubts, visit a typical home for fallen women. The difficulty faced by Magdalen homes in finding girls willing to be "saved" is quite marked.'

'Yes. But what of the present case? How does this get us any further forward?'

'Ah.' Henry gazed into the middle distance, which happened at that moment to be occupied by an enormous horsehair mattress; he had found it that morning rolled up in a neighbouring front garden.

'You have no theory?' I asked.

'At the moment, beyond speculation, no.'

'Then your speculation?'

'I would surmise that Mr Mbati is in some danger.'

'Why do you say that?'

'Any person who is held against their will is *ipso facto* in danger. The abductor might at some point wish to silence them.'

'Who might have abducted him, and why?'

'It is difficult to say. Mr Mbati was popular. It is possible that one of the hotel's clients nurtured an obsessive passion for the boy, spirited him away for his own exclusive private enjoyment, and paid the hotel handsomely to erase all evidence of his former existence.'

'Then how can this abductor be tracked down?'

'I have contacts in several of the Uranian brothels. They may be forthcoming where the Aeolian Hotel will not.'

'Let us hope that will be sufficient.'

Henry stroked his moustache. 'I have one further suspicion, however.'

'Go on.'

'I strongly suspect that the African element is significant.'

'In what way?' I asked.

'Mr Mbati's racial origin differentiates him from his fellows, does it not? He is an "exotic". Men will pay high prices for any new or unusual experience. The press at the moment is full of stories of African exploration. Clients excited by tales of colonial adventure might easily find appeal in the thought of an encounter with a genuine African boy. Mr Mbati was very probably expected to assume native regalia during his residence at the Aeolian.'

'I see.'

'Sexual conquest and geographical conquest are not so very different,' Henry continued. 'Throughout history territorial aggrandizement has invariably been accompanied by the forcible recruitment of sexual partners. Some of the brothels in ancient Greece were staffed, it should be remembered, by comely prisoners of war. The youth Phaedo was one such prisoner; and it is from Socrates' encounter with him that we derive one of Plato's most luminous dialogues.'

'Yes...'

'The key to understanding sexual selection is to look at the warrior trait in males as selected by females. However, this really forms no great part of the present enquiry. I would refer you to Clérambault, *Archives de l'Anthropologie Criminelle*, of December 1877.'

'Then –?'

'Then, in summary, it would seem at least a working hypothesis to suppose that our young man is being held by an obsessive Africanophile who is forcing him to re-enact symbolically the conquest of the Dark Continent.'

'Oh.'

'But I really have no proof of this idea. Unpalatable as it seems, we must simply wait and bide our time – for a few days at least. If there is any information it will find its way back to me.'

'I hope so.'

'The prize in this case will be to the one who hunts by stealth.'

But Henry, as I mentioned at the beginning of this tale, ultimately failed to bring the case to a satisfactory conclusion (even though subsequent events showed that his just-mentioned hypothesis was not so very far from the truth). Things moved very much more quickly than either of us had anticipated. The very day after the conversation I have just related, a singular story broke in that campaigning publication, the *Pall Mall Gazette*.

I had stayed the night at Dover Mansions, as was increasingly my custom, and in the morning, at around ten o'clock, Henry burst into my room. As I rose from my bed in a mental fog, he jabbed a newspaper at me.

'Here!' he cried.

I looked at the front page, which read, in two-inch-high letters: 'NEW ERA IN AFRICAN EXPLORATION'.

The article ran as follows:

The *Gazette* has learned that in the unseemly struggle for influence in Central Africa a new low has been plumbed. A group led by one 'Major' Richard Twite, formerly of the United African Company, a shadowy group operating in the Niger Delta, has mounted – with, the *Gazette* believes, the connivance of the present government – an expedition to the Congo, but without the expense and inconvenience of actually going there. The explorers have 'returned' with their treaties and their documentation, but the whole thing has been most invidiously faked. The motive is to lend credence to further actions by the British South Africa Company, operating from Zambezia to the South.

The *Pall Mall Gazette* has been at the forefront of exposing this hoax and can now report on the matter.

Failure of an Expedition

An expedition, it is true, was organized. It departed from Zanzibar in the June of last year under the leadership of 'Major' Twite, with the aim of seizing control of the regional capital of Bunkeya, home of the Yeke people, just west of the Lualaba River. Twite and his second in command, the ethologist WW Norris Coke, recruited around 400 Africans to take part, mainly Zanzibari in origin, and including around 200 'askaris' or African irregular soldiers, 100 porters or 'pagazis', as well as numerous cooks, personal servants, litter-bearers or 'imbaris', and other hangers-on.

Twite's role was to make contact with the various tribes *en route*, sign treaties, and pave the way for the British South Africa Company. However, three months into the expedition, through arid desert, treacherous swamp and baking mountain-top, leaving all the while exhausted stragglers to die with sun-blackened lips by the roadside, Major Twite encountered an enormous gorge which he found he could neither bridge nor circumvent. Mr Norris Coke had by this time died after a beetle had entered his ear, and more than two-thirds of Twite's askaris, pagazis and imbaris had also perished, leaving Twite only a small corps of loyal followers. These then carried him back to Zanzibar, which he finally reached, exhausted, in September. The very last native porter, alone of the 400 who had departed Zanzibar more than ten months previously, and who was carrying Twite on his back, died as soon as he had deposited him at the Governor-General's residence.

The 'Solution'

'Major' Twite, we learn, recovered after several weeks and was put on a troop ship back to Southampton, arriving in this country in January. His expedition, of course, had been an unmitigated disaster. The British South Africa Company neither had its treaties nor its photographic evidence, and were hamstrung in their pursuit of the annexation of Bunkeya. Moreover, the authorities feared that the Belgian Friendly Association under Aimé Baudruche would be the first to come to terms with King Msisri of the Yeke Kingdom and open the way for the enlargement of Belgian holdings.

The expedition was too important for the authorities to countenance failure. The requisite treaties were therefore most disgracefully forged; as for visual evidence, it was decided to fake the whole thing in a photographic studio.

Accordingly a warehouse in Virginia Water was converted to give a convincing representation of African conditions. Specially painted backdrops were employed and several tons of gravel and sand brought in. Africans were needed, many of whom were recruited from London's communities. A mock-up purporting to be the *boma*, or compound, of King Msisri in Bunkeya, was contracted to a local builder. Photographs of the *ensemble* with its personnel were then taken and circulated to the illustrated press in the form of photogravure engravings.

The *Pall Mall Gazette*, however, unlike other newspapers, was not taken in. The present reporter has seen the original photographs from which the engravings were made up, thanks to the co-operation of Mr David Blinkhorn, the photogravure printer concerned, who wishes to retire.

The discrepancies in the photographs are as follows:

- The colour and angle of shadows is inconsistent: shadows diverge from the subjects in the way they would if a source of light such as a spotlight had been placed close by to illumine them. These shadows could not have been produced by natural light, since the sun casts rays which, when they strike the earth's surface – or that of any other celestial body – are very nearly parallel.

- The backgrounds to the figures do not change, even when it is claimed that the photographs were taken many miles apart. The same range of coppies, for example, is visible in a photograph taken 'in the region of Motembe' on June 1 and in one taken 'near the Tsunangira Cataract' of June 4. The sand in both photographs is also suspiciously similar.

- The picture of 'Major' Twite playing golf near the *boma* of Msisri shows him using a grip that suggests that he has never played golf.

- There are reflections that suggest spotlights in the spectacles of one of the African askaris.

- The rocks seen to the foreground in some of the photographs look similar to rocks very commonly found in Berkshire, being of a very characteristic geological formation known as Berkshire oolitic limestone.

Sinister Development

In perhaps the most sinister development, it has emerged that several of the Africans hired for this purpose are now being kept prisoner in Virginia Water. They are being treated well, but are in reality no more than 'birds in a gilded cage'. This alarming circumstance came to light today with the confession of Mr Chikonkole Mbati, also known as 'Chiki' Mbati, a British subject who was involved in the plot. Mr Mbati, a boy of fifteen, was born in London of mixed African and English parentage, and says he answered an advertisement in *The Evening Standard* for photographic models, and took part in these elaborate attempts at deception in good faith. He was at first trusted, but later was suspected of 'talking', and was imprisoned, along with several others. He escaped, but alleges that a number, perhaps half of the original cast, are being held, and fears for their safety. He is currently under the protection of the *Pall Mall Gazette*.

'Good Lord, Henry!' I cried. 'Mr Wilde must be told immediately!'

'I have sent a wire,' Henry said. 'I have no doubt but that Mr Wilde is this moment hurtling toward the offices of the *Pall Mall Gazette.*'

'What an indictment of our African policy!' I gasped. 'This must surely mark the end of Britain's rush to acquire influence in the Continent.'

Henry raised his eyebrows. 'Unfortunately the *Gazette* does not represent the mainstream of opinion. Its rivals are unlikely to take up the story. This information will be countered at the highest level.'

'You cannot mean it!'

'I fear so. Who, after all, are the witnesses? A few African boys. Their testimony will be attacked. The *Gazette* will be denounced. Against them is the entire weight of the British Empire. Our international prestige, our pre-eminent place at the high table of nations – as well, of course, as the booty of conquest, that is, raw materials, markets for the industrial outpourings of our northern towns, et caetera et caetera – all are at stake.'

'Oh, Henry.'

Henry took the paper, walked slowly to the window, and stood looking out at Dover St in the morning haze. 'In our scramble for plunder,' he said, 'we have long since abandoned any rational engagement with the uncharted regions of the world. The significance of any unknown civilisation, after all, lies in the thousands of years of independent development that give it its character. Rituals of courtship; notions of maleness and femaleness; rites of passage; myths and legends; dance and song; the wisdom of the ages. Anyone who feels any concern for human progress must see these things to be of profound importance. But we, the colonizers, have no interest in any of this. No, we tread these things under our feet and obliterate them. We are willing to trade the true wealth, the enlargement of knowledge, the broadening of all humanity, for a mess of gold, ivory, tobacco, cotton, tin and rubber.'

CHAPTER FIVE

The Indentured Gourmet

❦

'The ingestion of excrement is a perhaps a rather neglected *leitmotif* in world culture,' Henry began one beautiful June morning as we were sitting down to breakfast.

It was shortly after the conclusion to the affair of the Stained Lieutenant, that scandal which had threatened, for a time, to blight the fortunes of one of our oldest English families. Henry had been closely involved in the case, and it had taken no little toll on his health. For a time afterwards I had attempted to shield him from any further involvement in the sphere of sexological detection, and, partly through my efforts – which included the daily destruction of all of his incoming post – no further appeals for help from Inspector FH Pelham Bias, of Scotland Yard, had come to his notice. I was gratified, therefore, that June morning, to see Henry's face a little less drawn than hitherto.

'How so?' I asked.

'Consider the religious mystic, who forces him or herself into acts of this kind as the ultimate proof of the rejection of the body;

or sexual athletes who extend their activities to the consumption of ordure in moments of supreme rapture; or the prescriptions of doctors who advocate its use as a medicine.'

'A medicine?'

'Certainly. Schurig has written a very detailed survey of the subject, "De Stercoris Humani Usu Medico". It shows the part the medicinal use of excrement has played in combating – with what seems to have been widespread success – a variety of disorders over the centuries.' He munched on some bacon. 'The faeces of menstruating girls, for example, is in Polynesia dried and smoked as a tobacco. It is apparently very good for headaches. And yet we in this enlightened age tend to regard such acts as bordering on insanity.'

'Is that not natural?'

Henry licked a small colony of crumbs from his moustache. 'I incline, as you know, to the idea that the phenomena counted "natural" make up a much smaller grouping than we are sometimes ready to allow. Would you be so good as to pass the marmalade?'

Such was our general mealtime chit-chat. It will seem quite repulsive to many, but close association with Henry had entirely inured me to it.

At that moment a knock was heard on the outer door. I rose to answer the summons, but before I had managed to extricate myself from the table (which involved pushing back my chair into the limited space behind me, rising and navigating past two large boxes marked 'Eonism'), we became aware of uncertain steps crunching in the hall and a nervous 'Halloa!' Many people, under the impression that the house was derelict, were liable to enter in this tentative manner.

'Halloa!' Henry sang out in return. And as the echoes of his salutation died away, the pleasant face of a young man made its appearance around the morning-room door.

'Dr Henry St Liver?' asked the head.

'Yes,' Henry replied.

Our visitor looked about him in polite amazement.

'I'm sorry if I disturb you, Sir, Miss.'

'Not at all,' I said.

'I saw the front door open and thought I'd see if anyone was at home.'

'Pray take a seat,' said Henry, indicating a tattered leather stool.

The young man expressed his thanks and, taking off a gray Derby, sat down. He was a youth of rather delicate build, not above five feet six inches tall, perhaps seventeen years old, with sandy hair and an open, lightly freckled face. His uniform was that of a city clerk, though his coat and collar were a little worn and frayed; the inside of his hat bore the initials 'E.W.' Henry, of course, was quite oblivious to these marks of the young man's profession and identity: our guest might have appeared quite naked for all the notice he took of them.

'Might I introduce my friend Miss Salter?' Henry said, gesturing toward me with a knife, which discharged a small quantity of *confiture* onto the tablecloth.

The young man bowed his head. 'Very glad to meet you, Miss. I've read your *Story of an Australian Barn*.'

'Oh,' I said.

'I enjoyed it very much,' the young man continued, rather unnecessarily. There was a brief silence. Henry is not always at his best, I had noticed, in drawing out petitioners, and tends toward long owlish pauses. The young man too seemed unwilling to speak: he almost certainly possessed some secret of an intimate nature, and was inhibited by the presence of a member of the opposite sex. The fact that he had read my *Story of an Australian Barn*, with its free descriptions of love between man and woman, did not seem to aid him. The conversation, therefore, languished.

'Will you have a cup of tea?' I asked, finally.

'No, thank you very much,' the young man said. He shot a look of appeal at Henry. 'I don't know if you can help me, Sir. All I know is I'm at my wits' end.'

'I will certainly try,' Henry said.

'Thank you Sir,' said the young man. 'I came because I knew your reputation for taking on all sorts of unusual cases, and the police would be no good to me.' He blushed. 'The only explanation, it seems to me, is that someone is having a joke at my expense. Otherwise...' he broke off.

'If you will tell us what troubles you,' said Henry, 'I will do my utmost to help. Please simply go over the main points from the beginning. You can talk before Miss Salter as you would before myself.'

'I'm sure,' the young man said, bowing slightly. He hesitated. 'Alright. I'll do my best. My name's Edmund Wolfe. I worked, until recently, at Bingham's in Leadenhall Street – the insurance concern – in the foreign currency department. That was until two months ago. Then one Friday afternoon, without any warning, I was dismissed.'

'I see.'

'I asked for an interview with my senior, Monsieur Guillaume, but he just told me that the business needed to reduce its staff. I was under the impression that we were short-handed as it was. We had business coming in night and day from the *Agricole* merger and were working fit to bust. But he only shrugged his shoulders and told me that I was the most recently arrived among the junior staff, so I should be the one to leave. There was nothing to be done.'

'I see. Go on.'

'Well... I began to look around for another position. At first I had some hopes, but as the days and weeks dragged by, and my savings got less and less, I started to see that for someone like me it wasn't going to be easy. I lived at the time in digs in Camden, and the rent was three shillings a week. I realized that at this rate my money would soon give out, so I left for a place in a rooming-house in Clerkenwell. This is where I live at present. And then one day I received a letter. I've brought it with me.'

Mr Wolfe reached into his right inside pocket and produced a worn piece of notepaper which he flattened out on the table. The letter, judging by its dog-eared and grimy condition, had long since lost its envelope. The paper was heavy, with a watermark; there was a small orange stain on it, which, however, had almost certainly been acquired that moment by contact with Henry's tablecloth.

Henry took the letter and read it slowly. Henry is a slow reader, though he has a highly retentive memory.

'May I pass it to Miss Salter?' Henry asked the young man at length.

'Please do.'

I took the paper and examined it: the letter was unheaded, and written in a fluent masculine hand. It read as follows:

To Edmund Wolfe Esq.

It has come to my attention that you have recently been discharged from your duties at Bingham's and are looking for work. Although I cannot furnish you with a position, I am willing to help. If you will go to the L'Oeuf D'Or corner house restaurant in the Strand every morning for breakfast, I will ensure that they have instructions to give you anything from the menu, free of charge. I would ask you to respect two conditions only: firstly, due to financial constraints, I must ask that you restrict your orders to the period between the hours of nine and half-past ten in the morning (though within this period you may order whatever you wish); and secondly, that after having eaten your fill, you remain at the L'Oeuf D'Or throughout the whole day until five o'clock in the evening. The second condition is, I admit, self-interest: I own a small stake in the L'Oeuf D'Or, and the restaurant has in recent weeks attracted rather less custom than I and the other proprietors would wish. We are looking, therefore, for persons such as yourself to be present throughout the day to give the appearance of brisk business. This information, of course, is given in the strictest confidence.

If these conditions meet with your approval, please apply to Monsieur Bernard, the manager, at any time after the receipt of this note.

Sincerely,

'A friend in need'.

'May I ask whether you took up the invitation?' Henry asked.

The young man laughed briefly. 'I was suspicious at first, as I'm sure you'll understand. To sit in a corner house all day, just to make it look busy, seemed an odd sort of job. And to be paid just by a single meal! How would I pay for my other meals? If I took up the offer I wouldn't have time to look for work! But – as the days went by, I found the idea of a free breakfast and nothing to do all day but sit in a restaurant more and more appealing. I soon realized that if I took full advantage of the offer it might be a better look-out for me than I'd first thought. If I could eat enough between the hours of nine and ten-thirty to last me for the whole day, I'd get rid of all my grocery bills at a stroke. Nor would I have anything to pay for heat and light during the day. I could use the restaurant as an office. I could write hundreds of letters from my table.

'It was only a matter of days before I began thinking seriously about the proposal, and it was about a week before I applied in person at the L'Oeuf D'Or in the Strand. Monsieur Bernard was a pleasant man, of foreign extraction, who seemed pleased to see me. He knew all about the letter. He had no objection to my using the table to carry out correspondence. And so I began my duties.

'At first it went rather against the grain to stuff myself – if you'll pardon me, Miss – so early in the morning, but I soon became accustomed to it. I've a healthy appetite, and by the time nine o'clock came round, it was pretty sharp, as a result of not eating through the previous day. I'd generally begin with a double order of sausage, ham and eggs, with plenty of toast. Around half past nine, I'd have pancakes, and at ten kedgeree and black coffee. At twenty past ten I'd get in a final round of cakes and tea. By the half past ten deadline I was very full, uncomfortably so, and could do little but sit: by midday the feeling had worn off and I was able to address myself to business. I'd generally pass the late afternoon in writing, reading or chatting to the waiters or other customers, and at five I'd leave and return to my digs. I'd no expenses except my lodgings, at a shilling a week; and my savings, I reckoned, would last me four months more. And I'd not given up hope that I might find a job. Twice I was asked to attend interviews, but on both occasions I was unsuccessful.

'Then the blow fell. One morning, after six weeks at the L'Oeuf D'Or, which I'd come to regard as a sort of second home, I arrived to find Monsieur Bernard looking rather gloomy. He explained to me that he'd been informed by the proprietor that business had now picked up sufficiently for him to dispense with my services. They were very grateful but they had no further use for me. They wished me well, and hoped that I'd gained some benefit from the previous month and a half. So, again, I was dismissed.

'But this time I suspected that there was more to the matter than met the eye. There was something about Monsieur Bernard's manner... it was suspicious. Nothing I could put my finger on, you understand, but it didn't seem to me that he was telling the truth. And that's why I came to you, Sir.'

'It is a remarkable case,' said Henry.

'Can you see rhyme or reason to it?'

As I waited for Henry to speak I felt I must ask a question of my own. The solution to the mystery, it seemed to me, was obvious: the unnamed 'friend in need' wished to find some method of persuading Mr Wolfe to vacate his lodgings during the day, with the object of carrying on some intrigue at or near those lodgings. The offer of breakfast was nothing less than a blind.

'May I put to you a question?' I asked quickly of the young man.

'Of course.'

'May I ask whether you were the only person so employed at the L'Oeuf D'Or?'

'Yes. I'd certainly have noticed if there'd been anyone else.'

'And was the restaurant, as the letter here says, rather sparsely visited?'

'Yes, it was not very busy.'

'How did you manage to attend the interviews you were asked to?'

'I made sure they all took place after five o'clock – though that wasn't always easy.'

'Is the place where you board in Clerkenwell next-door to a bank or other financial institution?'

'No, I never noticed one.'

'And one final question. Please think carefully. Have you

discerned anything unusual recently at your lodgings: any new tenants, any unexplained events or unusual sounds, perhaps the sound of digging? Or anything out of the ordinary?'

The young man considered briefly. Then he darted a glance at Henry. 'No. I don't think so.'

'Thank you. I have no further questions.' I sat back in my chair. 'Well, Henry, what do you make of it?'

Henry paused, with a slightly startled look, in the mastication of a tomato. 'It has some features of interest, certainly,' he said.

'Do you incline to the obvious theory?'

My companion's eyes clouded over. 'I do not see anything at all obvious in this case, though I have formed some ideas. I would recommend, first of all, that we visit this establishment, the L'Oeuf D'Or. I feel that it is at the L'Oeuf D'Or that we are likely to clear up this mystery.'

'The L'Oeuf D'Or? Should we not visit this young man's lodgings in Clerkenwell, as a matter of priority?'

But the young man had sprung to his feet, rushed to the table, and was pressing Henry's hand. 'Oh, thank you Sir!' he cried. 'You don't know what this means to me! I know you can help me.'

'It is a most interesting problem,' Henry said, also rising. 'But although I think I can promise some clarification, I must counsel you against too great hope. There are elements in this case that lead me to believe that never again will you eat breakfast at the L'Oeuf D'Or.'

'It is the injustice of it, Sir, that grates,' the young man said.

'Yes. That is understandable. Well, if you will meet me at this restaurant at three o'clock this afternoon, I fancy we might take the first steps to ensure that justice is done.'

It was, I must admit, with some puzzlement that I accompanied Henry by brougham to the Strand that afternoon, having first donned a disguise. (On this particular occasion I had decided to represent myself as an out-of-work porter, and was dressed in overalls and a battered wide-awake. My adventures with Henry in the seedier corners of the capital had convinced me that a man could penetrate into places where a woman would always be remarkable.) I was convinced, as I have said, that the solution to the mystery lay not at the L'Oeuf D'Or, but at the lodging-house. Nevertheless it was with the familiar thrill, half visceral, half ratiocinative, that I stepped from the brougham that afternoon, and stood with Henry in front of the premises that had played their part in this little story.

The L'Oeuf d'Or looked to be a pleasant establishment with, in the window, a goodly arrangement of red-and-blue bowls filled with salads, as well as French breads, bottles of vermouth, and so on. Outside stood a number of tubs full of brined gherkins and olives. A menu card posted on the doorway advertised 'saucisson', 'radis', 'escargots à la Grecque' and 'paté d'Italie'. Mr Wolfe was on the pavement; after exchanging a greeting, we entered to find ourselves in a cosy restaurant with red leather benches and much in the way of dark panelling and mirrors.

No sooner had we pressed through the restaurant's doors than Mr Wolfe's mouth fell open in surprise.

'Bolt!' he exclaimed.

There, at one of the tables, sitting in a leisurely pose, was another young man. One remarkably similar, in fact, to Mr Wolfe: a fresh, handsome, ruddy youth of about seventeen, of slightly under average stature, wearing a threadbare suit of navy-blue tweed.

'Wolfe!' the young man cried with equal surprise. 'What the devil are you doing here?' He looked at Henry and myself.

'Allow me to introduce my friends,' Mr Wolfe said. This is Dr Henry St Liver, the famous police consultant. And this is Miss Salter, his assistant.'

I was a little annoyed that Mr Wolfe had introduced me in such a thoughtless manner, revealing at a stroke my sex, true identity and relationship to Henry. The young man, Mr Bolt, regarded me with a frank grin.

'Delighted,' he said. 'Won't you join me?'

Henry looked at his watch. 'I think we are in time,' he said, abstractedly.

Mr Wolfe and Mr Bolt began to arrange the chairs that we might sit down, but at that moment a fat, balding man, wearing a white apron with, I thought, liver stains – though why liver stains in a restaurant that served mainly pastries and light meals I could not understand – approached us, hovering over us with an ingratiating manner.

'Mr Wolfe! Well, well!' he cried, addressing our young man in what was either a French or a Belgian accent.

'Monsieur Bernard,' replied Mr Wolfe, not without a touch of reserve.

'It is very good,' the manager went on, 'to see you. You are always welcome here. You found another job, eh?'

Monsieur Bernard seemed, to my eye, uneasy, and it was not difficult to guess why. The young man, Mr Bolt, to whom we had just been introduced, was obviously the replacement for Mr Wolfe. Here, then, was the solution to the mystery. The 'friend in need' had decided to bestow his charity on another recipient, but, lacking the financial resources necessary to support two young men of healthy appetite, had instructed Monsieur Bernard to dismiss Mr Wolfe, yet without furnishing him with the real reason for the dismissal. Now Mr Wolfe and Mr Bolt were face to face. The next few minutes, I thought, would prove interesting. Soon the whole thing would become evident to both of them – if it had not already.

'I am at present considering a number of offers,' Mr Wolfe replied.

'Good, good, I am pleased to hear it,' the proprietor said, smiling with unpleasant lips. 'Well, then, let me extend the compliments of the house to you and your friends.'

As he spoke the word 'friends', he glanced at me, and I saw bewilderment on his features as he sought to understand why a humble porter would keep company with an ascetic-looking older man, and why both (or either) would keep company with a young clerk.

'Thank you,' Mr Wolfe replied, still with a touch of asperity. 'Will you have a cup of tea, Dr St Liver?'

'Certainly,' Henry replied.

'And Miss Salter?'

Again I was annoyed at the disclosure of my name and

identity, this time in front of Monsieur Bernard, but nodded briefly in assent. And as the *patron* scuttled away, I began formulating a few terse questions which would, I was certain, clear the whole matter up.

Before I could speak, however, Mr Bolt rose to his feet.

'Please excuse me for a moment,' he said. 'I will return very shortly.' He glanced at Mr Wolfe. 'We must talk about Bingham's. I was dismissed just last week, you know.' He laughed gaily. 'We have plenty of time. I am here until five o'clock.'

I saw with some surprise that Henry too had risen and was standing beside Mr Bolt, regarding him with a strange intensity. 'May I accompany you?' he asked.

The young man looked at Henry in slight puzzlement. 'Why, of course,' he said. 'But... I really will not be long. I must just wash my hands.'

The lavatorial euphemism was obvious. Henry, however, remained beside him, with the same queer, intense look sparkling in his eye. 'Of course,' Henry said. 'I will accompany you. Perhaps Mr Wolfe too would like to join us.'

'Me?' replied Mr Wolfe in some astonishment.

'I think you will find it instructive.'

Mr Wolfe, after a pause, rose from his chair. 'Certainly, if you wish it,' he said.

'In fact,' Henry said, making a small gesture, 'it might be best if all present at this table accompany us.'

'I?' I said.

'Certainly.'

The quiet command of the man who had salvaged the

reputation of more than one European royal family – and irretrievably demolished that of as many others – was quite irresistible. Within moments the four of us, under the astonished eye of Monsieur Bernard (at that moment returning with a tray), had begun to make our way to the rear of the restaurant, down a small passage and toward a door marked 'Gentlemen'. Opening this masculine portal, Henry led us – followed by an excited Monsieur Bernard – into a small room that rather shocked me with its squalor. The floor was of rough concrete and there was a powerful stench of excrement. A small window, boarded over, was inset high up at the back of the room; the only illumination was from a weakly fluttering gas lamp. A row of three urinals lay on our left flank, while to the right was a single box stall.

Henry, however, did not take the time to note these various points. He marched straight to the stall and flung wide the door. Nervously we crowded around. Henry rushed forward into the empty cubicle and began running his fingers rapidly over some planks that formed its rear wall. Then, taking hold of one of the planks by a knothole, he gave a savage tug.

The plank came away – and a more amazing sight I have never before beheld.

Behind the plank was the face of a man in middle-age, with blubbery cheeks and a small, oiled moustache.

'Monsieur Guillaume!' shouted the two clerks in unison.

The face of the blubbery man disappeared, and, in a flash, a little form shot from the void behind the planks.

'Hold him!' Henry shrilled. A brief, frantic struggle ensued.

Mr Wolfe grasped the fugitive by the coat, Mr Bolt by the right arm; I slipped and found myself on my knees, clinging to a leg. In the space of a few seconds we had entirely subdued our man, who, pinioned by three limbs, now regarded us with a mixture of fear, shame and hatred.

'Ah! Ah! You have me!' he cried, shivering. 'You have me!'

'I think so,' remarked Henry.

'I will not resist you! Be so good as to release your hold!'

At a nod from Henry we three slowly let go the little man, and we six (that is, including Monsieur Bernard, who was regarding the scene hysterically from the doorway) stood breathing heavily in the small malodorous room.

'May I ask,' Henry enquired, 'what you were doing hidden there, Monsieur Guillaume?'

The Frenchman darted a sidelong glance at him. 'Am I in the presence,' he panted, 'of Dr St Liver, the celebrated police consultant?'

'You are,' Henry replied.

Monsieur Guillaume took a deep, shuddering breath. 'Then I see that it is all up with me. I will confess. But I think this is not the proper place, Doctor. I will tell all, but I make one condition. Only yourself and such persons as are necessary for transcribing a record of what passes between us may be present when I do so. This is not, I believe, a criminal matter.'

Henry looked at the two young clerks. 'I hardly think my clients would be happy to accept such a settlement,' he said. 'They have, after all, been dismissed, by you, from their posts at Bingham's. Unless I am very much mistaken, they will require clarification of this matter and of why, subsequently, they were engaged here at the L'Oeuf D'Or.'

The two clerks, such was their residual deference to their former chief, and even though they had that moment helped to apprehend him in grotesque circumstances in a filthy latrine, did not move to confirm the supposition.

'I am willing to restore them to their posts at Bingham's,' the little Gaul breathed after a space, 'on an increased salary, in return for their forfeit of the right to hear my confession.'

Henry turned to Mr Wolfe and Mr Bolt. 'I think the terms are generous. You two gentlemen will understandably wish to know more about the happenings here this afternoon, but, as Monsieur Guillaume has said, it is unlikely that this constitutes a criminal matter. If you will accept these terms I will hazard that you will have no more trouble from this gentleman.'

Mr Wolfe stared fixedly at the floor for a short time, and then turned his gaze on Henry. 'I would give a great deal,' he said slowly, 'to learn the true meaning of the events here today, but my livelihood is worth more to me even than this knowledge. I accept the terms. Thank you, Dr St Liver, for this amazing display of your powers.'

Henry turned to Mr Bolt. 'And you, my young friend?'

'I don't know how you did this, Dr St Liver, but I too accept the conditions. My heartfelt thanks to you.'

'Very well,' said Henry. 'We will leave you, then. Let us three – Miss Salter, Monsieur Guillaume – return to Dover Mansions.'

Henry leant back in his chair, his legs stretched out lazily before him, and pressed the tips of his index fingers together. 'It is not infallibly the case,' he began, 'that a mystery such as the one presented by our friend Mr Wolfe this morning has a sexological link. However, as the great Iwan Bloch himself said in *The Sexual Life of Our Time*, sexology must be treated as the unifying science, subsuming all other sciences – general biology, anthropology and ethnology, philosophy and psychology, the history of literature, and the entire history of civilization – and therefore the sexological approach to any problem is the one most likely to furnish the requisite tools to bring about its solution.'

He reached for an Abdulla from a box at his elbow. Monsieur Guillaume had been installed in a blue wicker chair among numerous piles of books, periodicals, pictures, *objets d'art*, ashtrays, souvenirs and other bric-a-brac. It was only now that I had a chance to observe him more carefully. He was, as I have mentioned, a man of around forty years of age, not above five feet five inches tall, with a smooth, cherubic, fat-cheeked face, marked only by a small manicured moustache and a livid red spot above the right eye. He had two gold teeth, both on the right side, one upper and one lower. As befitted his position as head of the foreign currency department at Bingham's, he was dressed soberly in a black coat and waistcoat, and his brogues had evidently that morning been polished to a high shine, though they were now somewhat bespattered. He seemed completely to have recovered his equanimity after the torrid activity of the afternoon, and was himself engaged in an interested examination of Henry as he reclined in his armchair by the large fish-tank.

'And in Mr Wolfe's case,' Henry continued, 'with its many suggestive elements, it was comparatively soon after perusing your letter, Monsieur Guillaume, that I saw that here was something that cried out for sexological explication. Consider the facts. A young man, of attractive mien, is dismissed from his job for no convincing reason. Some time later he is offered a mysterious position which involves the public consumption of large amounts of food. The manager of the establishment that proffers these large amounts of food is of French extraction, the same nationality as his former employer; there is, therefore, the strong possibility that the two are in league, and that the dismissal and subsequent offer are connected. Now, the concordance between the appetite of hunger and the sexual appetite has been thoroughly explored and documented. I do not think these basic facts need detain us. I refer you to Rafael Salillas, "An Introductory Survey of the Food Paraphilia" – you will find the applicable journal in that higher stack to your left under the small bronze – in which the obvious parallels are pointed out. Those between the mouth and the sex organs of a woman, for example; or between various soft foods that do not require mastication and the spermatic fluid; or between the introduction of foods into the body and coitus itself. Once we consider how oral play may in some cases entirely substitute for the act of coitus, how pregnant and lactating women have irresistible desires for various food delicacies, how children, especially little girls, crave for sweet things such as oranges or bananas, and how, in the sphere of religion, the sacrament of Communion itself may stand as a simulacrum of the ecstatic interpenetration of human and divine, we can no longer doubt the relations between the two phenomena. But one detail troubled me. Why was Mr Wolfe permitted only a single meal, and why must that meal be breakfast? Why was it imperative that the meal be consumed between nine and half past ten, and why – more pertinently – was it necessary for him to remain in the restaurant until five o'clock? Why not two, or six?'

Henry paused. I looked at Monsieur Guillaume, whose face and neck seemed to have distended a little, and gained colour.

'A large meal,' Henry continued, 'takes an average of five hours to be digested and for its waste products to be present as faeces in the bowel. After five-and-a-half to six hours, the pressure is insistent and must be relieved. Any person who has eaten a large meal will therefore be compelled to defaecate within six hours – given an average, healthy digestion. The pieces were coming together. It was evident that the anonymous author of the note was interested less in ingestion than in digestion, less in absorption than in excretion.'

'Yes!' broke in Monsieur Guillaume excitedly. 'Yes!'

Henry held up a forefinger. 'If I may be allowed to finish, Monsieur. The reason that five o'clock was chosen as the hour of Mr Wolfe's departure was that the evacuation of the bowel would be inevitable before this time. The young man would not be physically capable of waiting – without injury – until any later. He would be forced to satisfy this natural urge there in the L'Oeuf D'Or. Of course, in consuming only one large meal *per diem*, his digestion would soon be tuned to produce a healthy stool at a predictable time every day – "on the dot", so to speak. And it was at that time, at around half past three in this case, that you would be waiting for him in your hiding-place in the latrine, Monsieur.'

'I admit it unreservedly.'

'If one wished to give this complex of feelings and activities a name – and I trust I do not give offence, Monsieur – one might term it, in medical parlance, coprolagnia. This may manifest itself either as an attraction to excreta itself, or as a desire to witness defaecation, or both. Occasionally there is a purely olfactory fetichistic aspect. Coprolagnia is perhaps less common than its sister, urolagnia, as may be imagined: urine is generally less offensive, and is more readily associable with the primary organs of sexual activity. Bourke's *Scatalogic Rites of All Nations* gives a useful overview.

'But it seems that after a few weeks had elapsed, Monsieur, the spectacle of Mr Wolfe defaecating had begun to pall. You required new excitements. You had him removed from the L'Oeuf D'Or, and, after a decent interval, installed Mr Bolt in his place, having first engineered Mr Bolt's dismissal from the foreign currency department. And so you would have continued, had not Mr Wolfe applied to me this morning. In short, Monsieur, the dismissal of Mr Wolfe, your letter, the offer of breakfast at the L'Oeuf D'Or, et caetera, et caetera, were, I hazard, all part of an elaborate ruse, the object of which was to allow you to witness a young man in the act of defaecation. The "need" of the "friend in need" was not the need of the young men on whom you appeared to lavish charity, but your own need, an urgent and overmastering need, and one which you would stop at nothing to satisfy.'

Henry calmly regarded the little broker, who, for his part,

was sitting with his hands clasped in front of his chest in a gesture of homage.

'You have covered the cardinal points brilliantly,' the Frenchman said. 'Quite brilliantly. I congratulate you, Doctor. I see now that it would have been difficult for a logical mind, remorselessly applied as yours has been, to have reached any other conclusion.'

'Well. Perhaps that is true,' Henry replied gravely.

'Yes. And I, of course, I am cast as the villain. Yes, yes. That is inevitable.' He glanced slyly at us. 'Though I do not see who was harmed in this case.'

'The dignity of the young men, who counted themselves unobserved?' I put in.

'And their position at Bingham's,' Henry remarked. 'You must admit that in this respect you rendered them a very great disservice.'

Monsieur Guillaume smiled, a little wanly. 'Perhaps in that regard I am guilty. But... you have allowed me to come here to present my side of things.'

'That is so,' Henry replied.

'Then I would like, if you will indulge me, to tell my story. You – Sir, Mademoiselle – are perhaps in an unique position to appreciate it. And yet even such as yourselves will, I feel, be surprised at some of its facets.'

'You have our full attention, Monsieur,' said my companion.

The room was now growing dark, and I rose with the aim of threading my way through Henry's accumulated detritus to the wall-lamp; but the Frenchman held up a hand.

'Please, Mademoiselle,' he said. 'I wish to let the shades of evening cast their cloak around me as I recount my tale. It is, I think you will agree, a murky enough one.'

'Very well,' I replied.

'First of all,' Monsieur Guillaume began when I had regained my seat, 'I must tell you that although I was born in France, I have now taken British citizenship. My mother and father are both still living, in the place of my birth, a small village near to Chamonix at the foot of Mont Blanc, in the Haute-Savoie département. It was there that I attended school, moving to continue my studies – as an accountant – to Grenoble. I worked throughout my twenties and thirties in Paris. I came to this country at the age of thirty-two, seeking advancement in my career, and have now lived here for the better part of a decade.

'I was a serious child. I took an interest in poetry, in music, in mathematics, and excelled in the latter. I would have liked to have been a teacher, but for this I had no aptitude. My family were very religious, and I was expected to attend church several times a week. I do not now have any religious feelings, but I retain a strong moral sense: I am attracted to the good, the beautiful and the noble, and I delight in poetry and music, which seem to me the finest creations of the human brain. I do not willingly cheat or dissemble. Of course such a statement must seem strange to you.

'I am not a paederast, and neither have I ever used male prostitutes. It is true that my desires are directed toward very young lads, of twelve or older – rarely older than eighteen – but I seek not base physical contact, rather what is pure and perfect, a deep, noble spiritual affection. What I seek is to be in the position of father to a lad I love. I would wish to set such a young man on the right track in life and instruct him in the avoidance of the errors and false paths of my own.

'But having persisted in these feelings since my schooldays, and having suffered great pain because of them, I never encountered any answering soul. I listened to the ribald jokes of my schoolfellows and later my workmates, and saw the coquettish behaviour of young ladies, but found both equally incomprehensible. I did once, it is true, form a connection with a superior young lady, but was never able to reveal my true feelings, and she, for her part, must have been much perplexed by me. I am afraid I ill-used her. We drifted apart. Life resumed, a dreary and meaningless round, always the same. I felt myself to be the butt of some obscure and futile joke.

'But even that weight of misery was not all. I knew that even if I found a young man who was, like myself, an invert, my specific desires would in all likelihood be met with incredulity, perhaps repugnance. Through my reading – where I could find anything of relevance – I came to believe, with no little horror, that I was an invert almost of an unique variety. It may even be that what I am about to describe to you falls without the sphere of sexological enquiry.'

I glanced at Henry, wondering whether such a thing were possible. Henry, however, said nothing. By his head a black and brown carp turned slowly in the gloom.

'I remember at the age of eight or so first looking into a medical book and seeing a picture of the human digestive system. I was in transports at the superb economy of the organisation of stomach, gut and bowel: these organs seemed to me to be the crowning glory of creation. Yet I soon found that society wished never to speak of them. A veil was drawn over these most delightful things: digestion, the processing of food, excretion. I saw that people in public would sooner injure themselves by retaining the urine or the stool than admit to this need and seek relief. This seemed to me shockingly ungrateful, almost blasphemous. I felt as a normal man would if the Venus de Milo had been pronounced an ugly old crone, spat on and broken up with hammers. And I found as I grew older that I was only attracted to those parts of the exterior body associable with digestion, that is, the belly and the buttocks. To witness a fairly compact stool emerging from the anus was the *ne plus ultra* of my imaginings. But I could find no person, no text, no work of art or science that would explain these feelings. Occasionally I would come across passages such as those in Swift, regarding excrement, but these left me depressed for days, since a quite natural and beautiful function had been made to represent all that was base, disgusting, low and unspiritual. For me it was precisely the opposite, and the condition of the stool became to me an emblem of the condition of the soul. I think even my choice of career was directed by my desires: I was attracted to the world of finance because money is so well described in terms of movement and flow, liquid and solid. I ranked clients according to the health of their accounts. Those with prodigious cash flow I considered virtuous, while those with accounts that sat idle and stagnated for years I regarded as almost wicked.

'Here I must make one thing clear: digestion, excretion and excreta itself do not excite me sexually. On the odd occasion I experience erection while contemplating these things or indulging in what you have termed 'coprolagnic' behaviour – the term is new to me – but this is unwelcome and in fact causes me discomfort. Perhaps I have never experienced true sexual excitement.

'The design, situation and everything to do with public conveniences fascinates me. I have spent considerable time studying the provisions made in other countries and cultures to see how our own could be improved. Personally, I favour the squatting commode, or 'elephant's foot' design, as found in Turkey and other Middle Eastern regions. I have had one installed in my own house next to the conventional type, so that I may choose which suits me best on any particular day. My ritual is always the same. First I examine the distension of my belly to estimate the size and condition of the stool – I regret very much that advancing corpulence in latter years has rendered this more difficult – before defaecating with maximum control and concentration. Nothing pleases me more than to bring off a large, firm, healthy stool. If my digestion is unsettled, then I am unsettled. Heaven help my clerks or business associates on those days.

'As a young man I would often plan my defaecations – which meant, of course, carefully scheduling my meal-times – so that I was at liberty to visit some outdoor location, perhaps the woods or mountains, where I could defaecate *en plein air*. If unable to do this I would indulge in fantasies in which I was the main character in some Robinsonade, and had an entire archipelago at my disposal in which to defaecate, on sandbar, hilltop, grove or river-bank.

'Now, I must have given you the impression that my desires are somewhat solipsistic. Not so. Above all things I desired a companion who would understand these urges and who would himself experience satisfaction in the activities I have described. The highest ecstasy would be for us to spend time in the pursuit of some noble ideal – perhaps the reading of poetry or the contemplation of natural objects – before defaecating simultaneously and copiously. Beside this, the pleasures of defaecation *à seul* could never be more than a shadow. Again and again my thoughts would turn on that moment when I would witness my beloved's anus dilate and I would see the stool, with a gentle crackling sound, emerging into the world.'

Monsieur Guillaume paused, took a handkerchief from his waistcoat pocket, and mopped his brow. The day had been a warm one and even at this late hour the room was rather close.

'No boy came, however, and I fell increasingly prey to moods of self-disgust and shame, once the orgiastic reverie had passed. I attempted abstinence, but within days was driven back to my imaginings. I felt the encroachment of madness as I wrestled with thoughts that had never, so far as I knew, occurred to another living soul.

'By this time I had entered my fortieth year, and by a combination of good fortune and long years of service, had risen to become the head of the foreign currency department at Bingham's. Under me, naturally, I had several young men. Of course they were all normal, healthy young men who had the same interests as my own coevals when they were boys: young ladies, socializing, and so on. One in particular took my fancy – Edmund Wolfe. Although seventeen years of age he looked somewhat younger, and seemed a serious and sensitive lad, as I had been. I did not show him any particular marks of favour, but felt my eye irresistibly drawn to him whenever I looked up from my desk. I soon began to have shameful thoughts.

'Then, one day, a terrible plan formed itself in my mind. I would dismiss him, the one I liked best. I would prevent his gaining any other employment; and then I would ask Monsieur Bernard – a compatriot, who had received from me some years ago a small favour of a pecuniary nature – to play host to him at the restaurant in the Strand. I would enter the restaurant via the side door at around half past three in the afternoon every day, and conceal myself behind the partition in the lavatory. My knowledge of the physiology of digestion suggested to me that it would be at this time – as you have correctly surmised – that Edmund's physical needs would demand satisfaction.

'You can imagine the excitement of that first occasion. My whole body was squeezed closely against the rough planking. There was no sound in the latrine: the slightest noise would have given me away. I had only a limited field of vision, through a crack approximately an eighth of an inch wide. I wondered whether my loved one would see me through the crack, and had no way of knowing, that first time, whether or not I would immediately be discovered. When Edmund came in and took his breeches down I felt myself in the grip of a hurricane. I thought I would faint. He removed his breeches and discharged himself. I could not, unfortunately, see much on that first occasion, though by widening the crack later, as I became more confident, I was able to see more. On two occasions I was privileged, by a fortuitous placement of Edmund's buttocks, to witness the emergence of the stool. They were moments of terrible pleasure and great grief.

'So began my new life. Each day, at three o'clock, I would leave Bingham's, rush to the L'Oeuf D'Or, and secrete myself behind the wall. Each day I would be terrified I would be discovered before I had managed fully to conceal myself, or that I would meet Edmund coming into the latrine. On some days I would be forced to abort my plans when another customer met me as I entered the latrine; on other days there would be customers already in the latrine when I arrived, and, because I could not afford to wait there until they had left, had to make my exit immediately. Once secreted, I would sometimes have only a minute to wait before Edmund entered. At other times, I waited an hour or more; and if Edmund failed to appear I would return to Bingham's much disappointed. On many occasions I was forced to witness acts by other customers, many not very prepossessing, that I shall not describe to you.

'This went on for a few weeks with such success that I began to wonder whether it might not be possible to repeat the entire process with another young man. Edmund had not ceased to delight me, but I was greedy for a new adventure. Perhaps something within me also wished to be caught and exposed. Consequently I took another risk. Martin Bolt, who you have met, had begun to catch my eye at Bingham's. Accordingly I had Edmund dismissed – may he forgive me – and Martin took his place. I should not have done so. I should not have done any of it. I betrayed both of these young men. It was all madness. And you have outlined the rest of it very well, Doctor. Yes, it is all as you have said.'

Monsieur Guillaume fell silent. The room was now almost entirely dark.

'A very moving account, Monsieur,' Henry said at last.

'It is all true.'

'We could hardly doubt it.'

'What do you intend to do with me?'

'Nothing,' Henry said briefly. 'It is likely that if this matter came to the attention of the authorities you would be committed, not to prison, for your offence is comparatively light, but to an asylum.'

'Then...?'

'One probability that occurs to me is that now, having to some extent enacted your fantasies, you will find that a shift takes place within you that gives rise to a more genital expression. You might then find another who would reciprocate. I would recommend you search a little more fully than hitherto in the homosexual community. Make contacts among homosexuals – you might try my friend Horatio Tampe, of Chelsea. I will give you his address.' Henry took out a decrepit green notebook. 'By enlarging your acquaintance in this area you will discover worlds currently hidden to you. But I would strongly recommend that you do not repeat the behaviour of the last few weeks. I would beg you never to use the L'Oeuf D'Or, or any other establishment, for the covert observation of young men – to safeguard both your own liberty and the rights of privacy of the young men themselves. If you will promise me this I will be content to let this matter rest between these four walls.'

The little Frenchman sprang to his feet. 'Thank you, thank you!' he cried, tripping over two empty Salmanazar champagne bottles that Henry had recently acquired at a flea market. 'I will never forget the service you have rendered me here today! Perhaps, after all, it will be possible to live a normal life. You have given me hope. You are the only person in the world who has understood me – probably, could ever understand me. I thank God that Edmund came to you today!'

Such were the singular circumstances in the case of the Indentured Gourmet. But even after our guest had left that afternoon, and after we had turned up the lamps, and Henry was sitting comfortably in his armchair puffing on a cigarette and perusing the *Archiv für Sexualwissenschaft*, I found that I was still a little perplexed. I confessed as much, and Henry looked at me moonishly. It was difficult to tell whether or not a smile was forming under his moustache.

'My main area of puzzlement, I confess,' I said, 'is to do with the nature of this poor man's fancies. If, as he claimed, they had no power to arouse him sexually, and sexual arousal was unwelcome to him, then how can it be that they exerted such a powerful grip? Can it be true, after all, that there was no sexual component to these grotesque and bizarre compulsions?'

'That would depend on one's conception of the sexual,' Henry replied, tapping his cigarette carefully onto the carpet. 'Many things are sexual which do not necessarily involve the genital. The sounds, calls, odours, contests and mock-battles of animals, the singing, dancing and other rituals of human lovers in all societies; these, and much else, form the totality of the drama of sex. The slow accumulation of amatory excitement that we observe during these activities may even dwarf, in its psychic significance, the final crisis: that is, the orgasm itself and the associated expulsion of a teaspoon or so of seminal or vaginal fluid.'

'I suppose that is true.'

It is in this accumulatory phase that we must often seek the causes of sexual aberration. In courtship, the lover finds his attention drawn to the belly, buttocks and thighs of his beloved: those places in proximity to the genital regions. Monsieur Guillaume continues to linger in this phase, for reasons probably now undiscoverable, buried in the mists of his past, perhaps lost even further back in his heredity. He has elevated the accumulatory phase above its final end. He may not feel it to be so – he may, as he said, wish to spurn the base, aspire to what is pure and perfect – but in the grip of his cravings, he is yet another acolyte paying tribute to the gods of sexual love.'

Chapter Six

The Seven Spools

It had been some months since we had had a visit from Inspector FH Pelham Bias, of Scotland Yard, and I knew that our run of luck could not last for ever.

I find it difficult to explain fully why, in common with so many others, I felt such an aversion to Pelham Bias. It was not just his soft body, nor his slow and viscid movements – like something creeping at the bottom of a well – nor his bland demeanour, nor the fact that he profited by Henry's genius and gave nothing in return. No, his presence elicited a mysterious additional sense of repulsion that I could never quite put my finger on. But Henry, as I have mentioned, seemed positively to enjoy his company.

It was in the November of '94. Henry and I were sitting together one morning in the kitchen at Dover Mansions – somewhat hemmed in by Henry's collection of empty milk bottles – when suddenly I became aware of a series of sticky, scraping noises from the hall. My heart sank as I recognized the characteristic footfall of the just-mentioned detective. Alerting Henry to the presence of our visitor, I led the way into the morning room, where Pelham Bias already stood, motionless and slightly glistening.

'Bias!' cried Henry.

'How are you, St Liver?' said Pelham Bias, slowly taking off his hat.

'Very well, very well! Take a seat, my dear chap.'

I removed from the settle a quarter-size anatomical model of a mare's glutea, and Pelham Bias sank into it with an undulating movement.

'First, I must congratulate you, Miss Salter,' Bias panted, 'on your recent success. We are all surprised and delighted up at the Yard. Indeed I assure you we talk of nothing else.'

'Thank you,' I said.

'And I refer not just to your excellent Australian adventures. Your sketches of detection in the *New Age,* too, are fast becoming required reading. I was astonished to see myself depicted in one of them: the story of the Despoiler, I think it was.' He regarded me mucilaginously for a moment. 'Most instructive.'

'Thank you.'

'Then,' Henry interjected, raising an eyebrow, 'if you have the leisure to read Miss Salter, there are no unsolved cases currently taxing your wits?'

Pelham Bias smiled. 'I hardly like to trouble you.'

'Come along. Out with it, my dear fellow.'

'It is a trivial matter, quite trivial... But it holds some points of interest. I will tell you what I know of it, if you have the time.'

'Please.'

'It concerns the convent on Beddington Street in Hoxton.'

'The Discalced Servites,' said Henry. 'I know it.'

'Yes, the Discalced Servites,' said Pelham Bias. 'An odd name.'

'"Discalced", from *calceus*, shoe,' said Henry, 'and thus "shoe-less" or "barefoot". "Servites" needs no explanation. "Barefoot servants", then.'

'Yes. Exactly. Well, let me begin. About a week ago, a constable of ours was making enquiries in that area, with regard to a series of burglaries. Going from door to door, he found himself at the convent, and spoke to the Mother Superior. She told him that she had not seen anything suspicious. As he was about to leave, however, she surprised him by suddenly clutching at his sleeve. She then told him that she wanted to speak to a detective; she wanted advice, she said, but refused to confide in the constable there and then. Therefore the case came to me. I could hardly ask a venerable old nun down to the station, so I paid her a visit. Well... the essence of the case is that one of the nuns – the Superior knows not which – has been peculating.'

'Ah,' Henry said.

'The income of the nuns is mainly from sewing. They spend the morning in prayer and household chores, and after lunch go to the workroom. Here they engage in a rather unusual activity: they embroider sacramental cloths in gold thread. The thread is of purest gold, and very expensive.'

'Is the sewing by hand?' asked Henry.

'No, by machine.'

'Excellent,' said Henry. 'Pray continue.'

'It is the gold thread that lies at the centre of this case. The spools are large, and each spool is worth around fifteen pounds. It is these spools that are being stolen.'

'Why are the nuns under suspicion?' I asked.

Pelham Bias rotated torpidly to face me. 'Only one spool is ever taken at a time,' he said. 'So far, there have been seven such thefts, spaced over a period of three months. If the culprit had been someone from outside the convent, it is reasonable to assume that several spools would have been taken at once. Professional thieves do not generally take things in dribs and drabs.'

'Thank you,' I said.

Pelham Bias turned back to Henry. 'The spools are on permanent display in a cabinet in the workroom. The cabinet is never locked, even at night. Whenever a nun needs to change a spool, she simply walks to the front of the workroom and takes one. The Superior, whose machine is in the front rank near the cabinet, can see each time a nun takes a new spool. In addition she checks the number of spools each night, and again first thing in the morning. On seven occasions there has been a spool missing.'

'Has she considered locking the cabinet?' asked Henry.

'I taxed her on this very point. She refused to countenance the idea: she felt it would be corrosive to trust. For the same reason the workroom – accessed by an internal door – is also never locked. Any good it would do, she seems to feel, would be outweighed by the damage to the community.'

'I see.'

'The fact remains, however, that seven spools have now gone missing. This represents a loss of income equivalent to half of the entire profit the convent would expect to make from the embroidered cloths over the same period. If the thefts continue, therefore, the convent's very livelihood will be affected.'

'Has the Superior made any effort to speak to the nuns on this matter?'

'As far as I can see, she has not. She is a very highly-strung person – quite unlike what I had expected from a Mother Superior – and fearful of what might happen if the nuns became aware of this scandal. She is worried that if she makes her knowledge of the thefts public, no one will come forward to confess, and that the resulting suspicion and ill-feeling among the nuns will do permanent harm. Even if the offending nun – who is, I fancy, hoarding the spools out of some kleptomaniacal urge rather than profiting by their sale – were publicly exposed by this means, she would then likely feel compelled to leave the order. The Superior is eager to avoid this if at all possible. She would wish the offender to confess privately, do penance, and remain under the rule. But she sees no way of achieving this. She is quite at a loss.'

'She has not taken any other measures to discover the culprit?' Henry asked.

'She will not countenance a search of the rooms. Again, it would alert the nuns to the very thing she wishes to keep secret. And she will not think of searching covertly, I suppose for moral reasons.'

'What then of lying in wait for the thief?'

'The possibility has occurred to her. But these thefts take place very irregularly, and short of staying up every night for a fortnight, there seems little possibility of catching the thief in the act.'

'Hum.'

'So you see, St Liver, she has come to me hoping for a miracle. I am somewhat handicapped. The tools of the detective are interrogation; search; ambush. And all of these are specifically ruled out.'

Henry laughed and rubbed his hands together. The animation he habitually showed when in the presence of Pelham Bias was quite astonishing.

'Rather a puzzle,' he said. 'I am put in mind of the story of Rumpelstiltskin. You know the story – the princess, the golden thread and so on. The princess must weave a cloth of gold every night, and is helped by a dwarf who demands her first-born child. I cannot recall where I read it...'

'It is a children's story, Henry,' I said. 'Perhaps your mother read it to you.'

'Ah yes, of course.'

'Do you have any ideas?' asked Pelham Bias, bringing the conversation back to the matter in hand.

'The suggestive elements cluster so thickly,' Henry said, his moustache a little atwitch, 'it is an *embarras de richesse*, almost. I think I must first make an inspection of the convent workroom. I am sure then I will be in a position to give you something.'

'Excellent! Well, if you and Miss Salter would care to join me, I plan to visit the convent again tomorrow at around half-past one. Would that suit you?'

So it was that the following afternoon I found myself accompanying Henry and Pelham Bias to Hoxton – the scene of my first residence in London, of course – to the convent of the Discalced Servites. I was greatly looking forward to experiencing, if only briefly, the calm atmosphere of the convent, since my own affairs in recent weeks had been somewhat frantic, and I was moreover suffering from the headaches, chlorosis, asthma attacks and dyspepsia attendant on a literary life in London devoid of healthy exercise, sun and fresh food.

The convent was situated in the more genteel southern part of the suburb, and was built, to judge by its appearance, in the latter part of the last century. It was a large, rambling house of sandy-coloured brick, set in extensive grounds and accessed via a long, curving drive, so that it was invisible from the street. As our conveyance made its way up the drive, the first striking impression was of the nuns themselves, several of whom were at work tending the kitchen garden. In compliance with the rule of the order, none were shod, even with sandals; and I will admit – at the risk of sacrilege – that the effect in the wet weather was rather comical, since all were demurely robed and be-wimpled, yet covered in mud from the ankle down.

Pelham Bias rang the bell, and a smiling shoeless nun showed us into a simply furnished room on the ground floor. Within a minute the Superior of the convent entered to greet us. She was a slender woman of about fifty years of age, clothed in the dark habit of the order, with a cross about her neck and a bulky chaplet hanging at her belt. She too was bare-footed, her well-scrubbed feet and well-kept nails glowing an attractive pink, and there was an honesty and openness in her countenance that made a pleasant impression, though in the forehead there were lines of worry, and in the cheek, signs of paleness, which hinted that some personal trouble was gnawing at her (as in fact we knew to be the case).

'Thank you for coming again, Inspector Bias,' she said. 'May I welcome your friends?'

'Yes, this is Dr Henry St Liver,' said Pelham Bias, 'a specialist in criminal matters. And this is his assistant, Miss Salter. You may have read,' he added, 'her *Story of an Australian Barn*.'

'I am afraid I have not,' the nun said with visible consternation, 'though I will try to do so at the earliest opportunity.'

Pelham Bias's eyes roved slowly over her. 'I am sure you would enjoy it. As to the unfortunate events here at the convent, Reverend Mother, I am afraid I have nothing to offer you at the moment. My colleague Dr St Liver wishes to make a brief inspection of your workroom.'

The Superior's face fell. 'Oh, Inspector. When I heard you were coming again today I had hopes...'

'I fully understand. But please try to wait a little longer. We will do all in our power to bring this matter to a swift conclusion.'

'Thank you, I do hope so,' the Superior said. 'Well, then. If you wish to see the workroom, that can easily be arranged. It is empty at the moment. Will you gentlemen and Miss Salter follow me, please?'

She led us from the room into a white, unadorned hallway; we then descended down a queerly sloping corridor to a set of double doors, which she pulled wide. This was evidently the workroom. It was about five-and-twenty feet wide by twenty deep, lit on the left-hand side by a row of recessed windows covered in grilles. Filling the room entirely were thirty sewing machines, ranged in five rows of six. The machines were all of the treadle variety, and each had a plain wooden chair standing neatly by. To the left, underneath the windows, was a table with numerous bolts of white cloth and finished items of work, glinting gently with gold thread. At the far end of the room was an office desk, some shelves, and, at head-height on the wall, a cabinet containing several dozen large golden spools. The spools, even from a distance, were very conspicuous. They presented a flaming gold mass quite at odds with the spareness of the rest of the room, and indeed the convent in general. It was an effect almost Byzantine. Anyone with the merest tinge of the jackdaw in her would have felt the urge to touch, perhaps possess them, and it was not difficult to understand why one of the nuns had been led to covet them beyond reason, and had taken to secreting them in the poverty of her cell. Examining the room more closely, I saw that a single gold spool flamed also from the top of each of the machines.

'This is where we work from half-past two until mid-afternoon prayers,' the Superior said. 'Mid-afternoon prayers are at four. We sew, therefore, for one and a half hours a day. Our work is in sewing palls. The pall, as you will know, is the cloth that covers the coffin. The finished palls are here.' She indicated the long table under the windows.

Henry, Pelham Bias and I walked over to examine them. The topmost pall in the nearest pile was embroidered with an elaborate golden cross surrounded by a braided border; braiding was also visible on the folded edges of the cloths beneath.

'These palls are identical?' Henry asked.

'Yes,' the Superior replied. 'We work to a single design. We have done so for many years: there seems to be no appetite for variety.'

'And where do they go?' Henry asked.

'To Europe, to the Americas, and of course to parts nearer home. Our work is, I think, among the finest of this type. It is much in demand, and indeed the palls constitute our only income. That is why I must take action in this matter, even if...' – the Superior broke off, looked for a moment out of a window at the nuns in the garden below, and continued in lower tones – 'even if the consequences are very terrible.'

'I understand,' Henry said.

'I pray daily for the poor soul that has been tempted to this course. Perhaps it is not apparent to you, Doctor, what a breach this is of the principles of our order?'

Henry nodded, his moustache enormous.

'We live very simply, you see. We have no personal property. Everything is held in common. Even our pallets and the furnishings in our cells, our crosses and rosaries, are changed every year so that we never come to think of them as our own. These thefts constitute the grossest possible rejection of our shared life. They seem... almost insane.'

'Yes,' said Henry. 'Now, how much thread goes into each pall?'

'Each pall takes eighty-seven yards.'

'Exactly?'

'There are small variations, but no more than a yard or two. It is important to keep to the exact yardage if possible, because the thread is so expensive.'

'Very good. And how much thread does each spool hold?'

The Superior seemed a little surprised at the sudden materialism of the line of questioning, but went on stoutly. 'Each spool holds exactly two hundred yards of thread.' She walked to the nearest sewing-machine, neatly popped off the spool on top, and held it out to Henry, its golden strand trailing. 'You can see here,' she said, pointing to a manufacturer's legend on the base. 'Two hundred yards.' She wound up the spool and set it back on the spindle.

'Excellent,' Henry said. 'Now, if I may, to your books. I must see your books for the last three months, since the thefts began, showing the exact number of sewn items completed, as well as the number of spools received.'

The Superior regarded Henry for a few seconds. 'You are very welcome to do so,' she said gently, 'but the chief evidence, I feel, lies in the fact of the missing spools.' She gestured toward the cabinet. 'And I regret to say that for this you have only my word.'

'And I trust it implicitly, Madam,' Henry said. 'In fact I base this inquiry on it. Yet if you wish me to find the culprit, you must open your books to me. That is the only way, I assure you, that you can restore peace to your community.'

Again, it was remarkable to see the change in Henry as he took charge of the investigation. He stood more erect, he appeared more massy; his moustache quivered like a live thing, and the very air around him seemed charged. It was clear to me that the filaments of his mind were reaching out to things imperceptible to the ordinary observer, and I could not help wondering what orgiastic compulsion lurked at the root of these seemingly insipid crimes.

'I see,' the Superior said doubtfully. 'Very well.' She walked to her desk by the cabinet of spools. 'If you think it necessary.' She took a folder from a shelf, and opened it on the desk. 'These records show the palls we have sold, and to whom. They begin on this page, in August, and run to the present week. And here,' she continued, opening a morocco-bound notebook lying on the desk, 'are the records for the spools we have received during the same period.'

'Thank you.'

'Please call for me if you should need me. I shall be just outside.'

The nun strode quickly out through the double doors, and Henry sat at the desk. I watched as he began a careful study of the records. Knowing that this was likely to take some time, I walked to the window. I could not quite see what Henry intended, except to discredit the Superior's story. Could she have been responsible for the thefts herself? And if that were the case, what motive could she possibly have in calling the police?

Outside was the kitchen garden, and in it were three or four nuns engaged in trimming, composting, and so on. One young nun, about fifty yards off, caught my eye. She was attempting to uproot some species of large plant, perhaps a cabbage, though one long gone to seed. Obviously thinking herself unobserved, she had given herself up entirely to the struggle, with both heels dug deep in the November mud, and both horny fists wrapped around the stem, straining with all her might to wrench it from the soil. Her face was suffused with the fierce abandonment, almost, of Bernini's Cornaro Chapel. She was leaning so far back that had the roots given way she would certainly have taken a tumble into the mire. Just at the moment when it seemed that one or the other of them, nun or plant, must surely snap, an elderly conventual hobbled up and motioned that she should desist, and instead loosen the cabbage by digging around the roots. This the younger nun did, and the cabbage came up quite easily. I turned away from the scene to see that Pelham Bias had been observing the same events. Perhaps it was my imagination, but his attention seemed fixed rather hungrily on the cabbage.

After some little time longer, Henry rose from the desk and padded over to the cabinet of golden spools. Holding up a finger he began slowly counting off the spools, all the while muttering softly to himself. He took some time to make a calculation in his pocket-book; finally having completed it, he went to the door and called for the Superior. She came quickly and stood once more before us.

'I have it,' Henry announced.

The Superior's eyes widened. 'Indeed?' she asked.

'I think so. Unfortunately we have slightly mistimed our visit today. It will be necessary, I am afraid, to inconvenience you just a little more. Your embroidery work here begins at half-past two, in a half an hour's time, does it not?'

'Yes...'

'Very good. I will make one five-minute visit to you here this evening at six, if that is agreeable to you, and another tomorrow morning at ten.'

'A visit?'

'Yes. Here, to the workroom.'

'I see. But may I ask where is this tending, Doctor?'

'It will tend toward the solution of this mystery. One visit tonight, and one further visit tomorrow, both of five minutes.'

'I do not understand.'

'I hope I am not discourteous, Reverend Mother, but you must allow me to conduct this investigation at the pace it demands. I promise that you will have the solution very soon.' He paused. 'If it will help to put your mind at rest, let me tell you this: there is no thief here.'

The remaining colour drained from the Superior's cheeks. She seemed almost on the verge of fainting.

'Indeed?' she whispered.

'Please accept my assurances on that point. Well, then, Miss Salter, Inspector, I think we can take our leave. Until six this evening, Reverend Mother.'

Henry spoke little during the rest of that day, and, not wishing to disturb him, I did not ask him to reveal what he knew. To my mind, however, the solution to the mystery was clear. Henry had said there was no thief. If he was correct, that could only mean one thing: the records of the spools and the records of the palls had matched exactly. No thread was missing, and the Superior had, for some reason, made an error – or told an untruth.

I did not accompany Henry on his visit to the convent that evening, knowing that the culmination of the case would not come until the day after; but at half past nine the following morning I found myself once more riding with Henry through the streets of Hoxton toward the convent of the Discalced Servites. It was a gorgeous autumn day with a golden light, and, above, high chilly wisps of cloud. Leaf-smoke hung pleasantly in the air. We arrived and rang the doorbell, and this time were admitted by the Superior herself. She led us immediately to the workroom. She seemed paler and more hollow-cheeked than ever, and I was sure she had passed an evil night. I fully expected a confession there and then.

What she said was, if anything, more remarkable.

'Dr St Liver,' she began tremulously, 'you must know that after you left last night, I began thinking of what you had done — I mean, in your examination of the books. I fear I am not a very good book-keeper.' She gulped, touching her pectoral cross. 'At least, I had not thought to check the palls against the thread in the very careful way you did. I did not think it necessary, given the fact of the missing spools. However, after you left, I resolved to make the same calculation. I counted the completed and dispatched palls. Then I reckoned up the amount of thread bought in over the same period. I fully expected to find a discrepancy of seven spools, that is, 1,400 yards of thread – a considerable amount, and one that would have been readily discernible, even with a large margin of error. But I found, as you evidently did yesterday, that there was no thread missing. None!' Her voice rose to a squeak. She took a moment to collect herself. 'Nevertheless, I must tell you, Doctor, that I did count carefully – indeed I did so with increasing care, as more and more thefts took place – and I say again, that on seven occasions over the last three months there has been one spool fewer. There is no doubt in my mind. Yet they cannot have gone missing. Please tell me, Doctor. It is beyond me. What is the explanation?'

She gazed at Henry in frank supplication. Henry responded by lightly blowing out his moustache.

'I believe you, Reverend Mother,' he said. 'I am sure your observations were accurate. The spools were missing.'

'But you said –?'

'The explanation is quite simple. You have had a visitor.'

'A visitor?'

'A member of your own convent, who seeks to do good. Every night, for approximately a quarter of an hour, one of your novitiates wakes in the early hours and creeps down to the workroom. Here she does extra work on the palls.'

'Oh!'

'The workroom being at a remove from the main body of the convent, the noise of the machine would not necessarily be audible. In a quarter of an hour she uses approximately fifteen and a half yards of thread, or, to round the figures down, one yard per minute. Over the course of ninety days, therefore, this amounts to the full amount of 1,400 yards – that is, seven spools. The reason that the apparent thefts were at irregular intervals was that she required an additional spool only very infrequently during that nocturnal period, perhaps once every thirteen days or so, on average. The nocturnal spool-changes in fact followed a 42-day cycle, with a statistical clustering occurring in the first week of the cycle, given a notional setting of the thread at zero for the beginning of the nocturnal sessions. On the occasions when she found herself out of thread, she simply took a fresh spool from the cabinet, little thinking that you were keeping a careful count. The pattern of nocturnal as compared to diurnal spool-changes during the 42-day cycle – from which of course the pattern of the full 90 days may be easily extrapolated – I have drawn up as a graph, here.' He presented her with a crumpled piece of paper. 'You may well find the small black marks correspond to the days when you noted a missing spool.'

The Mother Superior stared dumbly at the paper.

'This became clear to me quite early in the investigation. However, the challenge was to discover which of the nuns had been doing good by stealth in this manner. In order to determine this, I returned last night, and, while you waited for me in the office, took the liberty of placing a small pencil mark on each spool as they were fixed here on top of each of the sewing machines. The pencil marks were orientated in the same direction in each case – east, towards the windows. If any one of the machines were set to run during the night, the spool would turn and the pencil mark would move round.'

'Oh, Doctor!'

'It would then be found pointing in a different direction the following morning. I have only now to examine each machine to find the one that was used last night.'

Henry started at the back row of six, walking past each machine and glancing briefly at each spool. He reached the end of the row, seemingly having found nothing, then walked on to examine the second row. Again he drew a blank. He moved to the third row.

Immediately, with a little ejaculation of triumph, he pounced on the machine nearest the window.

'Aha!' He pointed to the machine. 'Who sits here?'

The Superior and I rushed over. We looked at the golden spool. A tiny pencil dot on the spool-top pointed north.

'That is Sister Lawrence's machine!' the conventual gasped.

'Then Sister Lawrence is your benefactress,' Henry said.

'Oh, Doctor!'

'And no thief, as you can see.'

'Doctor, I cannot tell you what this means!'

'I hope your mind is now at rest.'

Oh, thank you! I will speak to Sister Lawrence. How blind I have been!'

'I hope you will not be hard on her, Reverend Mother.'

'No, never! I love her for it. But the work she already undertakes is arduous enough. She must not ruin her health by interrupting her sleep. She is an exceptionally hard-working young woman – faithful, dutiful – I will speak to her.'

'Then we will leave you,' Henry said. 'One last request: I wonder if it might be possible to speak to Sister Lawrence briefly before we go? I hope this does not seem irregular. I merely wish to clarify some details of the investigation. I would be interested to know whether my calculation of fifteen minutes' nocturnal activity, based on the amount of thread used, is correct – as well as a few other minor matters.'

'Well, I cannot see why not,' the Superior said, after a brief hesitation. 'Miss Salter will be present. Yes, that would seem to be quite in order. And you might take the opportunity now, if you wish. That is Sister Lawrence there.'

We looked out of the window at the nuns in the kitchen garden. I was surprised to see that the nun picked out by the Superior's forefinger was the very same I had observed the previous day pulling up the cabbage.

'I will speak to her first,' the Superior continued. 'Perhaps if you would be good enough to follow me, you might talk to her afterwards. I will broach the matter.'

We left the workroom and went through a door into the garden, where Henry and I stopped by an ivied wall in the soft sunshine. We watched as the Superior approached the young nun and bade her sit on a bench under the yellowing leaves of an elm. The pair conversed for a few minutes, the sister with head respectfully bowed. At length she looked up with rueful countenance, and the Superior, impulsively, it seemed to me, embraced her.

'A touching scene,' I said to Henry.

'Yes indeed.'

'But perhaps rather disappointing?'

Henry turned. 'What do you mean?' he asked.

'Henry, what has this to do with... your particular branch of science? If I may quote to you Bloch, as you have often done to me, on the "overarching science, subsuming all other sciences: biology, chemistry, poetry, archaeology, and so on..."? I am sure

I do not get it exactly right – but this is simply a case of poor book-keeping, is it not? What interest can it really hold for you?'

Henry now seemed to frown, although of course it was difficult to tell.

'How did you think I knew about the spools?' he asked.

'Why, by the accounts.'

'Solely the accounts?'

'I suppose so. What else was there?'

'Nothing else. But what made me look in the accounts, when no one else had thought to do so?'

'I am sure I do not know.'

'Ah.'

'What, then?' I replied with, I confess, a small degree of impatience.

'Sewing machines, my dear Miss Salter. Sewing machines.'

Before I could respond, the two nuns stood up, and the Superior beckoned gently to us.

'What do you mean?' I blurted out as I half-ran after him.

Henry did not reply.

We drew nearer to the pair under the elm, and I was now able to observe at close quarters the nun I had seen striving with the cabbage. Sister Lawrence, like her Superior, was unshod and was dressed in a black, sack-like habit. Her feet were large and dirty. On her head she wore a wimple with a black bandeau, and covering her neck was a bib of white linen, somewhat stained with green. Her pectoral cross had been slung behind her for convenience while she worked. She was, I guessed, about twenty years old, with a face neither beautiful nor plain; she had a snub-nose freckled like an eel, wide blue eyes and full lips. Small dark circles showed under the eyes. There was in the set of the chin and the expression in the eyes something rather unexpected – a touch of insouciance, perhaps, incompatible with the picture I had formed of the angel of mercy fired with nocturnal zeal for her cloister. But this small discordant note was lost in a general solemnity.

'This is Dr St Liver,' said the Superior. 'And Miss Salter.'

The nun bowed.

'Dr St Liver wishes, as I have said, to ask a few brief questions,' the Superior went on. 'Once again, thank you, Dr St Liver, for the inestimable blessing you have brought this community.'

'It was my great pleasure.'

'And thank you too, Miss Salter. I have not had much opportunity to speak to you – but I will certainly look for your book.'

'Thank you,' I said, a little hesitantly.

'Well, I will leave you together. Please take your time. Goodbye, then.'

We watched as she walked to the convent and disappeared though the small door.

'Well,' Henry began, turning to the young nun. 'Sister Lawrence. I asked to speak to you. I should say first that I understand that you were not at all at fault in this matter. But, if you will allow me, I have just a very few questions. Please tell me if you would prefer not to answer them: it is very far from my intention to cause you the slightest pain or embarrassment.'

The nun gave a brief nod, her eyes on Henry's moustache.

'Well, then, let us sit,' Henry continued. 'The Reverend

Mother will have explained to you my conclusion about the spools.'

'Yes,' the nun said simply.

'It was all a misunderstanding, of course – there was no theft. However, perhaps I should explain a little of how I was able to arrive at that conclusion. Again, please tell me if you find anything I say to be in the least distressing. I will, of course, immediately desist.'

'Very well,' the nun replied in a small voice.

'Excellent. Let me see, then. I was able to form the theory I did because of my particular work. My work relates to the study of the quite normal and natural functions of the body.'

A strange expression flickered across the nun's face, rather unlike the expression I would have expected in the circumstances. It was neither shock, nor surprise, nor outrage, but instead a look of suffering resignation, mixed, perhaps, with entreaty. She placed one dirty foot caressingly over the other.

'I have heard of your work, Dr St Liver,' she replied in a cultured voice with a trace of some accent I could not immediately identify. 'I have also read several of Miss Salter's stories in the *New Age* – before coming here to the convent, of course.'

I was utterly amazed, but Henry merely nodded. 'That is excellent. Then we understand one another. I hope I may be so bold as to present some of my thoughts to you.'

'Please.'

'Thank you.' Henry considered briefly. 'My investigation proceeded from my knowledge of certain aspects of the work you undertake here: I mean as regards the operation of the sewing machine. Perhaps you find yourself unable to exercise the perfect control you might wish for when engaged in this work? Perhaps, in addition, you do not have anyone to confide in? This is, perhaps, where I can help. I am a specialist in this area; and if I can be of any use to you, even if only to lend an understanding ear, please regard me – and Miss Salter of course – as being at your service.'

Now there was a further astonishment. Sister Lawrence buried her wimpled head in her hands and, with shaking shoulders, began to weep.

I put my arm around her to comfort her, and for a moment there were no sounds but her sobbing and the caw of some rooks in the trees on the other side of the garden.

At length Sister Lawrence raised her head and wiped away her tears, in the process muddying her face somewhat. 'Please forgive me,' she whispered. 'You are right. I have no one to talk to. There is too much within me that is dammed up. But now you are here, you two –' She broke off.

'Will you tell us, then,' asked Henry, 'something of your life?'

The few other nuns had gone inside now and we were the only three figures left in the grounds. A bonfire of wet leaves smouldered a little way off.

'I have not always been... like this,' Sister Lawrence said, gesturing towards her feet.

'Ah,' said Henry. 'Then you entered the convent recently?'

'I came here nine months ago. On my twentieth birthday. I felt I must break free from my former life. I thought that the best place would be a convent, in the company of women only.'

I began to wish I had brought a notebook. As I have

mentioned, I had really not expected much in the way of a *dénouement* in this particular case.

'I was born in Italy,' she began, 'to an English father and an Italian mother. I was raised a Catholic. When I was three my mother died and my father brought us to England – myself and my elder sister, that is. We were sent to the best schools, lived in a large house, had servants, and in fact had the best of everything. All was well, then, for a while; but then my father made a series of miscalculations in his business affairs. He was the proprietor of a string of small newspapers, and one after the other, they all foundered. We were left with terrible debts. The house was sold, and we moved to a tiny upstairs room in Woolwich, just big enough for three. My sister and I – I was nine and she thirteen – were forced to leave school. I worked at home, sewing, and my sister went out to a milliner's.

'My sister is four years older than I, and was more affected than I by my mother's death, I think. Perhaps that explains what came afterwards. She fell into evil company. By the time she was sixteen she was married, but her husband was a fool, and could not manage her. Soon she went altogether to the bad. Sometimes she would come home to us drunk. For myself and my father it was a nightmarish time. Indeed, I believe it affected my father's health, for when I was fourteen my father took to his bed with a stomach trouble. I nursed him for nine months. He died one week short of my fifteenth birthday, his hair snow-white, though he was only forty-one.

'I had nowhere to go except to my sister's. By this time she was no longer with her husband: she now lived alone, or rather I should say she lived in a house with five other young women. She had given up at the milliner's. You will perhaps understand what their profession was.

'I lived there for a year, and it was no place for a child. All night long screaming and fighting; songs blaring from the phonograph; pick-pocketing, drunkenness, every sort of immorality; men coming through the house in droves. I witnessed everything. I once saw a man almost battered to death by two women taking turns with a pewter jug. The constables would do nothing. It was a sort of miracle I did not join my sister, and become like her. But I felt nothing but disgust for her mode of life; and where there is no temptation there is hope for purity. Even after a year they had not succeeded in coercing me to join them. I was kept for one reason only: to cook and clean for them. Then I too was married. Like my sister before me, I was just sixteen years old.

'I will not tell you much of Alfred. He had raised himself through many trials to become a schoolmaster, and I thought selfishly that he could restore my fortunes. But I soon found he had no ambition beyond what he had already achieved. He knew nothing of good living, good clothes, fine houses, and so on: he was as a limpet on a rock. The real trouble, however, was something more fundamental. As a man he did not interest me. A week after our marriage I was already indifferent to him. God forgive me. Our marriage nevertheless lasted four years; there were no children.

'But I have skipped ahead too far. In our third year of marriage, when I was eighteen, I fell in love. He was a friend of Alfred's, a clerk. He came to the house to stay for a few days while he was in search of work in London. During that time I found myself, for the first time in my life, violently attracted to another human being. I expected him to notice me; I felt that our destiny must surely be together. But although I know he did notice me and divine my feelings, and perhaps even returned them, from motives still unclear to me, he never acted. Perhaps it was his sense of loyalty to his friend; perhaps, more difficult to contemplate, he was in truth indifferent to me. After those few days he took leave of us. It was the most terrible parting of my life.

'After this I fell into a dreadful melancholy for months. I prayed Andrew – that was his name – would write or find some excuse to call, but he never did. The pain was made worse by an accompanying surge in other feelings – my feelings as a woman, I mean.

'This part of me had now been awakened for the first time in my life. I was a prey to longings I had never before experienced; I became assailed at all hours of the night and day by strange and troubling thoughts. I began to understand my sister better. Her path in life had always been incomprehensible to me. Now, having wished for nothing more than to escape, I began to desire nothing less than to go back to that house.

'I have said that my feelings were awakened. But this does not begin to do justice to what had happened to me. Something that had been dormant had for the first time broken out and was able to flourish unchecked. I began to find stimulation everywhere.

'Anything could excite me. Newspaper stories about assaults and crimes fascinated me. I read a story of a man who dragged a young girl into a deserted house to violate her, and it gave me a powerful thrill of pleasure. Another account of how a man resuscitated a woman on a train – by blowing into her mouth after she had fainted when a goods train passed unexpectedly in the opposite direction – although seemingly innocuous, also affected me profoundly. If a young man who I liked the look of came close – I mean, within a few feet – I would begin to feel excitement. I must tell you though that I was never unfaithful to my husband. To this day he is the only man I have given myself to.

'The sound of men's low voices, or the sight of their beards, pleased me. I also felt terrible pleasure at seeing the naked statues in museums. I could not understand how the trustees felt it proper to allow the public to see such things. Any gossip or rumour concerning people fed my imagination for days. If I heard of a man who had impregnated a girl against her will, or if I heard that she had given birth to his child, I was excited; I longed to have these experiences for myself. If I went to the theatre, or the circus, I was always filled with pleasure at the sight of the men's bodies in their costumes, and with their magnificent moustaches. There was no object, it sometimes seemed, no work of nature or of men's hands, no gesture and no act that did not have some command over me. Train journeys excited me, as well as other forms of conveyance such as carriages or gigs; men swimming in a river, as glimpsed from a road or train; also sailors with tattoos on their arms, or any kind of tattoos; flies and wasps copulating; prostitutes in the street and their clients; anything to do with guns or weapons; the sight of a soldier in the street with a rifle; the feel of velvet or silk against my skin; a picture of a devil with a pitchfork; the mention of anything to do with desert islands (I think because of the four boys in *The Swiss Family Robinson*); the taste of anything acrid or unpleasant; a child's top being whipped up; elephants in the zoo; canvases in the National Gallery; a man sawing wood; a dog urinating; the smell of cooking offal. Even things that were not in the least sexual became mixed up in my mind with sexual feelings: fast and loud music; scenes of natural beauty such as mountains, sunsets, jungles, volcanoes, quarries, and so on. In order of excitement, I suppose I would put these natural scenes last, followed by paintings, weapons or guns, then tattoos, statues, then the sight of couples in the street, then the sight of men or boys swimming, then animals copulating, then circuses or dances, then stories in novels or the newspaper, and finally the proximity of a man I fancied.'

The list was comprehensive. I was struck both by her composure and her candour; Henry's ability to elicit the most detailed confession was astounding. Henry himself remained silent.

'You will wonder about the nature of the excitement,' Sister Lawrence went on. 'Well, I will tell you. These things I have mentioned were often enough by themselves to produce a powerful orgasm. I could in fact easily have an orgasm just by thinking about them. I could, if I wished, have twenty orgasms a day, just by listening to a man's voice or reading a novel. That was all that was required. I could do it "at the drop of a hat", as they say. I only had to make the small effort to think. At other times I would be taken over by these feelings quite independently of any effort. The excitement was literally spontaneous; it came out of nowhere and engulfed me before I could stop it, sometimes in actual defiance of my will. This was quite frightening, and would leave me shaking.'

'And throughout all this,' Henry suddenly put in, 'your husband remained an object of complete indifference to you?'

'Yes – it is astonishing, is it not? Like a stone. Perhaps, indeed, even less stimulating than a stone, for I can imagine all sorts of ways a stone could be stimulating. The rough feel of it in your hand, for example; or the massiveness and strength of a great cliff of rock. Or an obelisk.'

'Yes.'

'Finally I realized that I must take action. I must go somewhere where there were no statues, no animals, no novels, no newspapers, no zoos, no children, no dances, no circuses, and above all no men. Then I would regain control over this part of me – a part that had all but mastered me. I decided therefore to take the veil. I obtained a divorce from my husband – by mutual consent – and chose the convent of the Servites because of its extreme poverty. I am not, it must be said, particularly religious. But here there is not even a crucifix to distract me; and in fact the image of the crucified Christ had previously been a powerful source of fascination. It is for good reason that the Servites do not admit crucifixes: half the nuns in England are in love with Jesus, I think, though they will not admit it.'

'And did you experience any diminution of your feelings?'

'In some ways I did. I think the hard physical work was the greatest help. When one has been working for hours the whole body is exhausted; one wishes for nothing other than rest. The diminution of sex feeling is a sort of by-product of that, I suppose.'

'A very perceptive remark.'

'Here every moment is devoted to some duty. There is not even much time for personal spiritual contemplation. The day begins at five o'clock, with household duties and chores until breakfast. Then there is mid-morning prayer. Then there are more chores, then midday prayer, then an early luncheon, at twelve. Then there is a period of recreation for forty minutes in which the nuns may read or take exercise. Several of us choose to run around the perimeter of the grounds. After this there is gardening, then sewing, then mid-afternoon prayers, then household maintenance, then vespers, then our evening meal. Then there are further household tasks such as cleaning, sweeping, dusting, cooking and so on; then finally compline. By bedtime my energies are often utterly depleted. It is almost as if the conventual regime were designed to exhaust us. I fall asleep in an instant. The problem is the sewing, of course.'

'Yes,' said Henry, although I could not see why.

'The sewing machines are heavy and old-fashioned, and are worked by a heavy footplate. This requires an up-and-down movement of the legs. With the body at a certain angle on the chair, this leads to a very definite excitement. The great temptation is to work the treadle faster and faster. Thirty machines sewing funeral palls give out a deafening clatter, but if one machine suddenly starts working harder than the others there is a change in the overall sound. This happens quite often in the workroom. Suddenly the pitch of one machine is heard above the din, and, after continuing at a high rate for a few moments, it falls off and is lost in the general noise. If you look around you can usually spot the nun responsible: her head will be lolling down, her mouth open with perhaps a tear of saliva on her lip, her eyes heavy-lidded, her hands resting on the table, her work momentarily forgotten.

'Unfortunately this stimulation cancels out all the salutary effects of the convent. I came to dread these sessions, as for one and a half hours I would have to concentrate hard not to experience orgasm after orgasm. In the past I had only to see things or hear things to become excited, but this brute stimulation was something completely new. It began to take over my life. It was precisely what I had come here to escape from. And yet those ninety minutes held such indescribable pleasure, that in another sense they were the solution to the whole problem of my mania: I was left so shattered by the bliss of the sewing-room I desired no more stimulation for the rest of the day.

'Then, after perhaps six months, I found myself, much to my surprise, waking in the night, once again flooded with desire. I needed more. I felt that if I just had fifteen minutes I would be "right" again and would be able to sleep. And so every night I crept down to the workroom and did extra work on my pall. Then I returned to my bed, again at peace. I could manage until half-past two the next day. But now it seems that this is denied me. The Reverend Mother found the missing thread. And then she called you. And you, Dr St Liver, divined the truth.'

The nun finished, her eyes on her feet. Henry and I followed her gaze, and for a time we were all three of us contemplating them.

'A fascinating narrative,' Henry said at length. 'The case, if I may give it a name – and I trust this does not offend – is one of sexual hyperaesthesia.'

'But why?' cried the nun passionately, looking up at Henry. 'Why am I afflicted in this way?'

'I would offer as a hypothesis,' began Henry, 'that in your early life your normal development was somewhat cramped by the turn in your family's fortunes. Later you came to associate your sister's career with your father's illness and death, and felt a consequent revulsion from sexual things. When you came to marry you had still not divested yourself of this revulsion, and your husband was contaminated by association. You then experienced an ecstatic *colpo di fulmine*, but the blooming of your sexual life that might have taken place was checked when the affair came to nothing, and this unhealthy containment of the explosion generated a painfully exaggerated erotic hyper-sensitivity – that is, a severe hyperaesthesia. Naturally you found this bewildering. You came to the convent to escape from it, despite having little religious vocation. But this was not the wise choice it may at first have seemed. The ascetics have known the perils of this sort of life for thousands of years. The Desert Fathers, you will remember, were almost ceaselessly occupied in resisting auto-erotic temptation. Schrenck-Notzing considered that the ascetic lifestyle was apt to actually cause hyperaesthesia, and Nyström too wrote that it was responsible for numerous disorders, including, in men, orchitis and extreme priapism, and in women a list of complaints almost endless, among them neurasthenia, hypochondriasis, chlorosis, allergies, asthma attacks, and so on. You yourself found that heavy work dulled your orgiastic sense but could not extirpate it. That is not surprising: exercise only has the effect of dampening passion, as you correctly pointed out, after it has entirely crushed the healthy energy of the system as a whole and brought it to a state of collapse. But you are young: after nine months or so of this heavy work, you became accustomed to it. In fact it toned and invigorated you, and your system once again sent forth its insistent cry for satisfaction. You began to wake at night in need of stimulus. And at the heart of it all was the sewing machine. It was the presence of the sewing machine that first led me to examine the records and finally to divine the truth. The erotic significance of the sewing machine has long been noted. For instance, Fürbringer writes that in large sewing-machine shops the forewoman must take pains to ensure the girls all sit correctly, to prevent a decline in the quality of their work owing to the effects of frequent sexual crises. I came to realize that the apparent thefts of golden thread might be more easily explicable by postulating a novitiate who had found herself unsatisfied after her daily quota of pleasure, who was in doubt as how to act morally, and had decided that the line of least resistance was to satisfy her desires by stealth – while at the same time doing good to the community.'

Henry paused for breath. The nun fixed her eyes on him wonderingly. His moustache fluffed out slightly.

'Now,' he continued, 'you say that you have no real vocation for this sort of life. I would urge you to leave it. Get married again as soon as possible: join a marriage bureau, for preference. This is the obvious solution to your hyperaesthesia. The regular and harmonious performance of the sex act over a long period, with a man for whom you feel an intense, reciprocated attraction, has a strong anti-aphrodisiac effect. Moreover it will heal the psychic wounds of your upbringing and your early disappointment in love. A retreat from the convent will also remove the stimulation of the hermetic lifestyle. My advice to you, then, if you wish to re-establish equilibrium, would be this: go to your Superior and say to her, in the words of the evangelist, "Nunc dimittis servum tuum: Now lettest thou thy servant depart in peace."'

As Henry concluded this speech, Sister Lawrence sank to her knees in the mud before him. I supposed that his Latin climax, in combination with the repeated hammer-blows of Teutonic authority, was too much for her. The lower portion of her habit, as well as her face, feet and bib, were all now considerably begrimed.

'Dr St Liver,' she breathed, looking up at him, her eyes darting fire, 'No one before you has taken the trouble to understand me. I believe you are a saint. I know not how to repay you – except, perhaps, to do as you say.' She gave a sob. 'I must go now.' She rose to her feet. 'I will think of you sometimes.'

And with that she walked unsteadily toward the convent.

'I am greatly intrigued by the idea that self-restraint may actually be a cause of hyperaesthesia,' I said to Henry later, as we sat round the hearth at Dover Mansions. 'It does rather argue against the view that chastity is in itself a good thing.'

Henry threw a lump of coal onto the fire. 'Certainly it does,' he said. 'It would seem reasonable to assume that our convents are brimming with persons in the last stages of hyperaesthetic neurosis, passionately desiring that they be freed from this bondage, and indulging in ever greater feats of manual toil to subdue their passions.' He nudged at the coals with a poker. 'It calls to mind the justly famous passage in the writings of St Teresa, herself, of course, a famous anchoress. She describes how in her greatest ecstasy she was visited by a smiling boy-angel who thrust a fiery arrow into her bowels, causing a sweet, happy pain, and leaving her inflamed with divine love. St Teresa says bowels; we moderns would substitute a different part of the anatomy.' He withdrew the poker and gazed into the glowing depths. 'Perhaps it would be a more accurate one.'

Chapter Seven

Smith Ely Jelliffe

❧

By the early part of 1895 I had known Henry for over two years, and during this time my life had changed utterly. Not only had I made my home in London, and met all sorts of interesting people, and accompanied Henry on numerous of his investigations (publishing accounts of these in the *New Age*, including, in recent months, 'The Case of the Well-Born Client', 'The Case of the Sotadic Zone', 'The Case of the Boy Explorer', 'The Case of the Seven Spools', 'The Case of the Tontine Wedding', and others), but my *Story of an Australian Barn* had been adjudged by the public a success, and I was now hard at work on a sequel, which my publishers advised me should be entitled either *More Stories from an Australian Barn* or *Further Stories from an Australian Barn*. I had also begun a correspondence with Mr Oscar Wilde after the freeing of his African friend – it was astonishing how Oscar's personality bloomed when he was able to commit his thoughts to paper – and had been delighted to receive an invitation on New Years' Eve, 1894, to Tite Street, Chelsea, where Henry and I celebrated the year's end by meeting and conversing with a number of luminaries of the Aesthetic movement, among them Mr Ernest Raffalovich, Mr Ernest Shannon, Mr Arthur Symons, Mr James Kett and Mr Ernest Dowson.

When the case I am about to relate begins, in the third week of January 1895, Henry had been engaged for several days in a study of inversion in pigeons, and had been absent for long stretches while he observed these creatures in the London parks. It was one fine crisp morning, at around 11 o'clock, while I sat alone in the morning-room at work on some notes, that I became aware of a fluttering step in the hall at Dover Mansions. Soon there stood framed in the door a man of approximately thirty years of age, neatly be-suited, and with a small, mild face and a small beak of a nose. He was wearing a bowler hat.

'I do hope I am not intruding,' said the man with a timid smile, 'but I saw the door open. I was rather hoping to speak to Dr St Liver.' He looked warily about him.

'Dr St Liver is not at home at the moment...' I began, but no sooner had I uttered the words than I saw Henry, head bent, hurrying toward the house along the pavement. He was carrying what looked to be a small cage. 'My apologies,' I said. 'I spoke too soon. Here he comes now.'

A second or two later Henry strode into the room.

'This gentleman has just arrived,' I said, 'and wishes to speak to you.'

Henry, his face flushed with his efforts and the bracing weather, laid the pigeon-coop on a side-table, dislodging and smashing a small Ashanti bust. 'Certainly,' he said. He threw himself into his armchair. 'I am happy to listen.'

Our caller moved further into the room. 'I am sure I ought to have made an appointment,' he said hesitantly, 'but the matter was urgent and I was nervous of committing anything to paper.'

A solitary pigeon – possibly an inverted one – gave a low warble from its wicker prison.

'Please do not concern yourself,' Henry said.

'It is a rather difficult matter, I am afraid.'

'Will you take a seat? Miss Salter is my confederate. I hope you will feel as free to talk before her as before myself.'

The man looked in my direction as I removed a treatise on prostitution from the only available chair. 'I am a great reader of Miss Salter's stories in the *New Age*,' he said, 'as I am sure are many others. However I am here today on rather a personal errand. I feel that I must ask, if possible, that no one in this room make public what I have to say.'

'Certainly I will not,' I said. 'If that is what you wish.'

'Oh, that is a relief,' our visitor replied, sitting down and taking off his hat. 'I had feared it was almost a condition of obtaining an interview with Dr St Liver that the whole thing be published as a story. As I am sure you will see, such a course would be highly inappropriate. I am threatened with an exposure which would certainly mean the ruin of myself and my family.'

'Blackmail?' asked Henry.

'Yes,' replied our visitor. 'Blackmail.'

I took a closer look at him. He was, as I have said, about

thirty years of age, of medium height, slightly built, and with an aesthetic air, though not, I should say, with a capital 'A'. He was dressed neatly and simply in a pearl-gray suit with a five-button waistcoat and gold watch-chain, and on his ring-finger there shone a single ring with a modest topaz setting. Now that he removed his bowler, I could see that his hair was cut very short indeed, almost shaved, though not for the common reason that vain men in early middle age often cut their hair to the scalp: that is, that they are going bald and wish to lessen its appearance. He had, in fact, a very respectable follicular coverage, as well as a pleasingly-shaped skull.

'I see,' said Henry. 'Well, that is most serious. I will do all in my power to help.'

'My deepest thanks,' our guest replied. 'I hope there might be something in it of interest to compensate you for the trouble. Very well, then, I should perhaps begin by telling you my name. I am Smith Ely Jelliffe. I am a married man with no children, and I live quite close by you here in Shoreditch. You are a local celebrity, Doctor, and though I had heard of your work I never dreamed I would one day consult you. But now it seems that I must throw myself on your charity. Two days ago I received a note from an unknown person demanding money; my wife and I have not had a wink of sleep since. I am inclined to accede to the demand, since if everything were to come out there would be a dreadful scandal; but before I do that, I must know your opinion. Perhaps you will be able to speculate as to who would do such a terrible thing. But I suppose that is impossible.'

'Not necessarily,' said Henry.

'Do you wish to see the note?'

'Certainly.'

Our caller reached into his inside pocket and withdrew a square of paper. He handed it to Henry, who unfolded it and examined it for a little while. He then passed it to me. It read simply:

£1,000 IN CASH BY TUESDAY 8PM UNDER
BLACKFRIARS BRIDGE.

'The blackmailer does not say what it is he intends to expose,' I pointed out, handing it back.

'No,' said Mr Smith Ely Jelliffe.

'Do you feel able to give us some indication of what that might be?' Henry asked.

'Certainly,' said Mr Jelliffe, his eyes bulging slightly.

There was a pause.

'A little of your family history might help to start with,' Henry prompted.

'Yes. Excuse my hesitation, but I am not used to speaking of this before strangers.'

'Please think of us as your friends.'

'Very well.' Mr Jelliffe paused once more, then appeared to gather resolve. 'I will tell you a little of my early life, then,' he said. 'My earliest memory is connected with the case, I think. It dates from my third or fourth year. I was sitting underneath a desk one afternoon while my mother was writing something.

Perhaps it was the proximity of her skirts – she always wore yards and yards of frothy crinoline – but I remember quite clearly thinking that I was a boy, and was different to my mother, who was a girl; and that I wanted to be like my mother, and did not want to be a boy.'

'Yes.'

'Perhaps this is not uncommon in very young boys, who must make the journey from the maternal breast to a state of masculinity, whereas girls have no comparable journey to make; but I am afraid that as I grew older I was never at all attracted to the rough games of boys and was much more at home among teacups and dolls. At the same time, I was rather precocious, in a physical sense. You have asked me to talk freely, and, since there is little point in false modesty in a case such as my own, I will be as frank as I can. I began stimulating myself I think at the age of six. I used to delight in rubbing myself against the furniture or the floor until I experienced a surge of pleasure that I now know to be orgasm – though at the time of course there was no emission. I delighted in naked romps around the house, usually when my parents and brothers were out. I learned early on that these things had to be concealed – I am not sure how or why I learned it – and I suppose that the result of the secrecy was a certain degree of shame and resentment.

'I became aware of the essential physical difference between girls and boys at around the age of eight, having previously believed it to be entirely a matter of clothing. I once overheard a friend of my mother's say that women are more beautiful than men, and it struck me forcefully as true, though to my mind, again, the clothes that girls and women were allowed to wear constituted their chief beauty. A gracefully and charmingly clad girl I saw almost as a divine being. I felt that girls and women were quite aware of this advantage of theirs, and I imagined that the pride and hauteur of the female sex stemmed from their sense of superiority in the matter of clothing.

'Soon after I entered puberty I began a programme of masturbation that was probably rather excessive. Women's underclothing stimulated me particularly. If I saw women in the theatre revealing their underclothing I would dream about it for days; or if, at the beach, I saw girls in their frothy underskirts and white knickers, sometimes revealing a delightful patch of thigh, my feelings were intense: lust mixed with a sort of envy. As in my early memory under the desk, I desired more than anything else actually to *be* a girl, though I now knew that I had no chance whatever of achieving that state. I should perhaps say that anatomically I am male in all respects: my genitals are normally developed, and so on. Moreover, my sexual desires are directed exclusively towards women.

'Everything changed one day at around the age of fourteen. My mother and father had taken us on holiday in the mountains, and the whole family – I and my two brothers – were forced to share a single large cabin. The others went out on a hike, but I, having pretended to be ill, remained alone at home in something of a sulk. My mother had left some of her underthings lying carelessly in an open drawer in the room we shared, and in a sort of dream I picked them up and examined them.

Then, taking off my own clothes, I tried them on. I looked at myself in the mirror, and saw that I was utterly transformed, not just in clothing, but in my whole conception of myself. I took some more of her clothing from her travelling bag and tried that on too – it was, I remember, a pleated skirt with petticoats and a crimson bodice with ruched sleeves – and all of a sudden felt an enchantment that was entirely new. Through sheer luck I had stumbled on exactly what it was I wanted. I had spent all my time mooning over girls when all along there had been a girl at home I could have any time I liked – I mean, of course, myself. In girls' clothes, I *was* a girl, one that would uncomplainingly adopt any attitude or do the most silly things just for my benefit. From that moment on I became a sort of hermaphrodite. I had the normal desires of an adolescent boy but the sensibilities and feelings of a girl or woman. I really felt I *was* a woman when I put on female clothing, and with it came a completely new feeling: that of contentment, for the first time in my life, in the body I had been born with.

'I now began to spend all my time in my new hobby, which I carefully and successfully concealed from everyone. I began to collect garments secretly, ordering them in the post, and spent hours poring over magazines, relishing advertisements of daring décolletés, frilled drawers, foamy petticoats and exquisite underthings of all kinds. Soon afterwards I left the parental home – I took a job as a solicitor's clerk – and had some liberty to indulge myself without fear of interruption. I spent entire days as a woman, sometimes in dainty lingerie, other times in corsets with silk stockings, occasionally in full evening wear with cloaks, wraps, jewellery and handbags. I remember my excitement the first time I bought a real fur with sable cuffs and a shawl collar.

'All of this was done inside, in secret, but occasionally I plucked up the courage to walk out in public dressed in my finery. I loved the summer particularly, because at four or five o'clock in the morning, after dawn has broken, the streets are deserted, and yet it is broad daylight. I would put on perhaps a simple skirt and frilly knickers and a sleeveless bodice, or lace myself up tightly in a corset (I am a confirmed tight-lacer), with a blonde wig, high heels, sheer silk gartered stockings and suspenders, my undergarments frothing deliciously around my thighs. At these times I was so lost in my femininity that I do not think I cared much whether anyone saw me. On one of my walks I found myself at a tennis club and was surprised to find the door of the clubhouse open: it was the day after a big garden party and no one had locked up. I recall standing in the deserted clubhouse as the warm sunlight slanted through the windows, and then climbing onto the stage convulsed in giggles – needless to say I was not in the least intoxicated, except by my own delicious sense of fun – and spending some time in a sort of striptease, half hoping the caretaker or his wife would come in. I ended by falling to my knees and rolling over and over on the floor, more than half out of my mind, rubbing myself against some velvet curtains in a frenzy of excitement until in a terrific wave of excitement I spent with agonizing pleasure into my silk knickers.

'Perfumes, jewellery, pretty ribbons and bows, silk underwear, rings, baubles and bracelets: all of these attract me more than I can say, and naturally I am attracted to women who share my love of these things. Perhaps the closest one might come to it would be to say that I am a Sapphist in a man's body; but that does not really cover the ground entirely, because my desires relate chiefly to the female form as it is covered by clothes, and the most intimate aspects of intercourse, while not unpleasant to me, are not essential to my enjoyment. The male role in the sexual act has never been one that I have adopted with any degree of enthusiasm – it seems so unfeminine – and yet I worship the female form, and am utterly repulsed by the thought of touching a man; neither a man's clothes nor his body strike me as at all aesthetically pleasing, and the male genitals strike me as utterly absurd. In some respects my body is rather like a woman's – I am as you see quite small in build, and have the sort of face that might pass for a man's or a woman's, especially if heavily made up. My only defect is in not having much of a bust, though my breasts are very sensitive, like a woman's. I have bought pads and bust improvers and the like, and tried all sorts of creams and preparations for improving the bust, but to no avail; and nothing, in matters of dressing, can compensate for the lack of full, swelling breasts. With that proviso, I enjoy the sight of myself as much as could be expected. I have never reached that pitch of narcissism where I would be completely fulfilled merely by caressing my own body: like any other human being I require another person for the fullest delight. And so my greatest pleasure is to be dressed as a woman, in front of another woman similarly dressed – "up to the nines" in yards and yards of petticoats, tightly-laced corsets that push my breasts out at the front, exquisitely high heels, charming French lingerie, bodices cut low to the ultimate inch, pretty blouses and dainty nighties, and so on – and worship her as she worships me.

'This leads me onto matters perhaps more relevant to the problem at hand. In 1889 I met a charming young lady on a sea-trip. She and I got on famously, especially when I discovered she knew a great deal about clothes and could cast an educated eye over both male and female apparel. It turned out that she had once been a model for clothes, though this had been cut short when her father, who is very strict, forbade it. She is not what I would describe as a very feminine girl, in the way I am, but she loves dressing-up and she has a great sense of fun. By the end of the voyage I did not want to lose her and asked to call on her when we landed. You will have guessed how it all ended up – we were married, and she is now my much-adored wife. I was very reluctant to ask her to marry me, since I was conscious that, with my peculiarities, I might be doing her an injustice, but I knew that she doted on me, and I hoped that it would all come right. On our wedding night I confessed to her that I could not perform without the added stimulus of all my feminine wear, and she, knowing nothing else of men, agreed; to my joy it all went off delightfully well, and, dressed in a corset, I was able to have full sex relations. She later found out by reading books that her young husband was rather unusual, but luckily she is broad-minded, and in addition I suspect – though I have never put it to her quite in this way – she is not particularly strongly sexed, and thus does not demand coitus very frequently. However, I know it is important for her to be treated as a woman, and I make a point of showing my love to her now and then in the way nature intended.

'And so began a life of pleasure I had not fully imagined possible. My wife insists I go into an adjoining room to change every night, and then I emerge, butterfly-like, into her boudoir. She compliments me on my outfits and we spend a long time chattering over my latest acquisitions; soon, however, our words have turned to kisses and I am moulding one of her delightful breasts. I meanwhile am attired in French knickers and tucked and ruffed lingerie, or in a lace dressing-gown with an immaculate long blonde wig. Sometimes she will admire my own breasts with many kisses and caresses, and I will finish either by spending in her hand or we will attempt a connection, after which we both lie dreaming, surrounded by acres and acres of creamy lace.

'My wife is in this matter my only confidante, and though in the past I have been very indiscreet, going out dressed in all sorts of gorgeous and outrageous outfits, that is all many years ago. We have since then moved house more than once, and I have not kept up with any of my former acquaintance – and in fact I have no close friends. I obtain most of my clothes either through the post or through my wife, who knows all my sizes and says they are for her sister. I suppose I spend half our income on clothes. I have often wanted to go out in feminine attire and promenade, or do something mad, but I know how rash that would be as regards my wife and my career. I should have said that I am a partner in a small firm of solicitors. No one at work has the least idea of the transformation I undergo in the evenings. It is all kept completely private and concealed with the utmost care. It is utterly unfair, of course, since women who are masculine in appearance and desire to adopt masculine clothing are tolerated as eccentrics, and if they go out wearing a three-piece suit, cut their hair short, smoke a cheroot, and converse in loud raucous voices, they are not hounded to death or put on a police register: and yet if I went out attired in a pretty dress, wearing stockings and heels, with a wide hat and a parasol, trailing yards and yards of lace petticoat, I would be dragged off and locked up for the protection of public morals.'

'Indeed,' said Henry. 'It is regrettable. However, may I ask a few brief questions?'

'Please.'

'You say you have no other confidantes. You truly have no friends, male or female, with whom you have talked about these things?'

'No. My wife wanted me to go to a doctor, but I persuaded her that it would be counter-productive. She later came to accept that I could not change, that I will always love stockings and frills and petticoats and exquisite things, and I think is now happier in her mind, since in all other respects I am completely sane.'

'So you have no clue as to who might know of your secret life?'

'None at all.'

'Do you have any household staff?'

'Only a maid, and she is beyond suspicion. She is a girl of nineteen who has been with my wife for two years, and is of excellent character.'

'I see. And do you have sufficient funds to satisfy this demand, if it came to it?'

'I am afraid I do not. The only place I could possibly get such a large sum would be from my aunt, the wife of my father's brother, Miss Agatha Jelliffe, of Walthamstow, Essex, who has often told me in the past that I could come to her for help. I am, I believe, her heir. She and I have always been especially close. Her husband, my uncle, made a fortune in wrapping paper.'

'Have you spoken to her?'

'No. I am extremely reluctant to do so. My wife is all for asking her, but I must make sure first that it is my only hope.'

'Concerning the demand: you received it two days ago, on Wednesday?'

'Yes.'

'It is now Friday, so we have four whole days at our disposal. I think, Mr Jelliffe, you might leave this case with me for a day or two. If you will return on Sunday at eleven o'clock in the morning I will lay my conclusions before you.'

'Then you have some hope?'

'I think you will not be required to pay the £1,000.'

'Oh, that is wonderful!'

'If you would leave some note of your address, I can call on you if I need further information. I ask one thing only of you, Sir. I am very partial to a type of French cheese known as "baratte".'

'Indeed?' our visitor asked with a surprised look.

'Baratte is a goats' cheese, usually presented in small roundels.

It is best ripened, though sometimes eaten fresh.' Henry's moustache quivered as if with appetite. His words were, to me, entirely baffling.

'I see,' said Mr Jelliffe.

'It is something of an addiction. However, the best baratte is to be found at Hirschfeld's, a cheesemonger's in Finchley.'

'Yes.'

'If you would consent to fetch me a batch from Hirschfeld's this afternoon, I would regard it as equivalent to a fee in this case. Unfortunately Hirschfeld's is closed at the weekend, and so now is the only time.'

'Oh! Certainly.'

'That would be excellent.'

'Well – I can go immediately if you wish.'

'I would be most grateful.'

'Well, then,' Mr Jelliffe said, getting up, 'I look forward to our meeting on Sunday. Here is my card.' He presented Henry with the object in question, then made uncertainly for the door. 'I am much heartened by your confidence.'

'Until Sunday,' Henry said, also rising.

'Yes indeed.'

Our visitor departed, looking a little mystified, though not more mystified than I was myself. Henry watched him through the window for a few seconds, then dashed over to the bookshelf and began stuffing some papers into his pocket.

'Quick!' he cried. 'There is not a moment to lose!'

'But where are we going?' I asked.

'To solve this case,' Henry said, with a stern look.

Noting the masterful set of his moustache I did not attempt to resist, though I confess I was puzzled.

'Henry –' I whispered, as we hurried, crouching, out of the house and down Dover Street in the wake of Mr Jelliffe. 'What on earth are we doing?'

'Surely it is obvious?' Henry said.

'Not to me, I am afraid,' I said. 'I have never known you to have a partiality for goats' cheese.'

'Hush!' he said. He pointed ahead to where Mr Jelliffe could be seen hailing a cab. We then watched as Mr Jelliffe climbed aboard. The cab set off, turning the corner into the High Street. 'Excellent,' remarked Henry. 'Our unusual solicitor is as good as his word. He is off to Finchley.'

'To buy cheese?' I asked.

'Yes,' said Henry, straightening. 'It unlikely, of course, that he will actually succeed. He will find it rather difficult to locate Hirschfeld's, I think. I admit I made that establishment up on the spur of the moment. Magnus Hirschfeld is the author of a celebrated study on transvestism, and his was the first name that came to mind. With luck Mr Jelliffe will spend some time trying to locate the shop, and will be much delayed as a result.'

'To what end?' I asked.

'Consider the facts,' began Henry as we walked up the road and turned into Shoreditch High Street. 'The unfortunate Mr Jelliffe is being threatened by an unknown person. He has been extremely careful in recent years to keep his secret from prying eyes. He has all the while worked conscientiously as a solicitor, unadorned by a single stitch of lace, wearing the drabbest of clothes, which must chafe him like the bandages of a mummy.'

'Yes.'

'He is a notably unmasculine man, whose psychic make-up closely parallels that of the opposite sex, and yet his sexual impulses are normal, in that they are directed toward females. His is a case of sexo-aesthetic inversion, in which he identifies closely with the object of his desire. The high degree of identification in his case is possibly explained in terms of a perversion of that instinct of courtship that is found in all normal males, that is, that leads them to identify closely with the beloved, and develop an exaggeratedly passive and sympathetic understanding of her, for the final biological purposes of seduction.'

We turned left off the High Street into a tree-lined road of terraced villas.

'To sum up, then,' Henry continued, 'We have before us a quiet, hard-working man whose feminine sensibilities far outstrip those we would expect to find in any invert, who would not hurt a mouse, and who has no known enemies.'

'You have said so, yes.'

'Cannot you see where this is leading? But here we are, on the right: Glebe Road.'

'Surely you do not intend to leave me in suspense?'

'Now, number three...'

I found that we were standing before an ordinary suburban villa with, in the front garden, a well-trimmed lavender-bush and a tree-peony. Its general air of good upkeep gave it the appearance of the home of a modest professional man, perhaps a rather fastidious one.

'Well, then,' said Henry, 'there is no sense in putting it off.' He strode up the path and rang the bell. A plump maid answered the door.

'May I speak to Mrs Jelliffe?' asked Henry.

The maid took our names and asked us to wait, and in a moment a young woman came to the door. She was quite tall, and of pleasing appearance, but with a decidedly mannish air.

'Please come in, Dr St Liver, Miss Salter. I apologise for leaving you waiting,' she said in an agreeable tenor.

'That is quite alright,' Henry replied.

'Essie is a little silly sometimes and doubtless did not recognize your names.'

'No offence, I assure you.'

Mrs Jelliffe looked over her shoulder at the retreating maid. 'John,' she said, rather more quietly, '– I call him John, since "Smith" seems a strange name for a man – told me he intended to visit you. Is he not with you?'

'No,' said Henry, 'Mr Jelliffe went to Finchley a moment ago on a brief errand, at my request.'

'Oh?' asked Mrs Jelliffe, raising one sculpted eyebrow.

'Yes. He will return shortly.'

'I see. Well, please come in.' She showed us into a violet-papered drawing-room decorated with boxed fans. She indicated a settee.

'Mrs Jelliffe,' said Henry as soon as we had made ourselves comfortable, 'I must tell you that your husband has shown me the note.'

Mrs Jelliffe glanced quickly at the drawing-room door, then rose and closed it soundlessly. 'Indeed?' she said in a low voice. 'Can you throw any light on it? Who could have sent it?'

'I believe I know, Madam,' said Henry.

'Oh! Indeed?'

'Yes,' said Henry. 'I believe you sent it.'

Mrs Jelliffe fixed Henry with a granitic stare.

'Then you are wasting my time,' she snapped. She rose from her chair. 'Kindly leave.'

Henry remained seated. I rather uncertainly half-rose, and then, as Henry began to talk, slowly sat down again.

'I do not make this accusation lightly, Mrs Jelliffe,' he said. 'Let me explain. I believe that your husband has starved the household of money as a consequence of his insatiable appetite for clothing. You knew that his salary would never provide you with anything other than a modest allowance, and yet you also knew that Mrs Agatha Jelliffe had agreed to supply him with a loan at any time – a loan that would probably never need to be paid back, since that lady would name your husband in her will. You knew further that he would never ask for the money if left to himself. You therefore concocted this plan to extract the money from Mrs Jelliffe. Mr Jelliffe of course would never have agreed to any of this, and so you were forced to deceive him.'

Mrs Jelliffe stood uncertainly by an ormolu cabinet, her chiselled features thrown into high relief. Henry's accusations had been disquietingly specific. But she was a woman of some obvious mettle. Even as the ghost of indecision passed across her face, it was supplanted by a sneer of contempt.

'Ridiculous,' she said. 'You have no proof.'

'Then how do you explain these?' cried Henry, springing to his feet, and thrusting at her a mass of screwed-up papers. They were the same, I saw, that he had hastily crammed into his pockets as we left the house.

Mrs Jelliffe took one look at them and recoiled in horror. 'Where did you get these?' she gasped.

'You recognize them, then?' Henry asked.

Mrs Jelliffe seemed unable to speak.

'Your words, and your silence, are both eloquent,' Henry declared. He snatched the papers back. 'I have the information I came for. I will present my findings to Mr Jelliffe at our next meeting.'

He strode past her and opened the door to the hall.

'Wait!' cried Mrs Jelliffe in tones of agony. 'Wait! Please do not tell John! He would never understand! Please!'

Henry turned and puffed his moustache at her. 'Are you willing to make a full confession, Madam?'

'Yes, yes! But do not tell John. It will break his heart!'

'Very well, then,' said Henry, his hand relaxing on the knob. 'Mr Jelliffe will be detained for another hour or so. Let us begin again.' And turning, he returned to the settee.

Mrs Jelliffe closed the door once again behind us, and tremblingly sat. For several moments she held her head in her hands. Finally she looked up, her cropped brown hair somewhat rumpled.

'I will tell you the whole truth.'

'Please.'

'I could still deny everything, you know, but given your reputation, Dr St Liver, I hardly think it worthwhile.'

'Quite.'

'Well, then. You are right. John will end by ruining us. He is
obsessed. I do not say that this is any excuse for my actions.'

'No indeed.'

'May I ask how you obtained these papers?'

Henry took one of the documents – a creased yellow fools-
cap – and smoothed it out on his lap. I looked at it. To my astonishment it read as follows:

£1,000 IN CASH BY TUESDAY 8PM UNDER
BLACKFRIARS BRIDGE.

My head span. It was exactly the same form of words as in
the blackmail letter Mr Jelliffe had shown us. And yet it was not
the same note.

'I was given this by Mr Ernest Dowson,' Henry said, 'this
New Year's Eve. The other two notes in my possession were also
passed to me on that same occasion, by Mr Ernest Shannon and
Mr Ernest Raffalovich. Both also employ the same rubric.'

'Do you mean –,' I cried, unable to contain myself, 'that Mr
Dowson and the others –?'

'Yes,' said Henry, turning to me. 'Mrs Jelliffe is one of the
most prolific blackmailers in London. Today I learned her name
for the first time.'

'Oh!'

'And yet,' Henry continued, turning back to Mrs Jelliffe, 'though she is distinctly energetic, she is not our capital's most efficient practitioner. I will not distress you, Mrs Jelliffe, by describing in detail Mr Dowson's or Mr Raffalovich's reaction to your demands. Suffice to say that they laughed. Their lifestyle and habits are known to all. They certainly had no intention of paying £1,000 to prevent you from telling everyone what everyone already knew. Your targets are singularly ill-chosen. If you were present under Blackfriars Bridge on any of those Tuesdays, I have no doubt that they were not. They gave me the notes because I am meditating a little monograph on the prevalence of the blackmail of inverts.'

'Oh!'

'When I saw your husband's note I knew immediately that it had come from the same clumsy blackmailer as that of our notorious London Urnings. But how to discover the source? The clue was in the recipients. Mr Raffalovich is a noted scholar and authority on Walter Pater, who lives most of the time in Italy, where the law cannot touch him. Mr Dowson is a poet and disciple of Whitman. Mr Shannon is the celebrated portraitist, miniaturist, needlepoint artist and friend of Mr Wilde's. Mr Jelliffe, by contrast, is a humble solicitor. Either the blackmailer had suddenly changed his or her method of working, and had decided to move his or her focus from prominent inverts to obscure toilers in the legal profession, or there was another reason: the blackmailer had moved rather closer to home for victims. The identically worded notes bespoke a singular lack of imagination. The fact that these other targets were homosexuals, and your husband is by no means a member of this distinct group, represented, of course, yet another departure, deriving from a crass misunderstanding of sexological categories. So. The victim, Mr Jelliffe, was very well known to the perpetrator. Who was this perpetrator, then? Given that Mr Jelliffe had been extremely careful in recent years to conceal his private life, and had no close friends, the obvious candidate was yourself – his wife.'

Mrs Jelliffe gulped.

'Now we move to motive. What might that be? Clearly you resented Mr Jelliffe's high spending, and wished to tap the easily available funds of his aunt. A final matter was rather technical, and I will not go into it in detail. Add it all together, and the answer was not hard to come by.'

'What will you tell John?' groaned Mrs Jelliffe.

'Nothing,' said Henry, rising.

'Nothing?'

'In return I will ask that you cease your activities once and for all. As far as I can see, you have never made a penny from this unpleasant trade. Let it stop while no one has been truly harmed. I will simply tell Mr Jelliffe that I have identified and cautioned the criminal, and that he, Mr Jelliffe, should have no fear.'

'Oh thank you, thank you!' cried Mrs Jelliffe, gazing at Henry with tear-stained cheeks.

'I am inclined to be charitable on this occasion,' said Henry, 'out of respect for Mr Jelliffe's sensibilities, which, as we both know, are finely tuned. But if I find that you have continued in this course, I will not hesitate to report you to the police.'

'What was the technical detail that you mentioned, Henry, but did not elaborate upon?' I asked as we munched on some cheese that evening. The cheese, though it gave off a distinct whiff of goat, was surprisingly good. Mr Jelliffe had been unable to find Hirschfeld's, but had shown himself to be a person of some resource: after scouring most of north London, he had finally succeeded in locating some 'baratte' at a cheesemonger's in Hampden Square.

'Ah,' said Henry, waving his cigarette. 'You will remember that Mr Jelliffe told us that Mrs Jelliffe had once been a fashion model, but had been persuaded to give it up by her father, who was very strict.'

'Yes.'

'That was the clue I spoke of. A father must indeed be strict to be able to control a full-grown daughter's choice of career, especially a woman of spirit such as Mrs Jelliffe. Mrs Jelliffe, then, was accustomed to the presence of a strong masculine authority in the home. And yet, when she married, she found herself presented with a man who, above all else, wished to be a woman. The outcome was predictable. While her husband persisted in his sexo-aesthetic inversion, or as Hirschfeld puts it – and these are excellent cheeses – transvestism (an inexact term, to my mind), Mrs Jelliffe filled the gap by becoming increasingly masculine. The role of pliant and passive wife slipped away, and instead of merely resigning herself to Mr Jelliffe's spendthrift ways, she took the reins and endeavoured to become herself the breadwinner, though in a rather unusual and unethical manner.'

'I see,' I said. 'One thing puzzles me, though. How did Mrs Jelliffe intend to collect the money from her own husband?'

'It is difficult to say,' Henry said. 'Perhaps by adopting a disguise. The adoption of alternative identities was so rife in the household that this would have been the obvious choice. Or perhaps she would have sent the maid, disguised as a gypsy or seaman.' He popped a roundel of 'baratte' into his mouth. 'I certainly hope not. Blackmail of the sexually unconventional is no career for a young girl.'

CHAPTER EIGHT

The Thief of Potchefstroom

When I look at my notebooks for the first half of 1895 I see a number of singular cases. The affair of the Moist-Handed Madonna falls into this period, as does the strange case of the Fifteenth Ewe, for which Henry was awarded the freedom of the town of Lampeter. But perhaps the most remarkable of all Henry's cases of this time was that of the Thief of Potchefstroom, for reasons which will soon become apparent (the reader will understand that it would be counter-productive, from the point of view of narrative suspense, to reveal these in the opening paragraph).

It was March, and the weather all week had been blustery and unsettled. On the day that this case begins it had taken a turn towards the stormy, and we had therefore been indoors since about six o'clock, Henry in his armchair by the large fish-tank, turning over the pages of *The Times*, and I in front of the fire, perusing a volume of poems by Mr John Gray – though somewhat distracted from it by the lashing of rain at the windows and the howling of the wind in the grate. Around ten I was about to throw the book down and retire to bed, when from the outer door there was a sudden loud thump. After a lull there came a second, and then a third loud report, as of a hand slowly and nervelessly beating itself against the wood.

'A visitor?' I wondered aloud to my friend.

'If so,' Henry remarked, 'his errand on a night such as this must be of some urgency.'

But no sooner had he spoken than there was a deafening crash from without. Henry, I recalled, had propped against the door – in an effort to seal it against the elements – a large cheval mirror, and this, it seemed, had been pushed roughly over and dashed to pieces. As we rose to our feet there came a further tumult from the hall, as of fragments of silvered glass and wood being trampled underfoot. Then, as we stood there, undecided as to what to do next, the door of the morning-room was flung wide.

To my utter astonishment, in the doorway was a man identical in almost every respect to Henry himself.

'You!' Henry cried.

Our visitor emerged from the murk of the hall, dripping rain from a black cape. The flickering firelight threw his shadow high up on the bookcases.

'Yes, I,' the apparition replied. 'I hope I find you well, Henry? You would not throw out your own brother on a night such as this?'

'Brother?' I cried involuntarily.

The middle section of *The Times* fell from Henry's fingers onto the floor.

The visitor turned to me. 'Will you introduce me, Henry?'

My friend made a small noise in his throat. 'This is Miss Olive Salter,' he said. 'Miss Salter, Jack St Liver.'

'A great pleasure,' Mr St Liver said, offering his hand.

My mind, as readers will guess, was racing. Henry had never talked of any brother. And this man before me was almost certainly not merely a brother, but an identical twin. Jack St Liver had the same tall and bony physique, the same unkempt chestnut hair, the same moist hazel eyes, the same wide and enquiring nostrils. Only one feature set the brothers apart. On Jack St Liver's lip was no moustache. It was hairless.

Henry, meanwhile, had collected himself.

'What do you want of us, Jack?' he asked sternly.

'Henry, Henry!' cried our visitor. 'You have not forgiven and forgotten after all this time?'

'You ask me that?'

'You do not wish to know how I have fared these five years?'

Henry said nothing.

'I had hoped for your help,' Jack St Liver said.

'You can expect no help from me.'

Jack St Liver flashed his brother a malevolent look. 'I think you will not say that after you have heard me out.'

'The time for a hearing was in the kraal of Gosi.'

'True enough. But I have paid for that lapse. You do not know, I think, that I have been in a Boer jail these past five years.'

Henry blenched visibly.

'Aye,' Jack St Liver said. He thrust out his hands toward us. On the wrists was evident a pattern of livid circular scars, much as are produced when an animal is carelessly tethered. 'Manacles,' he said, grim-faced. 'Manacles – and shackles.'

'In Pretoria?' Henry asked.

'In Potchefstroom.'

'Great God.'

'I have paid, brother.'

Henry motioned to a packing case by the fire. 'Then sit,' he said.

'My grateful thanks,' Jack St Liver replied, doing so a little gingerly on the case, which bore the word 'Coprolalia'.

'But be warned,' Henry said. 'If you lie, Jack, I shall know it.'

In the light of the fire I was able to observe our visitor more closely. His resemblance to Henry was truly startling. Aside from the lack of a moustache – and aspects of his clothing, which, unlike Henry's, seemed to be of fashionable cut, and unstained by remnants of food – the two were as alike as it is possible to be. But as I looked still more closely I was able to see something very remarkable. In the region below the nose and above the lips, that region where a moustache would have been present had there been one there, were a number of raised bumps, rather like moles, though of a fleshy colour, and all of equal size, three on the left-hand side of the face and three on the right, following the downward curve of the lip a little beyond and above the corners of the mouth on either side. The effect was odd, to say the least.

Seeing the direction of my gaze, Jack St Liver threw me a grimace.

'Miss Salter must be quite taken aback, Henry,' he said. 'You have done nothing to prepare her for our meeting.'

'I did not know you were coming.'

'True. Well – now I am here, and perhaps Miss Salter would care to know about me. She is, after all, is the chronicler of our family's adventures.'

Torn between loyalty to Henry and my own very great curiosity (I had in recent weeks been meditating a book of Henry's cases, to be titled something such as *The Oxford Despoiler and Other Mysteries from the Casebook of Henry St Liver*, and was eager for any small piece of biographical detail I could get), I did not reply. Henry too remained silent. Jack St Liver, however, did not seem the least bit put out.

'Henry has his reasons for not making me more welcome,' he continued. He stretched out his hands to the fire, once again showing the livid scars on his wrists. 'My behaviour has sometimes fallen a little below what might be expected of a loving brother. But even a man such as myself may change. I hope you may be convinced of that, Henry.'

It was surpassingly odd to see Mr St Liver speaking with what was, essentially, Henry's mouth. Mr St Liver's teeth, I noticed, were very discoloured, and I wondered if Henry's too were such, or whether this was a consequence of his sojourn in prison, where, I imagined, he had had little opportunity to clean them.

'Go on,' Henry said.

'Thank you, brother.' Mr St Liver turned his moist orbs on me. 'You will not have failed to notice, Miss Salter, that we are twins, Henry and I. Identical twins. Unless you have a twin, you are unlikely to know what that state entails.'

'No, indeed,' I said.

'From an early age Henry and I were the closest two human beings can be. Each of us knew exactly the other's thoughts and feelings. Each could instantly detect any falsity in the other. Each was constantly mistaken for the other. We delighted in our close resemblance, and played up to it on every occasion. Children with a similarity as close as ours often have an unnerving effect on people. On one occasion, I remember, we surprised a man at the Greenwich Observatory eating his lunch: he was so alarmed by our sudden appearance – from behind a tree – that he choked and fell writhing onto the grass. He almost died, I think. Those were sterling times, were they not Henry?'

Henry gazed unspeaking at our visitor.

'But, notwithstanding this intuitive mutual sympathy, there were differences in temperament. Early on Henry showed a talent for study; I was a sluggard who distrusted letters. Henry was the favourite of my father, and the ideal companion on my father's merchant trips; I chafed at home with mother. Henry was level-headed; I sought pleasant diversions. I dragged Henry more than once into one or another of my schemes, and it was sometimes Henry who was blamed when I, in reality, was at fault. Henry will remember the case of our uncle's tabby-cat, which died when I pushed it off a bridge – by accident, of course.

'In brief, while there were close ties between us, there were also resentments and rivalries. As time went on, our parents thought it advisable to send us to separate boarding-schools. Of course we were both much upset; perhaps I more so than Henry. Without the influence of my brother, I fear I fell into bad ways.

'On leaving school it was Henry who took the first steps away from the nest. He went off to his medical training, and then set out travelling. I too went tramping around the world. Finally I fetched up in the Klein Karoo, in Ndelele country, and called in on him. I stayed for a while.'

'About a year,' Henry said.

'Yes. The people seemed to like us. But then an unfortunate incident occurred. The Ndelele live by the re-use of human detritus, as I am sure you know, Miss Salter. Their clothing, their shelter, and so on, is wrested from the great waste-mounds of what we are accustomed to call civilization. Our rubbish and refuse – scrap paper, tin cans, vegetable peelings, or whatever it may be, they see as furniture, compost, decoration, bedding and so on. About five months after my arrival – I had taken a compound in the village – it so happened that one of the villagers, foraging on the tips outside Potchefstroom, found a number of artificial limbs, thrown out after the end of the Transvaal War. I don't know what he intended to do with them: perhaps make them into a table or something. The Ndelele are very inventive. Anyway, he stocked up his hut with them. But one day it was discovered that these legs had gone missing. A council was held and accusations were made against the fellow's neighbour. This neighbour was disliked (I never found out why: perhaps he had conspicuously failed to recycle some object); but I knew him to be entirely innocent. Henry was perhaps the only one who knew the truth. And that truth – that melancholy truth – was that I, his brother, was responsible.

'Yes, Miss Salter, it was I. I had taken them. I cannot quite say why now. I am sometimes something of a compulsive... collector.

But my brother grasped immediately what had occurred, and, I am glad to say, took the decision to keep the information to himself. The fellow under suspicion was arraigned for the crime, proven guilty – despite the legs never turning up – and beheaded. Incidentally, the Ndelele always conduct executions during eclipses of the sun or moon, which they predict with great accuracy. So: I escaped justice. Henry, finding his position compromised, left the Karoo, and came here to London. So far, of course, Henry is well acquainted with the story.'

Henry continued silently regarding his brother.

'A melancholy tale, then. But I am afraid there was a sequel: I fell into a further little difficulty. Another theft, I am afraid – I hope you will forgive me if I do not say of what. This time I was caught red-handed, and, in a search of my compound, the missing limbs were discovered. There were immediate demands for my execution, of course. But there are advantages – I mean apart from those of natural endowment – in being a white man. I saw that my one chance of escape was to throw myself on the mercy of the Boer authorities. However antipathetic they were to the *uitlander*, they would not countenance a fellow European being hacked to pieces. Accordingly I claimed my right to a trial by my own people – or as near my own people as possible in the circumstances. My sentence was commuted to a term of five years in the Victor Verster Very High Security Gaol in Potchefstroom.'

'I see,' Henry said.

'Yes, brother. Five years. And not in the most comfortable of accommodations. Dutch prisons are rather severe, I think. My cell was six feet by eight, with no bed nor furniture of any kind. I was manacled and shackled to the wall with chains just long enough for me to lie down on the stones. I was utterly alone. How often have I wished for warmth such as that of this hearth as I lay there at night, shivering like a beast, watching the rime creep up the walls – and in the day, how often I wished for night, as I baked in the pestilential heat. Unvisited, except by the guard once a day with a bowl of mealies, I languished in my chains, the featureless days soon blurring into one another. I felt the springs of my mind begin to loosen. But then a miracle occurred. One day my cell door opened, and instead of a guard with a bowl, I beheld an angel, clad from head to toe in shining white. But this was no hallucination. Before me was a young woman, a missionary worker, clothed in a white silk dress. I had neither shaved, washed nor changed my clothes for months. But however filthy, matted and verminous I had become, she knew me for a child of God.

'On that first visit she called for water and washed my body with her own hands, paying particular attention to the sores underneath the cruel bands on my hands and feet. It was the first visit of many. Gradually she overcame the obduracy of the Boers and secured some improvements in my conditions. In my third year I was allowed straw, for example. My chains, while not removed, were lengthened: she saw personally to that. But these material improvements were as nothing beside the knowledge that another human creature cared for me and wished me well. Though she could not remove my chains, the fact of her presence seemed to melt them away.

'She told me a little of herself. She had been born in London, and after study at Cheam had received a proposal of marriage from the brother of a fellow-boarder; deciding she did not yet possess the materials for an informed decision, she travelled extensively abroad during the next six years, always visiting the poor and needy. The previous year, she had been to Sakhalin Island in Russia; she had also investigated certain mines of South America, and worked among the oppressed peoples of the Basque country, in a place called La Folletta. The Boer penal system, she told me, was among the harshest she had yet encountered.

'As the months and years passed in Potchefstroom, she never left my side, and my love for her – for such it was – at length found an echo in her own breast. We began to talk of spending our future lives together. On my release we would quit the Transvaal and make our home in the Cape Colony – or in the mother country. The fellow waiting on her decision could be informed by letter. On the day of my release she promised to meet me, a free man, outside the prison gates, and thence quit the hated Dutch dominions forever. But when that day arrived –'

Here Jack St Liver paused, his face haggard.

'Surely,' I stuttered, 'surely she kept her promise?'

'No,' Jack St Liver replied. 'I doubted my own sanity. I stumbled into the town to find her, but no one knew her. It was as if she had never existed. After six days I traced her to her lodgings, which were no more than two hundred yards from the prison gates, in one of the poorest districts. The hag from whom she had rented rooms told me that she had departed Potchefstroom on the morning of my release, for an unknown destination.'

'You never found her?'

'I searched in Pretoria, in Witwatersrand, in Bloemfontein, all through the hubbub of the mining towns – in a thousand places. No one knew her. After many months, at my wit's end, I came to London. I knew she had a brother, though I did not know his name. I resolved to seek him out. But I have found neither.'

'You have tried the missionary societies in London?' Henry asked.

'Yes.'

'The police register?

'Yes – nothing.'

'The newspapers?'

'I placed notices everywhere my means would allow.' Jack St Liver reached into his cape and withdrew a small bundle of clippings. From these he extracted one and handed it to his brother. Henry examined it in his characteristically slow and intense manner, and for the space of a minute there was no sound save for the crackling of the fire and the faint noises his moustache made as it brushed the paper. Then he handed the clipping to me.

It read:

MISSING

Miss Joy Keane, missionary, late of Potchefstroom, South Africa, sought by Mr Jack St Liver, also late of Potchefstroom. Anyone with any knowledge of Miss Keane or her whereabouts should apply to Box No. 2402. Reward.

I was much astonished. 'Joy Keane!' I blurted out. 'But I know her!'

'What?' cried Mr St Liver.

'Joy Keane – she is the sister of Mr Karl Keane!"

'Karl?'

'Yes. Yes, Mr Keane and I – are friends. Mr Keane mentioned her to me, now I recall it. She was in Southern Africa.'

'Yes!'

'She returned to London I think in May last year. She bought a large house, where her brother joined her.'

'Where?'

But Henry, to my surprise, was sitting forward, one finger raised. 'One moment,' he said. 'Miss Keane may not wish to be found.'

'But you must tell me, you must!' howled Jack St Liver. 'Henry! Give me a chance to see her! I must know what stands between us – from her own lips. Who knows what goes through the mind of a woman in love? Perhaps it is something utterly trivial.'

Henry considered. 'If I or Miss Salter could first sound out Miss Keane, then perhaps something might be done. We could then pass on any reasons she may feel ready to give to you.'

'Yes –!'

'But you must respect those reasons, whatever they may be. That must be the end of it.'

'You have my solemn word,' said Jack St Liver eagerly. 'I will

---

* Readers will remember Mr Keane from the story of the Well-born Client in Chapter Three.

wait in a hansom while you speak with her, and if she agrees to see me, you can give a signal – wave a handkerchief or some such.'

'No,' said Henry, whose experience of these things was large. 'That would not do. If we were to take you to her house you would, I have no doubt, be back later on. You must wait elsewhere while we conduct our investigations.'

'But I know I can persuade her!'

'That is precisely what I wish to avoid.'

'Then – perhaps some other location – the zoo, for example. If then she does not wish to see me, I need never know her address.'

'The zoo?'

'Or Queen Mary's Gardens. I will wait in one part of the Gardens while you conduct your interview in another.'

'That sounds sensible,' I put in.

Henry looked at me with some surprise. 'Possibly,' he said after a pause. He turned back to his brother. 'Of course you would have to give a strict undertaking that you would not intervene.'

'My word has been worth little until now, Henry,' Jack St Liver said. 'But let this mark a new covenant between us. If I break this most sacred oath, may I never henceforth be called your brother.'

And so ended that extraordinary night. Jack St Liver departed as suddenly as he had arrived – he had obtained lodgings in Highgate – and Henry and I were left to ponder the remarkable tale we had heard.

There seemed no doubt in Henry's mind that the story was true. His brother had indeed been rotting for half a decade in a South African dungeon. And Henry believed this despite the fact that Jack St Liver was an accomplished liar, thief and cheat. Such was the degree of mutual understanding between the brothers.

I was at first a little surprised that Henry had agreed to his brother's plan of an interview in the Gardens, knowing that Jack St Liver could not be trusted; but I soon saw the reason. Henry had, evidently, divined that I did not wish to encounter Mr Keane. Interviewing Miss Keane away from their shared home was, thus, first and foremost, convenient for myself. It spoke a great deal for Henry's sensitivity that he was ready to endanger the successful outcome of the case – and perhaps place Miss Keane in jeopardy – for my sake.

The following morning, then, in consultation with Henry, I fashioned a letter to Miss Keane, asking if she would consent to a meeting at Queen Mary's Gardens, on the following Thursday, the 20th, to settle an enquiry from an erstwhile friend, in confidence. This was duly dispatched to the address in Kennington where I knew that Mr and Miss Keane had taken up residence following Miss Keane's return from South Africa. We then sat back to await events.

Henry remained uncommunicative throughout the next few days, and, as I did not like to press him on the likely outcome of the affair, I returned to my own business. As well as putting the finishing touches to my memoir *Further* (or *More*) *Tales from an Australian Barn*, I was also at the time engaged in composing my account of the Falmouth Minnows, that notorious case that had led to the disgrace of three members of the cabinet, including the

Chief Secretary to the Navy, and which Henry had finally solved via his knowledge of Suetonius.[*]

I was at work proofreading some papers early on the Tuesday when I heard the morning post falling amid the rubble of Henry's hallway, and went down to retrieve it. Among the numerous items of correspondence, postcards of thanks, and so on, I found a letter addressed in a flowery hand and bearing the stamp of the Kennington sorting-office. I ran with it up the stairs to Henry's little back bedroom. Henry was already awake, sitting up in bed smoking a cigarette. He took the letter from me and tore it open.

I give the reply in full.

28 Verulam St

Kennington

17th March 1895

Dear Miss Salter,

I was much astonished and shocked to receive your kind letter. It can relate to none other than Mr Jack St Liver, with whom I developed a friendship in the Transvaal.

Mr St Liver helped to make my stay in that region of the world much more instructive and pleasant than it would otherwise have been. However – and there is no way to say this without seeming terribly cruel – I see from what you have said in your letter that he must have thought rather more of me than I of him.

---

[*] See *The Twelve Caesars*, III: 'Tiberius'.

I suppose what I am trying to say is that Mr St Liver, though very dear to me, is no longer so, for reasons I am afraid I cannot really explain. I did, I admit, see his advertisements in *Snowden's*, *The Pall Mall Gazette*, *Tit Bits* and the *Manchester Guardian*, but I am afraid I could not respond.

You ask to meet me at the Main Greenhouse. Of course I am willing to meet you but I do not really see what use it would be. Jack is dead to me now and however deep his desire to continue our friendship I am afraid it is impossible. I was much upset – as upset as he was, I think – but I knew our friendship could not continue.

I am much more articulate when I am talking than when I write because when I write I find I cannot find the means to quite say what I mean and I go off at a tangent. I am much more coherent in person.

Therefore, if you really want to meet and talk in Queen Mary's Gardens then I suppose I will do so, to put an end to this matter, but please on no account reveal my address to Mr St Liver. I do not wish to see Mr St Liver again. I must *stress* that. I have read your stories in the *New Age* and am looking forward to meeting Dr St Liver in person – not Jack, of course.

Until next Thursday then.

With very sincerest regards,

Joy Keane.

'An attractive communication,' said Henry, tapping ash onto the coverlet.

'Indeed,' I said. 'But I think it holds out little hope for Mr St Liver?'

Henry looked meditatively at some stains on the ceiling. 'That would depend,' he said.

'On what?'

'Consider Miss Keane's current address.'

'Yes... '

'Verulam Street is just off the Gray's Inn Road.'

'Yes.'

'You do not find that suggestive?' He exhaled calmly. 'Miss Keane is, I think, a somewhat complex individual.'

'You think so? I had formed quite the opposite impression. A rather brittle creature, I would have said.'

'Ah. You did not see what I saw then.' He prodded at the letter. 'You note the very great self-deprecation with which this is written.'

'Yes.'

'It is commonly a sign of immense self-assurance.'

And that, tantalizingly, was all Henry would say on the subject. He promptly buried himself in a study of the urethra in Iceland, and I was left to wait until Thursday for the full revelation in this case.

Readers will agree, I think, that it proved to be a remarkable one.

Miss Keane, it turned out, was a figure in a capacious white cloak with pink trimmings. Perhaps she was not so very pretty – her beauty was of the more obvious kind – and her dark hair was tied up under an unbecoming straw hat with a pink bow. On seeing us she swept in our direction, putting out her hand rather as if she expected it to be kissed.

'Dr St Liver, I presume,' she said, smiling extravagantly.

'Miss Keane,' Henry replied, taking the hand.

'And Miss Salter. I am so pleased to meet you. My brother too sends his regards.'

'He is well?'

'Never better.'

I was rather surprised at this, since ten months previously Mr Keane's doctors had given him a year to live.

'I have been here twenty minutes already,' she said. 'I am much taken with the bromeliads. Little prisons for the poor flies!'

'Yes indeed,' Henry said.

'Shall we walk or do you prefer the greenhouse?' Miss Keane asked.

'The climate indoors,' Henry said, 'is perhaps preferable to the drizzle. I hope only that we can find somewhere to talk undisturbed.'

'I have thought of that,' Miss Keane said. 'While I waited I found out a little corner in the upper gallery close to the brazier. It seems deserted. Will that do?'

'Admirably.'

We ascended a wrought-iron spiral staircase to the upper gallery, which was, as Miss Keane had said, unpopulated: the rain had put off all but a few visitors to the Gardens. At the far end, which was very steamy, a bench stood vacant, canopied by a vine which dispensed great cascades of wan-looking leaves.

We sat.

'Dr St Liver,' Miss Keane began, loosening the collar-ties of her cloak, 'I agreed to meet you today because I feel I do owe your brother some explanation.' She paused. 'I am sure I have not behaved very well. But a missionary works in a professional capacity, you know. The ideal is to retain a certain distance between missionary and client.'

'I can see that would be desirable,' Henry replied. 'May I ask, if it is not too great an intrusion, which missionary society you are currently attached to?'

Miss Keane plucked at her glove-buttons. 'I am a freelance,' she said.

'A freelance. Then that would explain it.'

What this explained I had no idea at all.

'Yes,' Miss Keane replied carefully. 'I find I do my best work when given free rein.'

'Of course.'

'And so, Dr St Liver, my message to Jack is simply this: I take full responsibility for all the remarks, undertakings and promises I may have made, and regret that I was, to an extent, swayed by his plight in prison, and did not wish to destroy the tiny shreds of hope that were enabling him to endure the wretched conditions in that terrible gaol.'

'I see.'

'Yes – it is hard of me I know, but my work must come before everything.'

'Your work – do you mean your work at present?'

'Why, yes.'

'And if it is not impertinent to ask, does that work involve visits to Coldbath Gaol?'

A flush crept over Miss Keane's face. 'Coldbath? Yes, but I see in that no relevance to the matter at hand.'

'Forgive me, Miss Keane, but I believe there is every relevance.' Henry fixed on her a steely gaze.

'What do you mean?'

'I mean that the reason you broke your vows to my brother – which, let us remind ourselves, were vows of the most solemn kind, pertaining to an engagement to be married –' he paused to let the words sink in – 'was that you could no longer countenance the idea of a connection unless your fiancé were imprisoned.'

Miss Keane seemed unable to reply. A leaf dropped from a plant and landed at her feet.

'I apologise for the directness of my tone, Miss Keane,' Henry went on. 'I act in this matter on behalf of my brother, and must defend his interests. Perhaps also I would not speak in this way if I did not think that he is now a finer man than when he entered into penal servitude. It is a transformation for which I believe you are, to a large extent, responsible. So if there is anything I can do to prevent what seems to me to be an avoidable tragedy, then I must try.'

Miss Keane looked at Henry at first with tight lips; but, perhaps realizing that she was in every respect out-generalled, she lowered her lashes, and briefly nodded. 'I should have known better,' she murmured, 'than attempt to deceive you, Dr St Liver. I know your work, of course.'

'And I yours,' Henry said.

Miss Keane glanced at him in confusion. 'Mine?' she asked.

'You are the "J. Keane" of the *Archives de Neurologie*?'

Miss Keane gasped. 'You have read –?'

'Certainly. Your study of the link between fettering and neu-rasthenia. Most interesting.'

The persona Miss Keane had adopted in her letter now seemed to have fallen away to some extent. She was now revealed as what she evidently was – a contributor to Henry's own arcane branch of science. I was, I confess, not a little taken aback. And looking at her, it was obvious that Henry's words had touched her professional pride: the beginnings of a small smile were struggling to emerge from her surprise and confusion.

I felt a little left out; but since I had no notion of what rela-tion penal incarceration bore to neurology, nor in fact what was going on, I had no choice but to remain silent. Moreover my asthma was a little affected, I think, by the steam.

'If I may, Miss Keane, I would like to make my train of thought clear,' Henry began, retrieving a cigarette from his case and lighting it with a sudden flare. 'You tended to my brother throughout four long years, were patient and loving all that time, and promised to be his wife on his release. Yet at the moment of his release – the very moment – you forsook him. What had changed? Only the fact of his incarceration. It was his incarcera-tion itself, then, to which you were profoundly drawn.'

Miss Keane appeared to weigh the point.

'You lived very close to the prison,' Henry continued, 'in a poor district. Could this be explained simply by want of funds? Evidently not, since on your return to London you took up resi-dence in Verulam Street, near Gray's Inn Fields, one of the bet-ter-appointed districts of North London.'

'Yes.'

'Verulam St is in close proximity to Coldbath Gaol. Coldbath has one of the most severe of all English prison regimes. The treadmill is still used there, I think.'

Miss Keane bit her lip.

'You wished, therefore, wherever you might be, to be close to a prison. You had been an indefatigable traveller, but only to places notable for their penitentiaries – and more specifically, for regimes of particular harshness. Sakhalin Island, where thousands die yearly in the bitter cold; or Vitoria-Gasteiz, in the Basque Country, notorious for the prison of La Folletta.'

'Yes,' Miss Keane said, a little penitently.

'The identification of yourself with "J. Keane" was, I admit, conjectural, but after putting the other points together I felt the inference might be made. And, if I may say so, your quick response to Miss Salter's communication and desire to meet in person – knowing that she and I were connected – bespoke a professional interest. Having severed your ties with my brother and ignored all his advertisements, you had nothing else to gain.'

Miss Keane smiled. 'I concede the latter point, Doctor. In fact I concede all your main points.'

'Thank you,' Henry said.

'But I ask nevertheless for a chance to explain my actions.' She glanced at me. 'I have no objection to Miss Salter taking down the relevant details, as long, of course, as she does not use my real name.'

'Naturally not,' I said, taking out my notebook.

'Yes.' Miss Keane folded her hands in her lap. 'As I say, you have covered the main points, Doctor. I am – and have been from an early age – deeply fascinated by prisons. All aspects of prison life engross me, though I suppose at the heart of it all is the conception of punishment. From an early age I loved to read about men and women being punished, fettered or tortured – for example in Butler's *Lives of the Saints* – and often, indeed, envied them.'

Miss Keane delivered herself of this astonishing statement with an equanimity I supposed born of the common relief felt by those who confess; perhaps also her own training in Henry's field of study helped diminish any embarrassment she might have been expected to feel in the circumstances.

'I remember these feelings beginning in early childhood,' she continued. 'One summer when I was aged about six, my father built a chicken coop, and playfully put me inside. I was utterly delighted by this new sensation and did not want to leave. Long after the joke had lost its savour for the rest of the family I insisted on remaining within, and my father had finally to drag me from it screaming.'

The picture painted was a momentarily arresting one.

'I would play at fettering and binding long before I knew that these were methods of punishment. I played at these games with my brothers and sisters, and of course often practised on myself. I would sometimes sleep entirely wrapped in rope. As I grew older I discovered that restraint, confinement, binding, fettering, manacling, punishment and torture were all employed as corrective measures for the criminal classes – and rejoiced in the knowledge. Images of punishment and correction haunted me constantly. If, for example, I saw elegantly-dressed gentlemen or ladies at a social function, I would imagine how their appearance would be improved if they were fitted with a ball and chain, or manacled to a rough stone wall. It seemed to me that elegantly dressed, fashionably attired and exquisitely made-up ladies needed but one thing for the perfection of their ensembles: to be savagely and repeatedly struck, and then dragged off, chained up and forgotten in a malodorous bastille. Dapper city gents walking to the office over Westminster Bridge I pictured shuffling along in chain-gangs.

'Soon I realized that if I were to avoid insanity I must put these desires to some good use: accordingly I became a missionary and prison visitor. You would be astonished how easy it is for a young woman to gain admittance to the most desolate and forbidding prisons. Similarly slave-ships and mines. I simply needed to tell the authorities that I was a missionary and they would allow me access to their charges, in what, to me, were the most delightful surroundings imaginable.

'You will wonder, Dr St Liver, whether my impulses were sadistic. I do not believe so. I have read de Sade, of course, and thrilled to his power and – perhaps you will find this a strange epithet – to his honesty. But I did not desire to see suffering. That was not it. I felt that the prisoners were often genuinely appreciative of their punishment. I often wished to change places with them, though I could never quite bring myself to the point of committing a crime. Am I then a follower of Sacher-Masoch? Again, I say no, though I have great admiration for the man and his work. Stcherbak perhaps comes closest: he mentions how some women will become excited by a declaration of love from a man who is physically repulsive, even though she does not wish to respond to his advances; and speaks of individuals who feel a definite physical arousal when they see disagreeable things, such as vomit, blood, filth, dead bodies, and so on. But that is to stray a little from the point, which for me was always exclusively penal.

'My interest was almost abstract in nature. I never desired, for instance, any physical contact with any prisoner, and liked to believe that they felt the same, though perhaps in the circumstances that was a little unrealistic – many of the men I encountered had not seen a female for several years, let alone a healthy and attractive one. Let me be frank. The primary element in my sexual make-up I believe is this: a fascination with restraint, imprisonment and punishment in and of themselves, in isolation from particular individual acts, perhaps instilled in me by early childhood experiences.'

Miss Keane brushed an invisible spot of dirt from her cape. 'And so to the matter at hand,' she said. 'I admit that Jack was different. I did admire him greatly and valued his company. We found ourselves fully in harmony on almost every question. Each to the other was the perfect companion. Rarely had I seen a man held in quite such abject squalor. The Boers really do hate the English, you know: Jack was little more than a chained and starving skeleton when I first met him. I was at the time living near the prison: as you have correctly surmised, I must live within sight of a prison's walls if at all possible, even if this necessitates taking up residence in a poor district. I began to visit him every day. But I soon saw, to my distress, that Jack desired above all to be released. I knew that I would have to face the terrible day when he would walk free, and yet I am afraid I dismissed the knowledge from my mind, and allowed things to run on without telling him of my true feelings. I hoped, too, that somehow I really would find myself able to marry him on his release, and live a normal life. But this was all self-deception. I am afraid I used him very badly. On the day of his freedom I abandoned him, and came to London. The truth is, I still miss Jack dreadfully. There is nothing like the Victor Verster Very High Security Gaol in Kennington.'

'Oh Joy!' cried Jack St Liver, bounding out from behind a fern, and somewhat covered with brownish dust. 'Joy!' He fell to his knees in front of Miss Keane and buried his head in her lap. Both Henry and I were considerably startled. Miss Keane gave a shriek of disgust and rose to her feet: Mr St Liver tugged at her cloak in an effort to restrain her. It came away. Beneath it she wore a brilliant white silk blouse with leg-of-mutton sleeves, a patterned white silk skirt and a cream bustle. Her hair under her hat, I now saw, was raven.

She flashed Henry a look of magnificent enmity.

'Dr St Liver,' she cried. 'I trusted you!' She tugged at her cloak, tearing it from the grip of the still prostrate and wordless Jack St Liver, and strode toward the staircase.

'Wait!' Henry shouted, rising to his feet, his moustache tossing off gobbets of wet. 'Miss Keane! I had no idea my wretched brother had followed us to the greenhouse!'

'It matters little,' Miss Keane snapped over her shoulder. 'The interview is at an end.'

'Joy!' sobbed Mr St Liver, scrabbling to his feet.

I felt the urgent desire to speak.

'Miss Keane,' I called out after her. 'Might I make a suggestion? What if Mr St Liver were to commit another crime here in London?'

Miss Keane paused for a moment, her hand on the stair-rail. Then she gave a curt shake of the head. 'No,' she said, beginning her descent.

But Mr St Liver, who had evidently heard everything from behind his fern, ran over to her.

'Yes! Of course!' he cried. 'I will – rob a bank! Or anything you desire! Please forgive me for hiding – it was my only chance. Please... please! Allow me to commit the crime that will bring us together.'

A look of great weariness came over Miss Keane's features, and for the first time I understood that she had not lied when she had spoken of her tender feelings for Mr St Liver. 'That cannot be, Jack,' she said. 'Miss Salter's solution, while superficially attractive... ' she trailed off. 'I will say only that in British prisons even the rudiments are no longer observed. Prisoners are allowed recreation – recreation! – in the form of oakum-picking. And fettering was abolished by the Prisons Act as long ago as eighteen fifty-six.'

'Then why not commit a crime in a foreign country?' I put in, strolling toward the pair.

'Yes!' ejaculated Jack St Liver, throwing up his hands. 'Name the country! A robbery or a murder committed in the Russia of the Czars would attract quite draconian penalties, I imagine.'

Miss Keane gazed at him wonderingly. 'You would do that – for me?' she asked.

'I? Can you ask it? I would spend our entire married life, if only you would say the word, labouring under the most dreadful penal conditions.'

'Oh, Jack!' cried Joy Keane, flinging herself into his arms.

'My darling!'

Henry touched my sleeve, and we left the pair in the steam.

Outside in the March weather my friend permitted himself a laugh. 'Well, my dear Miss Salter,' he said as we looked up at the panes. 'The palm on this occasion belongs to you.'

'No,' I said.

'Yes, certainly. The essential element, that of love, and what a man may do for love, had eluded me. I will not make the same mistake again.' Henry pulled his cigarette case from his waist-coat pocket, but, fumbling, disgorged its entire contents onto the wet grass; I knelt in the drizzle to help retrieve the cigarettes. 'My brother has never quite found his way in life,' Henry went on as he crouched beside me. 'But perhaps now, with the love of a good woman, in a new country, he might be happy. It is not the most conventional ménage that must involve a prison, but the sphere of the conventional must always contract to a dot once individual cases come under consideration.'

'I am still a little curious about one thing, Henry,' I said, pausing in my work. 'Please tell me if I intrude into what must be a most private and personal demesne.'

'Certainly.'

'Why does Mr St Liver have those queer markings on his lip?'

'Oh – the scars of the *bela*?'

'The *bela*?' I asked.

'The Ndelele rite of initiation. I told you about it, I think.'

'But – you said that you yourself had undergone the rite.'

'And so I had. Jack arrived six months before the *bela* was due to take place. He was thus eligible for the ritual at the same time as I. We underwent it together.'

I was dumbfounded. 'In that case – you too –'

'Yes. I too. I bear the same scars.' Henry's eyes smiled. 'But I felt it best, all things considered, to conceal them from the English gaze. I found many were unable to see the man beneath.'

I made some inarticulate sound.

'You find the notion strange?' Henry asked.

'No!' I cried. 'No – I was simply –' I paused. 'Naturally it makes no difference.'

'I am glad to hear it.'

'Then did you receive,' I asked, 'the exact same pattern of marks?'

'See.' He motioned to me. Already close to him, grubbing as I was for the spilt cigarettes, I shuffled closer, the wet turf staining my skirt. Henry parted the great masses of chestnut hair that streamed down over his mouth. And there, beneath, was disclosed a flesh-coloured scar, about the size of a small olive pit. His fingers moved; another scar was disclosed. The marks were strangely beautiful.

'May I touch them?' I asked.

Henry nodded.

'They are – quite hard,' I said.

Henry gently took from me the wedge of damp Virginians I

clutched in my free hand. 'Thank you, my dear,' he said.

Thus concluded the case of the Thief of Potchefstroom. Not more than a week later, Jack St Liver and Joy Keane married at the little registry office in Pentonville, quite close to the gaol: Henry and I acted as witnesses; and the same day we saw them off on their honeymoon to British Columbia, where the Canadians have instituted one of the most cripplingly severe of all the world's prison regimes. Henry requested that I keep secret the story of his brother, and so the events of that week in March, and in fact the entire affair of the Thief of Potchefstroom, could not form any part of my story-collection *The Oxford Despoiler and Other Mysteries from the Casebook of Henry St Liver*, which appeared under the imprint of Drebber and Drebber in March 1896.

As far as I know, Henry never again heard from his brother Jack. But to judge from the multitude of papers Mrs St Liver – née Keane – continues to submit to international sexological journals, the couple continue to enjoy a happy and productive married life.

❦❧

THE END